Island of

Promise

Praise for *Summer's Squall*

"The author obviously did a lot of research for the book and it showed, not in boring lists of facts, but in the way the book was fleshed out. In addition, the descriptions were beautifully done, not telling but showing the beauty of the area."

Among the Reads Review

"Good character development, plot, surprises, thought provoking with excellent descriptions of the Colorado mountain country."

Amazon Reviewer

Praise for Award-Winning, *Island of Miracles*

"A beautiful account of the love and the healing support of community!"

Chandi Owen, Author

"This is the kind of story that makes me long to run away from my perfectly fine life for the sole purpose of stumbling upon something magical."

Alex Jacobs, Author, The Dreamer

Praise for Award-Winning, *Whispering Vines*

"The heartbreaking, endearing, charming, and romantic scenes will surely inveigle you to keep reading."

Serious Reading Book Review

"Schisler's writing is a verbal masterpiece of art."

Alex Jacobs, Author, The Dreamer

"Amy Schisler's Whispering Vines is well styled, fast paced, and engaging, the perfect recipe for an excellent book."

Judith Reveal, Author, Editor, Reviewer

Also Available by Amy Schisler

Novels
A Place to Call Home
Picture Me
Whispering Vines
Island of Miracles
Summer's Squall

Children's Books
Crabbing With Granddad
The Greatest Gift

Collaborations
Stations of the Cross Meditations for Moms (with Anne Kennedy, Susan Anthony, Chandi Owen, and Wendy Clark)

Island of

Promise

By Amy Schisler

ISBN: 978-1-7322242-0-9

Published by:
Chesapeake Sunrise Publishing
Amy Schisler
Bozman, MD
2018

Acknowledgements

Writing a book is not an easy task. Though the words seem to flow effortlessly from my fingertips to my computer screen, there is so much more that goes into writing a novel than simply putting words to paper. Every character, every scene, every setting, becomes real to me, like family and favorite destinations. I pour my heart and soul into each story, character, and line, and I hope that is evident in the final work. But no work is final without a team of others to help me with the process.

Judith Reveal has been my editor since the publishing of multi-award-winning *Whispering Vines*. She is everything a wonderful editor should be and always makes my writing better. I am grateful that she continues to take me on as a client. Thank you, Judy!

Pat Woods is an outstanding graphic designer. His work on *Summer's Squall* and now *Island of Promise* is incomparable. Thank you, Pat, for making my books even better through their visual appeal.

My beta readers, Shannon Dolgos, Valerie Burd, Christina Holden, and Marian Grammer, are fabulous. They help me get everything off to a good start and keep me in line when I've failed to live up to their expectations. Thank you, ladies! My proof readers, Debbie Nisson, Mary Leve, and Cheryl Baummer, are phenomenal. If you find any errors, it is not their doing but mine. They have an eye for seeing even the most minute of errant details.

My friend, Valerie Burd, was my inspiration for this book. May God grant her a long life and continued good health. She has proven to many that a good heart, a strong faith, and a mountain of determination can slay a dragon.

Chincoteague Island is a real place, and I have tried to portray the island and the surrounding areas much as they are in real life. Though I have taken some license with geography, names, and businesses, what you read about is indeed the wonder of the island and its inhabitants. Thank you, citizens of Chincoteague, for embracing *Island of Miracles*. I hope that *Island of Promise* is all that you hoped it would be.

Finally, I am blessed with a rich abundance of family and friends who support my career, my crazy schedule, and my trips to visit and talk with readers. My husband, Ken, has been a stronghold for me since the day I decided to quit my job and write full time. I can never thank him enough. Our children, Rebecca, Katie Ann, and Morgan, are wonderful supporters, sharing my blog and books with everyone they know. My parents, Richard and Judy MacWilliams, are my biggest fans. If you have ever met my father, even for a brief moment, I am sure he has told you about my books. I would be nothing without their love and support.

I would be remiss if I failed to thank the others who have been there for me for the past ten years: my mother-in-law, Nancy Schisler; my aunts, Debbie Nisson, Mary Schisler, Mary Morgan, and Maureen Parkhurst; my friends: "The Anne's"- Anne Kennedy, Anne Novey, and Anne Warpinski; Debbie Swann; Tammi Warren; Michelle Zamora; Chandi Owen; Susan Anthony; Dan and Debbie Froelich; George Sprance; all of the ladies previously mentioned; and Ronnie Zollo who inspires me through her faith more than she could ever know.

I thank God for everything. May He shower you all with love and mercy.

PS All recipes mentioned throughout this novel are on my web page: http://amyschislerauthor.com. Enjoy!

To all women, everywhere, especially Valerie Burd and
Mary Morgan, who battled demons and won. I salute you.

Chocolate Chip Cookies
Origin: America

There is something about the chocolate chip cookie that
just says, "I love you." It's the quintessential recipe in
every mother's recipe box and the favorite of thousands of
children around the world. Though there are many
variations of it, the best recipe always seems to be the
simplest, just like the ones that came from the oven in my
mother's kitchen, baked with love and eaten hot off the
pan on a cold winter's day.

From *Around the World in Eighty Meals*
by K.Z. Middleton

<u>CHAPTER ONE</u>

The scope found its mark as Zach held the rifle steady, the crosshairs pinpointing the back of the head of one of the FBI's most wanted. The streets of Kabul were quiet as night set in, but something was off. Instead of desert sand, Zach smelled salt air. Where there should have been stifling heat and stillness, he felt a breeze and heard the gentle lapping waves of the ocean. He tried to concentrate on the man in the lens, but something else caught his eye. Just as he pulled the trigger, he heard Kate scream, and he watched helplessly as his bullet took down his sister, his best friend.

Jolted from his sleep, Zach sucked in the cool, salty Atlantic air that wafted in from the open balcony doors. Drenched with sweat, he tossed the covers aside and sat on the edge of the bed. He took several deep breaths, reassuring himself that Kate was okay, that the intruder who had stood on that very balcony was dead, shot by Zach's own rifle, and that Kate and her unborn child were saved. Shaking away the dream, one of many that haunted him often, Zach stood and walked to the balcony.

It had been a clear night, much like this one, but wrapped in the raw cold of a Mid-Atlantic February night. He remembered hearing the noise on the balcony that adjoined this room, his sister's at the time, and his room next door. He had been ready, he and Aaron, Kate's then-fiancé. They had known that Kate's ex was nearby, plotting and planning his way back into her life, his obsession with her growing more dangerous by the day. Zach took the shot the moment he had the chance, and he didn't regret it one bit. Okay, he regretted taking another life, but he didn't regret saving his sister and his niece. Mark was prepared to kill her if she didn't go with him, and there was no way on earth Zach was going to let that happen. Of all the kills he'd been responsible for over the past fourteen years, that one had been the only one that had been personal. However, it was not the only one that haunted him.

There was the one in that village in Iraq where the little boy stood silently in the shadows when Zach had shot the boy's father. Zach would never forget the look in the boy's eyes when he ran from his hiding place behind a curtain and dropped to the ground, cradling his father in his tiny arms. The boy couldn't have been more than seven.

Then there was the time that Zach had killed a woman. Granted, she was a high-value target on the Most Wanted list and had lured many U.S. soldiers to their death. Her urgent pleas for help became a cackle as she fled amidst the gunfire that took the lives of the men who went to her aid. Still, Zach had been raised to respect women and to treat them with care. He'd had to steel his mind to the job at hand and remind himself several times that she was a killer, no better than he was, even worse.

Zach inhaled the damp, September breeze and let the soothing salt air cleanse his lungs and his mind. That life was over. His role in the never-ending war in the Middle East was done. He had a chance to do things right, to make a real life for himself on Chincoteague, this sleepy little island that his sister now called home. He had hoped that it could become his home, too—a place where he could find peace, but the demons wouldn't back down, wouldn't go away, and he wasn't sure if he would ever truly find enough peace for any place to be a real home.

Looking across the marsh to the nearest house, Zach wondered about the family inside. He didn't know what time it was, but by the angle of the moon and the almost imperceptible light on the horizon, the inhabitants of the house next door would soon rise and start their day. When he first arrived on the island, Zach spent a lot of time with the family, but lately, he'd been keeping his distance. Kayla and the boys had their own history with a killer. Did they really need another one in their lives? If Kayla knew what he really was, what he had done for all those years, would she even allow him in her house, near her children? He was certain that the answer would be no, but what kind of life could they ever have together unless he told her the truth?

Zach closed his green eyes and turned away. She deserved more, so much more. She'd already lost her husband to a bullet. There was no way she would be able to accept Zach for who he was, for who he still is and always would be inside—a cold-blooded killer.

***

Kayla rinsed the breakfast dishes and enjoyed the quiet. The boys had eaten and been put on the bus, laundry was started, and now the cereal bowls and juice glasses were ready for the dishwasher. She ran her hand through her shoulder-length brown hair, still damp from her shower. Out of habit, she scrunched the ends with her fingers in an attempt to give it some volume.

Glancing out the window, Kayla wondered about her neighbor. She had seen very little of him lately and missed him. Too much, to be honest. She had become accustomed to his presence at the dinner table, sitting beside him at Mass, and their late-night talks after the boys were in bed. He had never touched her, never kissed her, or made any moves on her. For some reason, he always held back, but that was fine. While she wouldn't have complained if he had, she had two young boys to worry about, and though they had all talked about the possibility of her falling in love again, she worried she might carry things too far with Zach and that would go against everything she was teaching her sons. Still, she longed for something more, for a commitment, a man to share her dreams with. The boys had been so young when Eddie was murdered, still babies really. She never planned on being a single mother or living the best years of her life without a man by her side. She thought they would grow old together.

For years after Eddie was shot, she wouldn't even consider the thought of being with another man. Eddie had his faults, but his love had been strong and true, perfect really. It had taken her a long time to get over the loss, and Zach opened up to her the possibility of loving again, but as quickly as he came into their lives, he left. At the very least, he had stopped coming around. So much for thinking they might have a chance.

Sighing, she pulled open the dishwasher and filled the last remaining spaces before turning it on. She switched off the light as she left the room and settled in at the desk in her office off of the kitchen. Almost five minutes went by before she realized she was simply staring at her computer. And there was too much to be done to sit idle. Her new business venture, Second Helpings, was wildly successful, and she had quite a lot of emails to answer, calls to make, meals to plan, and shopping to be done.

The fall sports season was beginning, which meant that dinner orders would begin flowing in at a faster pace. There were recipes to be organized, menus to be updated, and bulk food orders to be processed. If things kept going at this rate, she was going to have to hire another cook. For now, she and her sister-in-law, Kate, had everything under control. Brilliant and beautiful, with long blonde hair and striking green eyes, Kate was the computer genius behind the website, brochures, marketing, and anything else that needed to be designed or written. Kayla handled the orders and, of course, the cooking. They had just decided to hire an assistant to take and organize the orders so that Kayla could concentrate on supplying busy families with home-cooked meals to go, and Kayla was in the midst of lining up interviews while trying to plan a special menu for the fall.

Somehow, Kayla and Kate managed to keep their personal lives and professional lives separate. It helped that Kate had a baby to care for, was writing a book, and did all the writing and designing for Second Helpings in her own home office. There was little time left for Kate to question Kayla about her personal life or for Kayla to ask about Kate's brother, Zach. Aaron stopped by the previous night to see his nephews and mentioned that he had been out with his brother-in-law over the weekend. Kayla had remained silent. She knew that both Kate and Aaron hoped that she and Zach would fall in love, but Kayla felt Zach distancing himself, and she wasn't sure why. Perhaps Zach detected an unknown signal from her. Maybe he knew that deep down, Kayla could never really love anyone else the way she had loved Eddie. Possibly he had decided that a ready-made family with eleven and eight-year-old boys was too much for him. Maybe he was enjoying his life of freedom, now that his time in the Army was over. Or maybe he had just decided that he wasn't really interested in Kayla.

Only, that's not how it seemed for the past several months. Whenever their families were together, he was attentive to her and the boys. He took over right where Aaron left off after Miren was born, taking the boys for ice cream, spending lazy days on the beach with the three of them all summer, flying kites with the boys in the yard. And then, it all just stopped. Excuses were made at dinner time, the 7:30am Sunday Mass suited his exercise routine better than their usual, later time, and his new job as a trainer with the island police department meant earlier evenings and busier weekends. Though disappointed, Kayla hadn't been worried at first, but now, she knew that something had gone wrong, something had changed. Zach was avoiding her, and she did not know why. She refused to ask Kate or Aaron. That would open a kettle of worms that she didn't want to open.

Resigning herself to returning to the life they knew before Zach entered their lives, Kayla clicked on the touchpad and watched her screen light up. She had wasted enough time and energy. She had a business to run. Any more thoughts of Zach would have to wait.

***

"No," Todd yelled as Kayla tried to convince him, later that evening, to put on his Scouting uniform. "I'm not going. I hate Scouts."

"Since when?" Kayla asked. "You've always loved it."

"No, I don't. I only went because Uncle Aaron went. Now he's too busy with that stupid baby."

"Todd Aaron Reynolds, don't you ever call your cousin, or anyone else, stupid. That's not nice, and you know it."

"Well, she is stupid, and I hate her. She took Uncle Aaron away from us." The little boy crossed his arms over his chest and held his ground as tears welled in his eyes.

"Todd, honey," Kayla said soothingly, sitting beside him on his bed. "You know that's not true. Uncle Aaron is still here for us whenever we need him. But Miren is a baby, and she needs him, too. He's doing the best he can to be there for all of us, but Aunt Kate isn't feeling well tonight, and Uncle Aaron needs to take care of Miren, so Aunt Kate can get better."

"Why can't we have a dad to do stuff with us? All my other friends have dads who take them to Scouts?"

Kayla's heart broke for the thousandth time. This was becoming an all-too familiar argument with Todd. EJ kept his feelings hidden inside, and though Kayla often saw the same questions in his eyes, he never voiced them. But Todd was a different child in many ways, and he was never one to hold his tongue or his emotions. She worried that he seemed younger than other eight-year-olds, and she wondered if losing his father affected him even more than she already knew.

"Sweetie, your dad is taking care of us the best he can. He watches over us every day and every night. He prays for us and makes sure that we are safe. He loves you, and I know he would be here with you to take you to Scouts if he could."

"Then, why isn't he? Why did he have to go to Heaven? Didn't he want to stay with us?" The little boy's tears ran down his face.

"Of course, he did," Kayla swallowed her own tears and pulled her son to her as he cried. "He wanted to be with us more than anything in the world. Daddy couldn't help what happened."

It was something Kayla had repeated many times, but the words always sounded hollow to her own ears. Eddie may not have meant to get himself killed, but he knew that he was putting himself in danger when he agreed to work as an informant. It still made her blood boil that his agreement to spy on his boss had endangered their whole family. She spent years learning to forgive him for putting himself in that position and leaving her behind to pick up the pieces. In the end, she forgave him. She loved him and knew that he was doing what he thought was best. Now, she had to trust that he was watching over them from above.

"Mom," EJ's quiet voice came from the doorway. "It's time to go. We're going to be late if we don't leave now."

"We're coming, EJ." Kayla looked at Todd. "Can you please get dressed, Todd? For your brother? It's a big night for him. He's moving up to a Boy Scout tonight. Can you please come with us to see his ceremony?"

Without a word, Todd nodded and reached for his shirt. Kayla helped him dress. The smell of freshly-baked cookies hung in the air as she raced to the kitchen and grabbed the plastic containers of chocolate chip cookies and snickerdoodles and hurried the boys to the car. For the second time that day, she glanced at the house next door as she buckled her seatbelt.

If only things had worked out, she thought, *then Zach would be going with us tonight.*

She shook away the thought and started the car. As they drove by the house, she thought she saw the front curtain move, but she dismissed it. Why would Zach be watching them? He'd made it clear that he was no longer interested in the comings and goings of their broken, little family.

***

Zach muttered an expletive as he moved away from the window. Tonight was the ceremony, and Aaron wasn't there to take the boys. He knew that Kate wasn't feeling well. Some days were hard on her. Having Miren almost killed her. Because of her heart condition, they lost her several times between the time that Mark broke in and took her hostage and when Miren was born hours later. It was touch and go for a while, but Kate pulled through the labor and the subsequent heart surgery thanks to Dr. Sprance, her real-life superhero.

Zach punched the speed dial on his phone and waited for Aaron to pick up.

"Hey, Zach, what's up?"

"I just saw Kayla leaving with the boys. Are you going to the ceremony?"

There was pause before Aaron answered. "No, I'm not," he sighed. "I had planned on it, but Kate's not feeling well, and Miren's teething. It's a brutal combination."

Zach nodded as if Aaron could see him.

"Is Kate okay?" While he had called about Kayla, his concern for his sister came first.

"Yeah, she's fine. She just needs to rest."

Zach chewed on the inside of his mouth for a moment as he thought about how disappointed EJ would be to not have Aaron there for him.

"Hey, man, how about I come over and take care of Miren?"

"That's really nice of you to offer, Zach, but you know how she is when she's hurting. It's going to be a rough night."

"I can handle a crying baby," Zach told him. "You should be with Kayla and the boys."

The line was silent, and Zach thought the call might have dropped, but then he heard Miren begin to fuss.

"Hey, Zach, why don't you go? I'm sure Kayla and the boys would appreciate you standing in for me. And I know it would mean a lot to Kate."

There he goes again, thought Zach. *Whenever Aaron tries to convince me to do something, he always manages to play the Kate card.*

Inseparable from the day she was born until the day he entered West Point, Zach always had a soft spot for Kate. It was why he devoted the entire last winter to move in with her and take care of her after they discovered her heart condition. He had to pull a lot of strings to be discharged, but she was worth every favor he had to call in.

"I don't know, Aaron. I think it should be a member of the family—"

"Don't give me that. You are family. You said you wanted to help, so, help. Stand in for me tonight. I'll owe you one."

Zach cursed under his breath as Miren's cries became louder.

"Hey, I gotta go. Do it for Kate, please."

Before Zach could protest, Aaron was gone. Grabbing his keys off the table by the front door, Zach turned off the light and headed out. He was still dressed from work in his khakis and button-up shirt. It would have to do. He cursed as he headed to his truck, expelling every word his mother taught him not to say.

"Always the damned hero," he said to nobody as he slammed the door and started the engine.

***

Kayla sat with the other parents and watched as EJ was ceremoniously escorted across the little wooden bridge. He turned to her and smiled, and she was struck by how much Eddie Junior looked like his father. He had Eddie's dark brown hair, brown eyes, and boyish dimples. Kayla's hair was a lighter brown, and her eyes were hazel. She considered herself average, but Eddie... now he was a looker. Kayla smiled as she pictured his face.

There wasn't a day that went by that she didn't think about Eddie. She harbored no illusions that he was perfect, but he was perfect for her. He was kind and gentle, a true family man, hard-working, and impeccably honest. And that was what led to his death. As soon as Eddie suspected that his boss was involved with illegal dealings, he contacted the authorities. He knew that Kayla would have worried, so Eddie kept it from her. He felt that helping the FBI was his duty to himself and to his country.

For a while, Kayla suspected that her almost-perfect husband had been having an affair. She threatened to leave him and take the boys, but he still didn't let on that he was part of an undercover operation, a pawn in a game of cat and mouse between the city mayor and the FBI. The same day Kayla threatened to leave was the day he confronted his boss—the day he was shot and his body placed in his car and driven into a nearby lake. The guilt she felt, when she was contacted by the FBI and told of his death, was almost unbearable.

Returning to the present, Kayla smiled at EJ. She became distracted by Todd who was sitting beside her, pulling at her sleeve.

"Not now, Todd. Eddie's about to receive his badges."

"But, Mom," Todd tried to whisper. "He came."

"Okay, Todd, that's nice," Kayla answered before thinking. She leaned down toward Todd without taking her eyes off of EJ. "Who came?"

"Uncle Zach. He came." The little boy pointed toward the back, and Kayla tried to nonchalantly turn around. Her heart began beating a little faster, and her throat went dry when she saw the good-looking man leaning against the wall at the back of the room. While Eddie was handsome, with his dimples and sparkling brown eyes, Zach was breathtaking in the way that action heroes are breathtaking. He had chiseled muscles, a hardened jaw, a single dimple that only appeared when his smile was at its widest, a scar under his right eye, and that look in his green eyes that made her think he could see right into her soul.

A ripple of excitement made its way down her spine, and Kayla felt heat rising into her cheeks. There was something about that man that got to her. She spent the entire summer watching him on the beach as he made sand castles with the boys and dove into the waves. His body was hard and toned. He seldom laughed or smiled of his own accord, but the boys had a way of bringing out the joy in him. She thought she did, too. At least, he always seemed happy when they were together, content even, in a good, *it feels right to be with you* kind of way. But then it stopped. She hadn't seen or heard from Zach in over two weeks, until now.

Once the ceremony was over, Kayla looked for Zach. She was raised to be polite and gracious and knew that Zach was only there to support EJ. She felt obligated to thank him for coming. Todd was the first to reach him, even giving up a prime spot in the refreshment line to hurry over to his newest hero. The big, strong man lifted Todd like he was weightless and wrapped him in a bear hug. Though Todd was small for his age, he wasn't weightless, but he appeared to be so when he was in Zach's arms.

"I missed you. Where have you been?" Todd asked, his little arms encircled around Zach's neck.

"I've been really busy, Todd. I'm sorry about that."

"It's okay, but we really want you to come back for our family dinners. They're not the same without you. Are they mom?"

Zach turned his gaze toward Kayla, who had followed Todd, and she felt as if a hot flame had been lit under her. Her cheeks turned rosy, and she reminded herself not to let him get the upper hand. His six-foot-three stature rose above her, and though she was a good five-foot-seven, his larger-than-life aura always made her feel as though he towered above her. Pulling herself up to her full height, she tried to shake his confidence with her piercing hazel eyes and firm set jaw.

"The boys got used to you being there," she said without warmth.

"I'm sorry about that. I didn't mean to let them down."

Kayla detected something in his voice and tried to find meaning in his clouded green eyes, but his defense shields were as high and impenetrable as hers. Refusing to admit that she missed him, too, she waited for him to say more, but he just held her gaze until EJ appeared at his side.

"Hey, Uncle Zach. Thanks for coming, man," he said as he reached out to shake Zach's hand, a gesture that made Kayla both proud and sad. Kayla smiled at her son. He was becoming so grown up.

Though she could see the gratitude in his smile and his fondness for Zach in his eyes, she knew that EJ was becoming a young man and was trying to keep up appearances. He was caught in that awkward place between being a boy and a man, and he was very protective of his mother. She could sense his conflicted feelings and wondered if it was because he felt awkward shaking Zach's hand rather than hugging him or if he knew there was something amiss between his mother and the man he looked up to.

Zach ruffled EJ's hair.

"I wouldn't have missed it," he said.

"Yes, thank you for coming," Kayla said, reminded by EJ of the reason she had sought him out in the first place.

"It's my pleasure," Zach said, grinning at EJ. "What kind of cookies do you think they have over there?" he asked in a conspiratorial tone.

"Does it matter? Mom baked most of them," EJ said with a wink, and Kayla saw a bit of her twin brother, Aaron, in him, too.

"Good point," Zach said, as he put Todd down on the floor. He turned to Kayla. "Shall we?"

Forcing a smile, Kayla nodded. She was too overwhelmed to speak. With Zach's left hand firmly being held by Todd, and his right hand on her lower back, Kayla felt too much like they were a family. She noticed the looks from the other moms and tried not to assume anything. Her eyes met those of her friend, Anne. Anne raised her brow in question, but Kayla shot her a look that said, 'don't ask.' Zach had been AWOL for more than two weeks. Not that she had been counting. And the more he smiled at the boys, and the more they reveled in his attention, the more irritated she became.

Shaking off his hand, Kayla made her way to the other side of the table. She refused to look at Zach, but she felt his gaze boring into her. She wondered if he would follow her, but he stayed in line with the boys.

Once they had their plates, the four of them found some chairs together and pulled them into a small circle.

"Who are those two men standing by the punch bowl? I've never seen them before," Zach asked.

Kayla turned and saw the two adults chatting by the drink table.

"The one with the beard is Mr. Urbansky, the principal. He comes to all of these events to support the boys. I'm not sure who the other man is."

"You know him, mom. He was at Meet the Teacher Night. That's Mr. Palmer, the new science teacher."

"Oh, yes, I recognize him now."

"He's awesome," Todd said, grabbing Zach's hand. "Come on, Uncle Zach, I'll take you to meet him." As they walked away, Kayla heard Todd prattle on about the things Mr. Palmer was teaching them in science class. She watched the men exchange greetings and a handshake. They spoke for a few minutes before Zach and Todd returned to their seats. Todd continued to talk non-stop about his new teacher.

Kayla ate in silence, ignoring Zach's glances. She smiled at the other parents and answered when spoken to, but the celebratory mood of the evening had been shattered for her. She didn't know what Zach was thinking by walking in and out of their lives like it was no big deal, but it was a big deal to her. After all, she was the one who would have to wipe the tears once he disappeared again.

***

"You're angry with me," Zach said quietly as he and Kayla walked out of the school cafeteria into the twilight. The boys were ahead of them and deep in conversation about a comic book hero.

"You're perceptive," Kayla said coolly.

"I'm sorry," was all he could think to say.

Kayla stopped and looked at Zach. He stood and waited for his deserved flogging.

"You waltz into our lives, making my boys think you are the next Captain America, with your military record and officer's rank. You pay attention to them, take them places, play with them, and act like you care. And then you just disappear. Now, all of a sudden, you show up on a very important night to EJ, making it seem like you've been there all along. And you think that's okay? That you can just show up when you want and then walk away without a word? How long this time? Will you stick around for a week, a month? Or is this a one-time thing?"

Zach exhaled and nodded his head, realizing only then that he had been holding his breath. What could he say? She was right.

"I really am sorry. I didn't mean—"

"To lead them on? To make them think you'd be there for them? They're little boys, Zach. They understand more than others how cruel this world can be, how sometimes people are there one minute and dead the next. What they don't understand is how someone they care about can just disappear without a word."

"I know, I get it. I'm—"

Kayla held up her hand. "Don't say it again. I heard you. You're sorry. Well, at least we both agree on something. You're a sorry excuse for a man."

With that, Kayla turned and walked toward her car. EJ narrowed his eyes at Zach, and Zach looked away. He wasn't sure if he was guilty or angry because, although he knew she was right, he had his reasons for keeping his distance. He stood motionless while Kayla and the boys climbed into her SUV. As the family pulled out of the parking lot, Zach closed his eyes and swallowed. He knew he should go after her. He wanted to. He wanted to be there for the boys, to be part of their lives. He wanted to share nights like this with them as a family. He wanted to… hell, he wanted to take her in his arms and kiss her until she forgot why she was angry. But he couldn't do any of those things.

Thanks a lot, Aaron. Why did you have to guilt me into coming tonight?

He didn't need any of this in his life. He carried around too much guilt as it was.

Zach walked slowly to his silver Chevy truck and stood by the door for several minutes. His head was pounding, and his thoughts were jumbled. He needed to think. He climbed into his truck and started the engine, but instead of heading to his house, he headed to the trail where he and Aaron ran every morning. He wasn't dressed to run, but he needed to clear his head.

Changing his mind, he headed toward Assateague, the National Seashore where the wild ponies roamed the beaches. Technically, the park was closed, but it was still camping season for a few more weeks, so Zach knew he could access the area twenty-four hours a day. He parked and walked to the beach. There were no tents set up along the shore. Most likely because it was a weeknight, and school was back in session. The moon hung low over the water, and the waves gently splashed along the shoreline.

Taking off his shoes and socks, Zach rolled up his pants and waded into the chilly water. Before long, it would be downright icy, but for now, it still felt good on his bare feet and legs. Zach closed his eyes and let his senses take over. The air smelled like salt and sand and goodness. His feet tingled in the cool water, and a breeze ruffled his untucked shirt and ran along his bare neck and the quarter-inch hairs that covered his head.

The gulls called to each other in the night, and the waves slapped the shore in a steady rhythm that seemed to match his slowing heartbeat. He took a deep breath and sucked the cool night air fully into his lungs.

This was peace. This was the serenity he sought. If only he could spend the rest of his life feeling just like this. No guilt. No demands. No taking or giving orders. No raising a gun. No teaching others to raise one either. No responsibilities.

But with that came loneliness and loss and the knowledge that he could have had something real. Something special. He saw Kayla's face in that blackness inside his closed eyes, and her words came back to him.

You're a sorry excuse for a man.

Yes, he was. There was no denying it.

Zach opened his eyes and looked out into the expanse of the ocean. It was time. He knew he needed help. He'd needed it for a long time. He didn't know if it would change anything. He didn't know if he deserved Kayla or if she would even want him. But he did know that she and the boys had suffered enough. They deserved to be loved, to be taken care of, to be saved from fear and sadness and loneliness. And he knew that before he could save them, he had to save himself.

Seafood and Spinach Fettuccini
Origin: Italy

If there's one sure way to get your children to eat spinach, it's in fettuccini. My mother's go-to recipe for picky eaters is a great alternative to spaghetti. Even my brother, Aaron, not the most adventurous eater as a child, could gobble up a whole bowl of this hearty meal in the blink of an eye. It's healthy but tasty and can be cooked in less than twenty minutes, so it's prefect for families on the go.

From *Around the World in Eighty Meals*
by K.Z. Middleton

Island of Promise

CHAPTER TWO

"It's good to see you, Zach," Father Darryl Millette said as he closed the door to his office. "It's been a long time since you came here to talk."

"Too long, Father. Thanks for making time for me," Zach said, taking a seat on the couch. The salty scent of the nearby ocean blew in from an open window, its gauzy white curtain blowing in the breeze. "I'm sorry if I'm taking you away from something important."

The young, red-bearded man shook his head and smiled. "What could be more important than meeting with a friend and helping him with a problem?"

Zach smiled. "I wish it was that simple."

"What's going on, Zach? More nightmares?"

"Some, but that's not what's bothering me today."

"Okay, then, what's on your mind?"

Zach took a deep breath and began at the beginning. "Well, you know about my job, about all the things I did."

"Yes, we've talked about your years as a sniper many times. Are you still struggling with forgiving yourself?"

"I think I'll always struggle with that, Father, but no. I believe you when you say that I've been forgiven and that self-forgiveness will come in time. I'm working on it." He gave the priest a lopsided smile.

"Then what is it, Zach? Is everything okay with Kate and the rest of the family?"

Father Darryl and Kate became quite close the previous winter when she arrived on the island and discovered she was pregnant with Mark's child. She considered having an abortion, but the young priest talked her out of it and convinced her to start going to Mass. It changed her life. Ironically, Zach had been going to Mass for a couple years now. It was one of the only places where he felt good about himself while he was in the Army. If a guy like St. Paul, who killed so many and even oversaw the stoning of St. Steven, could be forgiven and become a disciple, then certainly Zach could be forgiven.

"Kate's fine, Father. Thanks for asking. Everyone else is okay, too. Well, I assume they are. You see," he shifted uncomfortably. "I've been avoiding everyone lately."

"Ah, yes. I noticed that you've been coming to the early Mass alone rather than attending with Kayla and the rest of the family."

Zach looked embarrassed. "Yeah, I have. You see," he hesitated and stood. Sitting still reminded him too much of the old days when he had to sit still for long periods, waiting for the right moment to take his shot. Zach now fully appreciated having the freedom to move. Walking to the window, he looked out into the courtyard behind the church.

"I'd been spending a lot of time with Kayla, Todd, and EJ, you know, living next door and with Kate being married to Aaron and all." He turned back to look at Father Darryl.

Darryl nodded and waited for Zach to continue. Zach paced around the room as he talked.

"It was no big deal. The holidays were great, and the next several months went by in a blur. Kate was bedridden, and we were all trying to take care of her and be on the lookout for Mark. And then Miren was born, and Kate had to stay in the hospital for a while, then the wedding and the baptism. Well, you get the picture."

"Things were a bit hectic," Darryl said with a knowing smile.

"To say the least. So, anyway, when summer came, we were all comfortable with each other. It was natural to hang out with Kayla and the boys. They were family. We had a good time, and everything was fine. Until," Zach stopped pacing and tried to find the right words.

"Until you realized you have feelings for Kayla."

Zach was unable to speak. How did this young, unmarried man of the cloth know exactly what he was thinking? He blinked and swallowed.

"How?" Zach started to ask.

"I'm a priest, Zach, but I'm still a man. I've counseled many couples and married a good number of them. I've seen the way you look at Kayla and the way you act around her. It's obvious how you feel."

"Well, see, that's the problem. It wasn't obvious to me." Zach sat back down on the couch. "And then it was. And I knew I had to stop it before it was obvious to Kayla."

"And why is that, Zach? Are you afraid that you won't be good enough for her? Because, you're wrong if that's the case. You're a good man, Zach."

Zach put up his hands. "Whoa, I don't need a pat on the back. I've served my country. I go to church. I take care of my family. I get that, for all intents and purposes, I'm a decent guy."

"But you have a past," the priest said.

"To say the least," Zach agreed. "A past that involves killing dozens of people." He looked the priest in the eyes. "Hundreds."

"And? Kayla's brother is in the military, as was her father. She knows what happens in war."

"It's not the same, Father." Zach shook his head and looked down at his hands. The hands that pulled the trigger and condemned man after man after…

"Kayla's husband, he was murdered." Zach looked at his friend and let the words hang in the air between them for a moment. "He was shot and killed."

"And you're not sure Kayla will want to have a relationship with someone who shot people for a living."

Zach took a deep breath and exhaled it through his cheeks. "In a nutshell."

"And you know you have to tell her."

"I do. Even without you telling me. I could never even consider a relationship without full and complete honesty.

Father Darryl rubbed the whiskers on his chin and tugged on the tip of his beard.

"So, what are you going to do about it?" he asked.

"The hell if I know," Zach said and then winced. "Sorry about that."

Father Darryl chuckled. "I've heard worse."

"I guess you have. So, back to the question. What am I going to do about it?"

***

"Do you think I should suggest the lasagna?" Kayla asked Kate as they looked over the menu proposal for an upcoming party.

"I do," Kate told her. "It's one of your best recipes and in her price range. Plus, it's a good food for all ages, and I'm sure that a ninetieth birthday celebration will bring people of all ages. Of course, there's also your Seafood and Spinach Fettucine. It's always a winner and easy to make. And if there are allergies, we could substitute chicken."

"Yes, that would work," Kayla said absent-mindedly. "What about the lasagna?"

Kate looked at her sister-in-law and raised her brow in puzzlement. *Why is she so distracted?* "Um, isn't that what we just confirmed?"

"What?" Kayla looked up in confusion. "Oh, yes, we did. Sorry." She shook her head and looked back at her list of recipes.

Kate reached over and put her hand on Kayla's. Kayla stopped writing and looked back at the other woman.

"Kay, what's going on?" Kate asked. "You've been distracted all afternoon."

"I'm sorry. I guess I'm not much company today. I have a lot of things to take care of before I meet with Marian tonight to finalize the menu. I'm not used to doing events like this. Cooking for a single family is one thing. Cooking for a group of fifty people is another. I don't know why I agreed to do a big party."

"I don't think it's the party that has you distracted. Level with me." Kate peeked into the bouncy seat at her feet to check on Miren and then looked back at Kayla.

Kayla shrugged. "I don't know," she said, leaning back in her chair and throwing her head back so that she was staring at the ceiling fan above the kitchen table.

"You must know what's bothering you. Is there something wrong with one of the boys?" Kate asked, bringing Kayla back from distraction once more.

"No, well, not really." She looked at Kate and sighed. "Okay, yes. That's part of it. Todd hasn't been himself lately. He's moody and disagreeable. He refuses to do what I tell him to do, and he's started talking back."

"You mean he's finally acting normal instead of like the perfect child you've taught him to be?" Kate smiled and gave Kayla a knowing look.

"Believe me, neither of them is perfect."

"But up until now, they've put on a pretty good show, huh?"

"Yeah, I guess so."

"Do you think he's moving into some kind of phase? Exerting his independence, perhaps?"

"Maybe," Kayla considered the thought. "But I don't think so. I think there's more to it than that."

"What then?" Miren made a small, coughing sound, and Kate bent down and laid her hand gently on the baby's cheek before focusing her attention back on Kayla.

"I think," Kate watched Kayla, her brow furrowed, as she tried to phrase whatever was on her mind. "I think he's angry with someone."

"Who? You?"

"Well, yes, to a degree. But also his father, and Aaron, and…Zach." Kayla bit her lips together and looked at Kate.

"For what? Why on earth would he be angry with all of you?"

"I think he's angry that he doesn't have a father like the other boys have."

"Oh," Kate said quietly. She looked down at Miren and thought about her daughter's father. Someday, Kate would have to tell Miren that her father was a liar and manipulator and that he almost killed both of them. The eventuality of having to say the words was almost always on her mind. Fortunately, Aaron would be the only father Miren would ever know, and that made her a very lucky little girl. Kayla's boys hadn't been so lucky.

"I had to force him to go to Scouts the other night. He said that he wanted his father to take him like all the other boys' dads. He asked why Eddie had to go away."

"Oh, Kay, I'm sorry. That must have been so hard for you. And Aaron stayed home with me which must have made things even worse."

"It did, until…well, until Zach showed up."

Kate raised her brow. "Really?"

"Yes, and both Todd and EJ were overjoyed that he was there. They adore him, you know. And he fell right into place as the father figure, and everyone was so happy. But then, well, I kind of lost it." She looked away, her cheeks turning bright red.

"Why? What happened?"

Kayla swallowed. "I'm sorry, Kate, I know he's your brother, but he's been a real jerk lately."

"How? I mean, he's my brother, so I know he's not perfect, but you just said he was a father figure, and the boys adore him."

"When he's around."

"What do you mean?" Kate was surprised that Zach hadn't said anything to her about this.

Kayla stood and carried her mug to the counter. She opened a fresh tea bag, gesturing to Kate with a second bag. Kate shook her head, and Kayla proceeded to fill her mug from the instant-hot faucet that loomed over the stove and was a wonderful addition to the kitchen when there was a need to fill large pots. When Kayla sat back down, she blew on her tea before taking a sip and continuing. A spicy fragrance filled the air, a combination of pumpkin spices and black tea.

"We had such a great summer, Zach and the boys and me. Whenever Zach wasn't at the police department, he took the boys to the beach or the movies or wherever they wanted to go so that I could work. I'm sure you know that." Kate nodded, and Kayla continued. "And when I didn't have to work, we all did things together. Zach was a regular for dinner, and some nights, he'd stay even after the boys went to bed, and we'd talk or watch a movie. It was nice, comfortable even. And then, a couple weeks ago, he stopped coming. He didn't call or make excuses; he just stopped."

"Why didn't you tell me?"

"How could I? You and Zach are not just brother and sister. You're each other's best friend."

"Kay," Kate said, reaching over to lay her hand over Kayla's, "you're just as much my best friend. You could have told me."

Kayla shook her head and waved away Kate's hand. "No, I couldn't. If you had told me the same thing about Aaron, I would have felt like I was in the middle. I would have punched him and told him what I thought of him, but I would have been in the middle just the same."

"Okay, I get it. So, what happened the other night?"

"We were walking to the car, the boys in front, and Zach and I in back, and I was thinking about how unfair it was that we'd gotten so used to him being around, and then he stopped coming, and suddenly he was back, acting like everything was just fine. It made me really angry. What right did he have to mess with our lives and our emotions like that? I mean, not mine, but the boys. They want to have a dad so much, and it seemed like, well, like…"

"Like Zach was willing to take on the role."

"Yeah," Kayla exhaled and looked at Kate. "I know. That's wishing for too much. Zach needs to have his own life. Just because he lives next door, and he's your brother, does not mean that he's stuck playing daddy to my boys. I just thought…" Kayla looked away.

"That he might be the one?" Kate asked gently.

"Maybe," Kayla said quietly.

"Kayla," Kate began tentatively, "I've never asked this before, but, here goes. Are you in love with my brother?"

Kate was prepared for Kayla to deny it. She had never even hinted at the possibility that she might be in love with Zach, but Kate had seen the spark from the first day they met, right here in this very kitchen. Kayla was very good at keeping her feelings to herself and her emotions well-guarded, but Kate had gotten to know her sister-in-law pretty well over the past year, and she was sure she wasn't wrong about what she saw.

"I, I think I am," Kayla admitted. "Heaven help me, I don't know what to do about it."

Kate smiled. "I get it. Zach's not easy to reach. He's, how do I put it? He's got a lot of baggage."

"You mean from the Army? It can't be any more than Aaron has from his time in the Gulf of Mexico. He still carries the guilt of losing his best friend and Coast Guard brother to the underling of a drug lord."

"Well," Kate tried to find the right words. "It's different for Zach."

"I suppose it is," Kayla said after a moment of thought. "The only time Aaron ever spent in the Middle East was in Bahrain. He always said he couldn't imagine what it was like for the men in combat who saw people die practically every day."

You have no idea, Kate thought.

"Zach has a lot of issues, Kayla, big ones. I'm not trying to say my brother's a lost cause, but I think he has a lot to work out."

Kayla nodded and then looked at Kate. "Are you telling me to give him time and space to be ready, or that he's not worth getting my hopes up for?"

"To be honest, I don't think that's my call. But I can tell you that I think love might be the only thing that can bring Zach back from the hell he saw and the one he's still in."

Kate let that thought sink in with Kayla as she bent to wipe a bit of drool from Miren's cheek.

After an uncomfortable pause for both of them, they gladly changed the subject and settled back into looking at recipes and chatting about the business.

"Oh," Kate said suddenly. "I had the strangest phone call the other day from Megan, a girl I used to work with at Smithsonian Magazine."

"Isn't she the one who warned you that Mark was trying to find you?"

"Yes, and she feels terrible she couldn't do anything to stop him from finding me. She had no idea that he was abusive, but she knew I was in danger. Thank God she called me. We might not have known that he had found me until it was too late." Kate shuddered as she thought about the night that she almost lost her life and Miren's. "Anyway, she called for advice."

"About what?"

"I'm honestly not sure. She sounded upset, but she refused to elaborate. She said she just needed to talk to someone. She was asking me all kinds of strange questions about this guy we used to work with."

"Do you think she's into him and looking for advice on getting noticed?" Kayla asked.

"I didn't get that impression. He's not at all her type, and Megan has never had any problems getting noticed. She was grilling me about whether I'd had any encounters with him, did I ever feel like he was coming onto me, and other strange questions."

"Kate, did you ask her if she was safe?" Kayla asked, looking at Kate with concern. "Did she sound like he'd hurt her in some way?"

"Oh, my gosh," Kate said slowly, kicking herself for not being more in tune during the conversation. "Kayla, I was so surprised to hear from her, and preoccupied with Miren, I didn't really listen or think about it that way. Megan always had 'boy trouble,' so to speak. She likes to party and always has a new of guy. She isn't loose. She just likes to have fun. And she can hold her own with anyone, so I never thought of her as someone who would be put in a position to be hurt by a man, I mean physically."

"Had you ever pictured yourself in that role?" Kate bit her lips. "Before Mark? Never." She shook her head and remembered how frightened she was the first time Mark lost his temper and how stupid she felt after realizing how he had manipulated her in so many ways.

"Kayla, are you thinking Megan could be in trouble?" Kate was beside herself with worry. She had always thought of Megan kind of as a little sister. It was Megan who convinced her to go from Katherine to Kate and Megan who pushed her to get on with her life. Why hadn't she paid more attention to what Megan had been saying?

"She might be, Kate. How did you leave it?"

"I told her that she could call if she needed to. That was pretty much it. Oh, what a horrible friend I am."

Kate leaned her head back and closed her eyes. She felt terrible.

"You should call her," Kayla said. "I mean it. Check on her, and make sure she doesn't need help."

"I'll call her tonight. Hopefully I can get her to open up to me. She might just need someone to give her the courage to get away. If it's that bad, I mean." Kate turned introspective. "I can't imagine how my life would have turned out if I hadn't discovered that Mark was already married. I had no idea he was violent until I tried to leave. I was so afraid. Coming here, starting over, was the best decision I ever made."

"I understand. I knew, after Eddie's death, that the boys and I needed to start over again. We couldn't stay in that house, in Lakespring." Kayla shuddered. "It would have been awful."

"Yes, but you weren't really starting over. You had your family here ready to support you. It was different for me. Like it's different for Zach."

"How so for Zach?" Kayla asked coyly.

Kate wondered just how much Kayla knew or suspected about her brother's past. "Well, it's complicated. And not my story to tell," Kate said. "If you really want answers, to all your questions, I'm afraid you're going to have to ask him yourself."

Chicken and Shrimp Paella
Origin: Spain

My father was stationed in many ports before I was born and for the first few years of my life. While in Spain, he fell in love with paella, a mildly spicy dish with chorizo, chicken, and shrimp. Whenever I smelled it cooking, as a child, I always knew that mom was buttering dad up for something big. It is a delicious, hearty meal that is truly a comfort food and one that I make whenever my life seems to be spinning out of control.

From *Around the World in Eighty Meals*
by K.Z. Middleton

CHAPTER THREE

Kayla tossed and turned most of the night. She wasn't able to sleep well anymore, and it was really starting to get to her. She was exhausted all day but still couldn't rest at night. Why couldn't she have just one night where she slept for a solid eight hours? Or seven? Heck, she'd even take six. She turned to look at her clock and sighed. It was just after four, and she knew that she would never fall back asleep before her alarm went off at six.

Resigned, she shook off the covers and went into the bathroom to brush her teeth and throw on a robe. The days were still warm for September, but the mornings were chilly. She guessed that fall would show up soon.

In the kitchen, Kayla made herself a cup of tea and poured a bowl of Special K. She sliced a peach into the cereal and added milk. The horizon outside her window glowed with the faintest light, but the sun was a long time from showing itself over the water. As she dropped the paring knife into the sink, Kayla's eyes wandered to the house next door. She was surprised to see a light on inside and assumed Zach was up early, too. Dismissing thoughts of him, she went to the table and sat down with her iPad.

Kayla tried to concentrate on the daily news, but her mind kept straying back to Zach. Was it a mistake to admit to Kate that she was in love with him? She was sure Kate would keep her word and not tell him, but the two shared such a strong bond. Would Zach know something was up as soon as Kayla's name came up in conversation? Would he find a way to get the information out of Kate?

Shaking her head, Kayla pushed the questions from her mind. She doubted that her name came up very much in Zach's conversations with Kate. She and Zach were not an item. He had no desire to spend time with her. He showed up at the meeting because he knew the boys would need a father figure there. It had nothing to do with her. For whatever reason, Zach was not interested in her, and she would have to accept it.

***

Zach ate his oatmeal by the kitchen window. The houses weren't close enough for them to see into each other's windows, but he could see the light and the movement in the kitchen and knew that Kayla was awake. Why was she up so early? Was somebody sick? He kept watch the entire time he ate and was relieved that nobody left the house. No ambulance appeared, and no other lights went on. He knew Kayla was planning a big birthday party for one of the retired Coast Guardsmen on the island. Maybe she needed to get up early to work on that.

His thoughts turned to his last meeting with Father Darryl. When Zach first came to the island, he met with the priest on a weekly basis. In time, the man helped Zach overcome his guilt and understand that God did not harbor any offense against him for the killings he committed in the military. He even let go of the resentment he held for himself. Well, almost. He was still working on that. But all in all, his life seemed to be getting better. Even after he shot Mark, while defending his sister, the nightmares stayed away. It was only recently that they returned. Sometimes, Kate was the helpless victim of his shot, and sometimes Kayla was. Either way, he awoke, drenched in sweat, his heart racing, his mind reeling, and his body fully alert. Sleep would come no more that night.

Now, used to the intrusion of the dreams on his slumber, Zach woke early and went over his notes for the day's classes. He took his job seriously and worked hard, teaching the young men how to handle a weapon, but his heart was never in it. Many of these kids grew up duck and goose hunting and knew the mechanics of using a gun. They understood how to hold it, how to keep it pointed in a safe direction when not aiming to shoot, and all the other things one needed to know to safely operate a weapon. What they didn't know was how to handle the actual shooting of a person, and he prayed they never would.

While he spent a fair amount of time making sure they had all the rules down for the use of the weapons, he spent even more time talking to them about their fears, their assumptions, and their naïveté. To them, the thought of shooting a bad guy was the most exciting part of the job, and Zach hoped they would never know the flipside—the second-guessing, the realization that they had taken a life, the guilt.

Zach's mind drifted in a stream of thoughts until it came to rest on the same person as always nowadays—Kayla. She was always there no matter what else he tried to focus on. Father Darryl felt that Zach wasn't giving her enough credit. The priest was certain that Kayla would see past the things Zach had done to the man he is and that she would not associate his former life with her husband's death. But was Father right? And was Zach willing to take that chance?

He glanced at the house next door and made up his mind. He didn't have to go into the station until later in the day, so he had time to talk to her. He would wait until the boys got on the bus and then give her a few minutes to unwind before he went over. Zach took a deep breath and tried to dismiss his apprehension. Talking to Kayla was the right thing to do. Now he just had to do it.

***

Kayla's hand shook as she waited for the call to connect. Still standing in the bathroom, wrapped in a towel, she had wasted no time reaching for her phone when she exited the shower.

"Yes, this is Kayla Reynolds. Does Doctor Swann have anything available today?"

She waited, biting her top lip, while the receptionist checked the schedule. She could smell the strawberry scent of her shampoo as she twisted a strand of her wet hair.

"I'm sorry, not today. She can see you next week. I can make you an appointment for Tuesday at 9:30. What do you need to see her about?"

"Next week?" Kayla closed her eyes and took a deep breath. "I guess that's okay. It's just that, oh, never mind. I'm sure it's nothing."

"You don't want the appointment?"

"Well, maybe. I just thought she might be able to see me right away."

"Is this an emergency?"

"Well, not exactly. I just, I found something. This morning. When I was in the shower, and I thought maybe I should have it checked out." She bit her lip again, raking it through her teeth until it began to feel raw.

"What did you find, Kayla?"

"A lump," she choked out the words.

"On what side?"

"The left side."

"Okay, hold on." Kayla was put on hold for several minutes. While she waited, she slipped her hand inside the towel and felt the area where she had discovered the lump. Yep, it was still there. She supposed it was not her imagination after all.

"Kayla, can you come in now?"

"Now? Yes, I can come as soon as I get dressed." She thanked the receptionist and said goodbye. She thought about what she could throw on in a hurry. Catching her reflection in the mirror, she paused.

Taking a deep breath, Kayla put down the phone and let the towel drop to the floor. She wiped away the steam that stubbornly clung to the mirror over the sink and peered at her reflection. She didn't look any different. Everything still matched on both sides. There was nothing obviously different about her left breast. She felt the area one more time, then swallowed the lump in her throat. It was definitely there. Kayla closed her eyes and fought back the rising fear. She was young and healthy. This was nothing. Just a mass of tissue or some benign abnormality. Better to get it checked out and move on.

Kayla dressed quickly and grabbed her purse before heading outside. As she opened her car door, she saw Zach leaving his house. He stopped short when he saw her, and she thought she saw a look of surprise pass over his face. Certainly, he wasn't on his way to see her, she thought before shooing the notion away. That ship has sailed, she told herself. He made it perfectly clear that he had plenty of other things in his life more important than her. She turned the key and drove away, leaving Zach standing on his front step, watching her go by.

***

Dr. Swann's nurse asked Kayla several questions and typed the answers into her laptop. Once she was gone, Kayla tried to stay modestly covered by the paper top as she looked around the room at the posters showing healthy versus osteoporotic bones, the female reproductive system, and clear versus smoke-harmed lungs. The smell of antiseptic hung in the air. Kayla had been seeing Dr. Swann ever since she moved back to the island, and she trusted her. Not only because Dr. Swann was a good doctor, but because Debbie was one of her closest friends.

"Hey, Kay, what's up?" Debbie asked when she entered the room. Her smile disappeared when she saw Kayla's face. "Kayla, is everything okay?"

"You tell me," Kayla said with a forced smile.

The doctor sat down and took a cursory look at the notes on her laptop.

"When did you find it?" Debbie asked as she stood and washed her hands, the doctor replacing the friend.

"This morning," Kayla said. "I'm sure it's nothing. I don't even know why I came in. It probably could have waited until my next physical."

"Let's get something straight right now," Debbie said, leveling her gaze on her patient and speaking with a firm voice. "We don't fool around with things like this. The longer you wait, the worse it can be. I don't care if it turns out to be a figment of your imagination. You never, ever put off seeing me if you believe you feel a lump. You got it?"

Kayla nodded, unable to speak. Debbie was a good doctor, and Kayla knew she would have made this speech to any of her patients, but she was also a good friend who knew that Ronnie, Kayla's mother, had beaten breast cancer years earlier.

"Have you been tired lately?"

"All the time, but I'm not sleeping at night. I can't seem to make my mind shut down. I assumed that's why I'm so tired all the time."

"Well, let's take a look."

Ten minutes later, Kayla dressed as Debbie gave her instructions.

"They will do a 3D mammogram followed by an ultrasound. You will know what they find immediately. They won't wait around on something like this. After we know the findings, we'll proceed from there."

"What is the likelihood that it's cancer?" Kayla asked, surprised that she could say the word without breaking down.

"We won't know until we run some tests, but Kayla, with your family history—"

"I know. I'll be prepared."

"Do you want to call your mom to go with you? She'd be a great support system. After all, she knows what you're going through."

Kayla shook her head. "No, that's okay. Until we know more, I'd rather keep this to myself."

Debbie looked at her friend. "Okay, but if there's something there, you will tell her, won't you?"

Her friend knew her well. "When the time is right," Kayla assured her. Debbie frowned.

"That's not really an answer, Kay."

"It's the only one I have right now, Debbie. Please, let's just take this one step at a time."

***

Kayla was emotionally and physically exhausted by the time she met with Dr. Swann again at noon. The mammogram and ultrasound results were returned to the office, marked 'Priority.'

"We can have the MRI scheduled for tomorrow morning."

"That's fast," Kayla said. She was shocked that, without any prior appointment, she had been able to have the mammogram and the ultrasound done immediately. Now, she was to have an MRI the following day.

"We like to work fast in these cases. We've already contacted your insurance company. My office is faxing them the paperwork so that we can get an accelerated approval and get this taken care of." Debbie tried to smile, but Kayla saw the fear in her eyes. "It helps that you have great insurance."

"One of the few good things to come from Eddie's death," Kayla sighed. "Part of the settlement was that the boys and I were able to keep his insurance for life. It's been a Godsend."

"And one you might be very grateful for over the next few months."

"It's bad, isn't it?"

"We won't know until we run more tests."

Kayla had hoped that Debbie would be more forthcoming as her friend, but she was totally in doctor mode.

"What happens after the MRI?" Kayla asked.

Debbie sighed. "Most likely, we will schedule a biopsy. You'd have to go off-island for that and for any surgery that might be necessary. But let's not get ahead of ourselves. We need to take things one step at a time. For now, I want you to go home and try to relax. Have a good dinner, and spend a nice evening with the boys. Don't let this worry you. That won't help."

"Sure, that will be a piece of cake." Kayla frowned.

"Just get through tonight. Tell yourself nothing has changed. We'll figure out what to do next after the MRI tomorrow."

Kayla agreed and headed to her car. At least she would be able to keep herself busy all afternoon. She had lost the entire morning and had hours of work still to do for the party and for all of her regular meal orders. She checked her phone and saw that she had two dinner orders for that night. Sighing, she reminded herself that this was what she wanted—her own family-dinner catering business.

She thought about her business on the drive home. The party had been an experiment, and she already knew that it would be her first and last. She loved the small-scale catering, helping other parents feed their families healthy meals on busy nights. She didn't mind last minute orders and had a strict rule that all orders had to be placed before four in the afternoon. Her clients understood, and everything ran smoothly. For the most part anyway, which was why she agreed to take on the birthday party.

Kayla's head pounded as she went over, in her mind, all the necessary details for a successful party. If the diagnosis came back the way she feared it would, she was going to have to back out. She hated to do that, but she would have no choice. Things were going to move quickly, and she had no idea how she would be feeling by the end of October. Kayla felt terribly guilty about the thought of backing out of catering the birthday party for the father of her good friend, Marian, and she hoped Marian would understand.

As she pulled into her driveway, Kayla glanced at the house next door. The truck was gone, and she assumed Zach was at the station. It occurred to her that this situation could be even worse. If Zach hadn't backed off, they might be in a relationship by now. This certainly would have presented a problem. What man wants to be in a new relationship with a woman with breast cancer? What if she needs a mastectomy? He would never look at her the same again. Zach had never been married, never gone through a pregnancy with a wife, never experienced having relations with someone over the course of many years, through childbirth, aging, weight fluctuations, and illnesses. It would most definitely be a real turnoff and undoubtedly more than he could take. She released a long sigh and closed her eyes. Zach had really dodged a bullet on that one. At least she wouldn't have to worry about how she would look naked in front of him. He was probably never going to be interested in her again.

Shaking her head, she turned off the engine and gathered her things. She was getting ahead of herself. She didn't even have a diagnosis. And once she did, she would face it the same way she had faced everything for the past six years. Alone.

***

Zach was hungry when he put the truck in park in front of his house. He looked next door and wondered what was for dinner. Not that it mattered. If he showed up at the door, Kayla would probably kick him out. Then again, if the boys were home, she'd have a hard time making him leave. He'd planned on talking to her that morning, but she left the house in a hurry, and he never had the chance. He'd chalked it up as a sign. But after the day he'd had, he felt a strong need to be in her presence.

It had been a rough one at the station. The body of a little boy, missing since August, had been found in one of the many marshy areas on nearby Assateague Island, across the Maryland and Virginia state line. His death appeared to be a homicide. Though the boy wasn't local and hadn't been missing from or found on Chincoteague, everyone at the station was taking it hard. When he was first reported missing, over a month prior, the island police had partnered with the Maryland Department of Natural Resources Police, as well as Aaron and his Coast Guard crew, to scour both islands and the surrounding waters, but the boy wasn't located. This was Zach's first time dealing with a death that hadn't occurred naturally or in combat, so he wasn't sure what the protocol was or how long it would take to know what had happened to the boy and what led to his death. The many possibilities made Zach's stomach turn.

He looked back toward the house where Kayla was raising EJ and Todd. The pain of losing one of them would be more than Zach could bear. He sat for a minute and thought about what he should do about his neighbor and her boys; then, as if his body made the decision for him, he got out of the truck and headed across the yard. Before he could change his mind, he took the steps two at a time onto the back deck and knocked on the kitchen door. As the door opened, he was hit with the aroma of marinara sauce and what he thought was shrimp or some kind of fish.

A look of surprise was quickly replaced by a steel-set jaw and accusing eyes when Kayla saw Zach standing in front of her.

"Zach, what a surprise," she said evenly. "To what do we owe this visit? Are you out of sugar or just feeling hungry?"

Zach was taken aback by the tone of her voice and the sarcasm she threw his way. That was not like Kayla.

"No, I just. Never mind. I guess it's a bad time."

Kayla took a deep breath and blinked, her expression changing to guilt as she opened the door all the way.

"I'm sorry, Zach. That was rude. It's been a, well, a hard day."

"Tell me about it," he said under his breath. "Is everything okay?" Concern filled him as he noticed the bags under her eyes and the paleness of her cheeks. He reached for her but stopped himself, not wanting to push things.

"Everything is fine," she said with a wave as she moved aside to let him in. "I'm just in over my head with work."

"Anything I can do to help?"

She pursed her lips and shook her head. "No, but thanks. I can handle it."

Zach held her gaze for a moment. Something was off, but he guessed it would be after their last conversation. Maybe coming over was a mistake after all.

"Uncle Zach!" Todd squealed when he walked into the kitchen and saw the large, former soldier, standing next to his mom. The little boy ran to Zach and threw his arms around him. "I've missed you."

"I've missed you, too, buddy. What are you up to? Homework?"

"Nah, I'm done. EJ is still working, but he always has more than me. Come see my new Lego set."

As he was pulled away by Todd's small fingers clutching his large hand, Zach sent Kayla a look of apology and thought he saw relief wash over her face. His heart dropped as he realized she was thankful that he was being led into the other room. She used to enjoy being with him, but he blew it. Now, he was pretty sure she couldn't stand the sight of him.

Zach tried to listen to Todd as the little boy showed him the new toys and chattered about the spaceship he was going to build. Zach smiled and nodded and made the appropriate sounds, but his mind was still in the kitchen. It killed him that he had hurt Kayla. He knew he needed to talk to her, but when? He didn't want an audience, and he didn't want to catch her at a bad time.

"Dinner's ready," Kayla called from the kitchen. "Everybody wash up."

Zach caught the tone in her voice, and his heart leapt a little when he realized she was including him. He followed the boys to the bathroom where they all washed their hands. EJ kept glancing at him strangely, and Zach recalled the look the boy had shot him after the argument with Kayla the other night.

"We're having paella tonight," Kayla said when they entered the room. "Zach, beer?"

"No, thanks. Tea, please."

Kayla regarded him curiously but made him a glass of iced tea. She set the glass and the sugar on the table beside his plate before taking her seat. They said the blessing before everyone passed their plates to Kayla so that she could serve them the dish from the cast iron pan she had placed on the table.

"So, Zach," EJ began after they were all eating.

Zach glanced at Kayla, and she, too, seemed to be surprised. Since he first moved in with his sister a year earlier, Zach had been 'Uncle Zach' to the boys.

"Why did you decide to come over tonight?" the boy asked. He looked at Zach with a raised brow as he took a bite of his bread.

"I've missed you guys," Zach said. "I thought I'd see what you've been up to."

EJ slowly nodded, seemingly thinking about Zach's answer. "It would have been nice if you hadn't stopped coming at all," EJ said matter-of-factly.

"EJ," Kayla scolded. "Zach is a guest in our house. Don't be rude."

"I'm not trying to be rude. I'm just telling the truth. Isn't that what you always tell us to do, mother?"

Kayla looked shocked at her son's words and the bitterness of his tone. "Edward Steven Reynolds Junior, what has gotten into you? Do you want that dinner, or would you rather go to bed hungry?"

"Eat with him or go to bed?" EJ said as he put down his fork and stared at Zach. "I think I'll go to bed." He stood and left the room as the rest of the group watched in silence.

Zach could barely swallow the mouthful of rice and shrimp. "Maybe I should go," he said as he wiped his mouth with his napkin and started to stand.

"No, you don't," Kayla said in her stern, mom voice. "Sit back down and eat your dinner. EJ made his bed. He can lie in it."

Zach obeyed and sat down, but he had lost his appetite. He picked at his food and noticed that Todd, holding back tears, did the same. After a few minutes, Kayla spoke.

"I'm sorry, Zach. I don't know what got into him."

"Mommy, can I go to bed, too? I don't feel so well."

They turned to Todd who had managed to eat some of his meal and drink about half his milk.

"Are you sure, honey?" Kayla asked.

"Yes, ma'am. I'm full."

"Okay, baby. You can go, but please put away your Legos first."

"Yes, ma'am," he said as he stood. "Mommy?"

"Yes, Todd."

"I'm sorry for being mean to you the other night before the meeting. I didn't mean to upset you."

Kayla blinked a few times before nodding. "It's okay, Todd. We're all just having a bad week."

They watched Todd leave the room and sat in silence for a few minutes. Zach wasn't sure what was going on, but he had a feeling that it all had to do with him.

"Kayla, I'm sorry if my being here, or not being here, has caused problems. I never wanted to hurt any of you."

Kayla looked weary as she placed her elbows on either side of her plate and put her head in her hands. She took a deep breath, moved her hands to cover her mouth, and stared across the room for a moment as if trying to gain her composure. Finally, she crossed her arms in front of her and looked at Zach. The dark circles were even more pronounced, and there was a profound sadness in her eyes that broke Zach's heart. Was he the cause of her pain?

"It's not you, Zach. Well, part of it is, but I can't really blame you for it. For the past few months, things have been, well, they've been nice. With Aaron enjoying married life and a child of his own, the boys lost the only father figure they've had for the past six years other than their grandfather. Then you stepped in, and," she swallowed and let out a breath. "I think they hoped that... Anyway, they hoped you'd be around for a while, and that's my fault. I should have told them from the start that someday you would meet someone and get married like Aaron did and that they shouldn't get too attached. I should have known that once you settled into your own routine, your own life, that things would change."

"Kayla, I—"

"No, it's okay. I understand. You didn't move here with the idea that you would have to be responsible for the boys or have to give up your life to be with us. I know that, but the boys are still young. They imagined things that just aren't going to happen. In time, they will get over it, but for now, maybe it's best that you not drop in unannounced."

"Kayla, you don't understand. I want to be a part of their life. Part of your life."

Zach let the words hang between them as his eyes implored her to understand. Kayla's shoulders slumped, and she looked down, shaking her head. When she looked back up at him, the sadness in her eyes wounded his soul.

"Zach, it's okay. We're family now, and I get that we're going to see each other. But you don't need to feel like you have to take care of us."

He reached over and gently rubbed her cheek. Kayla froze but didn't move. Zach could feel her intake of breath and saw the fear in her eyes. Since when was she afraid of him? Granted, he had never actually touched her like that, but... He pulled his hand away and closed his fist. He pushed his plate away and placed his elbows on the table, folding his hands in front of him.

"Kayla, I don't want to take care of you because your brother is married to my sister. I want to take care of you because I have feelings for you. I know I should have told you sooner. I screwed up, but I can do better. I had a lot of things to sort out. I still have things to sort out, things that I hope you can understand and deal with, but—"

"Zach, stop," Kayla said, shaking her head. "I can't do this. I can't take a chance that the boys will get hurt."

"The boys or you?" Zach asked, sitting back in the chair and looking at her.

"Me?" Kayla faltered. "It's the boys I'm worried about. They're so vulnerable and scared and unsure about the future." Her lips trembled, and Zach noticed the tears she blinked away.

"Kayla, I won't hurt them." He leaned over the table, trying to get closer to her. "We can take it slow. Actually, we need to take it slow. As I said, there are things you need to know."

Kayla stood and began clearing the table. "Zach, I'm sorry," she said as she turned away from him. "I - don't - want - this." The words were slow and forced, and she refused to face him as she said them, but they still cut like a knife.

"You mean, you don't want me?" Zach asked quietly.

Kayla put the dishes in the sink and gripped the counter. "I'm sorry, Zach," she said, barely above a whisper. She slowly turned and held her hands out in surrender. "I'm sorry. I just can't do this. And I think you should go."

Unable to speak, Zach stood. He fought the instinct to go to her. He wanted nothing more at the moment than to take her in his arms and hold her until she gave in to him, but he knew it was too late. He had many opportunities over the past several months to do just that, but he held back. He'd never made a move to let her know how he felt, and now that he was ready, she wanted nothing to do with him. Feeling defeated, he headed toward the door.

"After you've had a chance to think about it," he started to say as he turned the knob.

"There's nothing to think about, Zach. I'm sorry, but this is the way it has to be."

Nodding, he opened the door and stepped onto the deck. A blast of cold autumn air hit him, and he shivered. As he walked to his house, a light rain began to fall, and the wind taunted him, reminding him that summer was indeed over, and all the promise that it held had blown away with the change of seasons and the cold reality that frost was in the air.

***

EJ's light was off when Kayla went to his room. For the first time, she noticed that it smelled like a teenage boy—a mixture of sweat, dirt, and the musky scent that pre-teenaged boys emitted. EJ was only eleven, but she was reminded that he was quickly becoming a young man.

"Are you awake?" she asked quietly.

"Yeah," EJ said, his back to her.

"Mind if I come in?"

"Sure," he said. Kayla took that as 'Sure, come in' rather than 'Sure, I mind.' She sat on the bottom edge of his bed and gently rubbed his leg.

"Zach left. He felt bad for upsetting you."

"He should," EJ retorted.

"You're right. He should. He let us down, and he knows it. But I let us down, too."

EJ rolled over and looked at his mom. "How? I heard what you said to him the other night. You were right. He just left without a word. You're the only one who's always been here."

"Yes, but I should have seen what was happening. I should have known that you boys saw Zach as someone who might be able to be there for you like a dad. I should have told you not to get your hopes up, or I should have told Zach not to come around so much."

"Mom, we're okay without a dad," EJ said, sitting up. His eyes shone in the glimmering moonlight. "It's you that we're worried about."

Kayla studied her son for a moment. "What do you mean?"

"Someday, Todd and I will be all grown up. We're going to have families of our own, like Uncle Aaron and Aunt Kate. But you're going to be all alone."

Kayla closed her eyes as a tear escaped from the corner of her eye and trailed down her cheek.

"EJ, I didn't know," she bit her lips and put on a determined face. "You don't have to worry about me. I'm going to be fine. I'll always have you and Todd, no matter what. We will always be a family." The reality of her situation hit her hard, and she had to bite back a sob. Would they? For how much longer would she be there for her boys? Without a father, what would happen to them if she….

"I know, Mom, but we don't want you to be lonely. We want you to have someone to love like Aunt Kate has Uncle Aaron. Like you used to have dad." The last word was almost a whisper, and Kayla realized that EJ was holding back tears, too.

"I mean it, EJ. You don't have to worry about me. I had a wonderful once-in-a-lifetime love. Your dad and you boys are all the love I'll ever need."

"Are you sure?" EJ asked.

"I'm sure," Kayla said as she reached out to pull him into a hug. She held him tight and said a silent prayer that he would always have someone to take care of him. She pulled away and lightly wrapped him on the chin with her knuckles. "How did you get to be so grown up?"

"I don't know. I guess it had to happen sometime," he grinned.

"I guess it did," she said, marveling at how lucky she was. No matter what the future held, God had given her the most precious gifts, and she was going to do everything in her power to be with them for as long as possible.

Wholesome Lasagna
Origin: Italy

When my brother and I were younger, lasagna was one of our favorite comfort foods. My mother is Italian-American, and she loves to cook her grandmother's recipes from 'the Old Country.' Mom can cook anything, but her lasagna beats all. I remember, as a young girl, watching her make her own pasta and being mesmerized as she created the perfect long, flat noodles. Today, I sometimes make my own, but it's just as good with store-bought pasta. I think because it's the love that goes into it that truly makes it delicious. When I walk into mom's house and smell lasagna, the first thing that comes to mind is, I'm home.

From *Around the World in Eighty Meals*
by K.Z. Middleton

CHAPTER FOUR

"It looks like invasive ductal carcinoma, or IDC," Debbie told Kayla the following afternoon. "But you will need a biopsy to confirm that."

"You don't have to go through the clinical definition. I know what it is."

Debbie nodded. "The same thing your mom had."

"Only hers was small and contained, detected very early by a mammogram, and easily treated. By the look on your face, you're going to tell me that I'm not so lucky."

"I'm not sure. My hope is that IDC is the only issue we are facing." Debbie looked back at the scan on the monitor.

"But we might be facing more than that," Kayla stated.

"It's possible," Debbie agreed. "We'll need to do the biopsy to be sure, and that has to be done by an oncologist. Until then, we're going to think positively."

Kayla took a deep breath. "Okay, can you point out to me what the MRI shows?"

Debbie indicated the original mass on the MRI. "I was surprised yesterday at the size. You've been getting annual screenings for years. Normally, we detect IDC much sooner than this with a mammogram; but, as you know, you have dense breasts, and the location of the tumor is not in an easy place to see."

"What are these patches?" Kayla asked, pointing to shading around the tumor that stretched across large areas of the breast.

"The mass has spread from the milk ducts into the surrounding tissue."

"That's bad," Kayla said. "Farther along than Mom's was."

"That does seem to be the case," Debbie agreed, "but, again, we really won't know for sure until you have the biopsy."

"So, we really don't know for certain that it's cancer."

Debbie shook her head. "Not yet. We won't know until we do the biopsy."

"And my prognosis? If it is cancer?"

"I'm afraid I can't answer that. If it's not cancer now, you have a high probability that it will be at some point. But, Kay, it's important not to get ahead of ourselves."

"But what if it's already too late? What if I already have cancer?"

"We proceed the same way. You'll probably have to undergo radiation or chemotherapy in either case, which you can do here at the clinic. But, again, let's not get ahead of ourselves."

"When do we determine whether my breast has to go?"

"*We* don't. That's up to the oncologist and the pathologist. Patty is trying to set up an appointment with Dr. Zink at Hopkins. She's the best. She will know more about what will happen and how to proceed than I do."

Kayla stared at the image and tried to imagine the monster that was living inside of her, destroying her cells. It was hard to believe that just forty-eight hours ago, she was baking chocolate zucchini cupcakes for her clients and planning a birthday party for a veteran. Her thoughts were broken by a knock on the door.

"Come in," Debbie called.

"Sorry to interrupt, but Dr. Zink can see Mrs. Reynolds on Monday."

"Thanks, Patty." Debbie looked at Kayla. "It's Thursday. You'll be okay until then?"

"What choice do I have?" Kayla smiled. "I'll be fine. I have a lot to do before Monday. If Dr. Zink works half as fast as you do, I'll have many lose ends to tie up in the next four days."

***

"What do you mean you're shutting down Second Helpings? It's been wildly successful, and it's something you've wanted to do for years." Kate's reaction was exactly what Kayla expected it would be.

"I'm not shutting it down," Kayla assured her on Friday morning as they sat in Kayla's office. "I'm taking some time off."

"Now? With school back in session, the days getting shorter, sports season kicking into high gear, and a string of holidays approaching?" Kate's eyes were wide with shock as she patted Miren's back.

"I know it sounds crazy," Kayla tried to reason with her, knowing there was really no good way to explain why she was taking a hiatus. "I'm just feeling overwhelmed right now. I think it's too much too soon."

She watched Kate as the new mother scrutinized her. Kayla knew she looked awful. She hadn't slept well in weeks, and the events of the past 48 hours hadn't helped. She felt as if she'd been hit by a train. Her body was betraying her in more ways than one, and her mind was having a hard time dealing with everything. Having an infant, Kate would be a expert at recognizing the signs of sleepless nights, unbearable stress, and the worry that comes with having children.

Kate shook her head. "There's more going on here than you're letting on. You do look tired and worried, but I know you've handled worse. You're not going to convince me that you're overwhelmed by the success of your business." Kate narrowed her eyes as she looked at her sister-in-law. "What are you not telling me?"

Kayla bit her lips together and thought about the ramifications of telling Kate the truth. Kate would be bound to tell Aaron. They had no secrets from each other. Aaron would tell their parents, knowing how upset they would be if left in the dark. Eventually, Zach would find out, and Kayla would never be able to stand him looking at her with pity. Taking a deep breath, she sighed and shook her head. She was not ready for all that.

"Please, Kate, trust me on this. It's for the best that I take a break for a bit. The boys are having a hard time adjusting to things right now. They're at that age when boys need a father, and I have to figure out how I can be both mom and dad to them." Kayla's voice caught at the thought that the boys might soon need both a mom and a dad, but she pushed the thought away.

The two women stared at each other for several seconds. Kayla was afraid Kate would find some chink in her armor, but Kate blinked once and sighed. She took the sleeping baby from her shoulder and cradled her in her lap before shaking her head.

"You're lying to me, Kay. I don't know why, and I won't press you about it for now. I'm sure you have your reasons, but you need to remember this..."

Kate leveled her gaze on Kayla and set her jaw in that determined way she had.

"Your family is here, including me, for whatever you need. You'd be a fool to not look to us for help. I know you're strong, and you've been through a lot, but so have I. So have Aaron and your mom. And, for that matter, so has Zach. There comes a time in life when you need to lean on those who love you. You taught me that, you and Aaron and Zach. Don't shut yourself off from us just because you feel like there's something you need to handle on your own. Whatever it is, we're all here to help."

Kayla fought back the tears as Kate's words echoed in her mind. Nodding slowly, Kayla offered a wary smile.

"Thank you, Kate. You have no idea how much that means to me. Believe me, when the time comes, I'm going to take you up on your offer. For now, I have some things to think about. Please, give me a little time."

"Okay," Kate gave in. "But don't wait too long, or I will find a way to pry it out of you."

Kayla laughed. She had no doubt that was true.

"My goodness," Kate said with a sigh. "Between trying to keep up with whatever you're hiding, Zach's constant moodiness, a teething baby, and almost daily updates from Megan, I'm beginning to feel like I majored in the wrong thing. I should have studied psychology."

Kayla laughed. "At least you're never bored."

"You can say that again," Kate agreed.

"How's Megan?"

"I finally got her to admit what's going on. This guy, Brad, who used to work in our office, just got promoted. He's now her boss. Figures. Megan has been there since she graduated, and he was hired right before I left. Anyway, he's been making passes at her, telling her that he will help her get a promotion if she goes out with him, things like that. I told her she needs to go to HR immediately."

"Is she going to?"

"I don't know," Kate said, shaking her head. "She says she's afraid she'll lose her job if she does."

"All the more reason to go," Kayla said.

"I completely agree. And if she does lose her job, she's better off."

"Sure, she is, but isn't that the real issue these days? *He* should be losing his job, not Megan."

"I couldn't agree more," Kate said.

***

Zach went through the motions at work on Friday, but neither his heart nor his mind was in it. As if a movie was playing on a constant loop in his brain, he envisioned the scene in the kitchen with Kayla, repeatedly throughout the day. She had been both vulnerable and rigid at the same time. He could see her back to him as she gripped the counter and told him to leave her alone. She was cold and distant, but he had seen pain and longing in her eyes before she turned away from him.

Zach's sandwich lay on the table in front of him, uneaten. Police officers roamed in and out of the lunchroom, but the mood was somber. Little Ryan Graham's death had been ruled a homicide. There were no suspects and no clues. One minute, the six-year-old was playing on the beach, his parents nearby; and the next, he was gone. It was thought, at the time, that he wandered too close to the ocean and was caught in the riptide, but the Coast Guard searched for hours to no avail. Eventually, the family left the island and returned home to Western Maryland, but Ryan's parents continued to visit the area every weekend, searching for their son. His photo was nailed to every telephone pole on the island. Zach couldn't imagine what the family was going through now.

Nobody was in the mood to talk. The sound of silence was deafening in the lunchroom, affording Zach the opportunity, or rather, the misfortune, to become lost in his thoughts. Zach closed his eyes and again saw the look in Kayla's eyes when he told her he had feelings for her.

Why the sudden change? Sure, he had hurt her, but she was a forgiving person. Why couldn't she forgive him?

Zach bolted upright in the chair. Had she learned the truth? Had Kate told her about his past? No, she wouldn't have. He had barely told her about it. Aaron? Zach shook his head. No, he didn't believe Aaron would say anything. There was a code within the military. They guarded each other's secrets and watched each other's backs. Zach couldn't imagine that Aaron would have told Kayla about his past.

Completely unaware of his motions, Zach swept up his entire lunch and threw it away before heading back to the classroom where a small group of new recruits were waiting for him. By the time the lesson was finished, Zach couldn't even remember what he had taught them.

He went straight to his boss's office to talk to him. Zach hadn't been happy at the station, and his desire to work on his relationship with Kayla, despite her dismissal of his feelings, had him thinking that he needed to make a change. His boss wasn't thrilled when Zach gave his notice, but he knew that Zach's position with the department had always been a temporary one.

Zach drove back to his house in a daze, trying to surmise how Kayla could have come upon the sordid details of his deployment. On the drive, Zach called Kate.

"Hey, sis, question for you."

"Hey, yourself, what's up?"

"Do you have any idea what's going on with Kayla?"

Her silence told him that she knew something.

"Come on, Kate, please. What's going on?"

"I honestly don't know, Zach. No lie. I've tried to get it out of her myself."

At least that answered his unspoken question. Kate had not told Kayla about his past.

"She won't talk to me, won't listen to me, and practically kicked me out of the house the other night."

"What night? Why were you there at night?"

"It was dinnertime. I wanted to talk to her, to tell her…heck, it doesn't matter. I just wanted to tell her I was sorry. But she told me she wasn't interested in talking to me and wants nothing to do with me. I know I was a jerk. I let her down, but she won't even let me apologize."

"She did tell me a little bit about that," Kate said without elaborating.

"What did she say?" Zach asked eagerly.

"I can't tell you, Zach. Just like I won't tell her that you called me and asked about her. Please don't ask me to betray her confidence."

You gotta love sisters, Zach thought. *They know how to lay on the guilt.*

"Fine, I won't go there. But please let me know if you think of something I can do to help. There's something wrong, and I don't know what it is."

"I'm right there with you, Zach. I think we just have to let Kayla come clean in her own time."

Zach thanked Kate and told her goodbye as he pulled into his driveway. He hated what she had to say, but he knew she was right.

He spent all day Saturday painting the spare bedroom. He wasn't sure what he would use it for. He didn't need an office, but he might need a guest room. Nothing had been confirmed, but he had a friend looking for a place to stay. Otherwise, working on the room was just a way to keep busy. At the age of thirty-six, one would think he'd know what he wanted to do with his life, but he had no idea. He always thought he would spend the majority of his adulthood in the Army, but that was before he was tagged to be among the elite soldiers whose sole duty was to take out the most heinous bad guys one at a time.

After Mass on Sunday, Zach took a run on the beach. A light mist was in the air, and he could sense the rain heading in off the coast. He spent the afternoon working in the spare room before cleaning up and grabbing his keys to run into town and pick up something for dinner. As he left the house, his phone buzzed. Hopeful that the message was from Kayla, he reached into his pocket and took out the cell. He read the text from his friend, Nick, crestfallen that it wasn't Kayla, and put the phone back in his pocket, vowing to answer his friend later.

As Zach climbed into his truck, he noticed that Kayla's car was missing from the driveway next door and hit himself on his forehead with his palm. It was Sunday. That meant dinner with the family. How could he have forgotten? Kate had texted him the day before, saying she expected him to be there. And though he was sure his was the last face Kayla wanted to see at the table, he had promised his sister he would attend. He wondered if Kayla might reveal whatever was going on with her.

Zach put the truck in reverse and backed out of the driveway, taking the island roads faster than he should have but feeling guilty that he was most likely holding up their family dinner. As he pulled into the driveway that circled in front of Ronnie and Trevor's house, he readied himself for seeing Kayla. With the other night's events so intensely burned on his brain, he knew he should have bowed out of dinner at Kayla's childhood home, but, as Kate reminded him, he hadn't seen his sister or the baby in a week, and he was looking forward to some family time. He missed his own parents and was grateful that Kate's in-laws had so graciously welcomed him into the family.

"Uncle Zach," Todd yelled when Zach walked into the house. Zach planted his feet and held steady, prepared for the little boy to slam himself into Zach's legs. His heart melted every time Todd hugged him or grabbed hold of his hand. Zach smiled to himself at the thought that even the deadliest soldier could become a puddle of jelly in the presence of a loving child.

"Hey, buddy," Zach said. "Where is everyone?"

The living room floor was covered with Legos. EJ sat on the couch, mesmerized by the Redskins game. None of the adults could be seen, but Zach heard Ronnie's laughter coming from the kitchen.

"They're all watching the game and talking in the kitchen. Booooring," Todd said.

Zach smiled and waved to EJ. "Who's winning?" he asked.

"Tied," was all EJ said, and Zach wondered if EJ was still upset with him. Not wanting to push it, Zach left the boys alone and wandered to the back of the house.

"Zach, welcome," Ronnie said, rushing to him and giving him a hug and a kiss on the cheek. "I'm so happy you came."

"Thank you for including me," he said, handing her a bottle of wine that he had thrown in his truck that morning before he lost track of what day it was. He caught Kayla's eye, but she quickly turned away and busied herself with taking her niece, Miren, from Kate.

"That's so sweet of you Zach. Thank you," Ronnie said, taking the wine as if Zach didn't bring her a bottle each time he came to dinner.

Zach shook hands with Trevor, Kayla's father, and the two fell into an easy conversation about the goings on at the police station. Zach maintained the dialogue while taking quick peeks at Kayla as often as he could manage without being conspicuous. At least, he thought that was the case, until he saw his sister watching him and knew she was on to him.

"Hey, everyone," Aaron said as he walked into the room in his crisp, white Coast Guard uniform. He went straight to Kate and gave her a hug and kiss before taking Miren from Kayla. Zach watched Aaron's face light up as he took the baby in his arms and wondered what it would be like to have a child of his own. His stomach lurched at the thought, and he instinctively glanced at Kayla. As if reading his mind, she blinked and looked away. Was it his imagination, or did her eyes glisten with tears?

"Sorry I'm late. I was meeting with your boss and some guys from Maryland DNR," he said to Zach, "about Ryan Graham. We're cross-checking everything we did that day, trying to figure out what we missed and how the boy disappeared. We don't know if he wandered off and was taken by someone, or if he was snatched right from the beach where he was playing." He looked lovingly at the little girl in his arms. "I can't imagine what I'd do if some monster did to Miren what that guy did to—"

"Now that Aaron is here, we can eat," Ronnie interrupted, sending a harsh look toward her son. "And talk about happier things." She opened the oven, releasing the tantalizing scent of homemade, Sicilian-style lasagna—her signature recipe and a family favorite. Kate told him it was the same recipe that Kayla used for Second Helpings.

Wanting to make sure Kayla was comfortable, Zach waited until everyone else took a seat around the dining room table before choosing his own. He ended up on the far opposite side of the table from Kayla, on the corner next to Todd and by Trevor, who was at the end. Holding hands, they bowed their heads and said grace before digging into the meal.

Conversation floated around Zach, and he participated as necessary, but his attention kept diverting to Kayla. She answered when spoken to, smiled now and then at what was being said, and admonished Todd for talking with his mouth full; but she was not herself. She contributed very little to the table chatter, and her smile was forced. She pushed her food around her plate and told her mother how good it was, but Zach didn't actually see her take more than a few bites. His heart ached at the thought that his presence was the cause of her pain, or perhaps it was the news about the little boy; he had no way of knowing. But as he pondered Kayla's distant gaze and the slump of her shoulders, he began to wonder if something else was wrong.

"So, Kayla, what's this nonsense Kate told me about you shutting down your business?" Aaron asked as Ronnie and the boys cleared the dinner dishes. Ronnie stopped and looked at her daughter.

"You're shutting down Second Helpings? Why?"

Kayla's cheeks turned red, and she looked toward Kate, her eyes pleading for help.

"I told you, Aaron," Kate said sternly, "Kayla needs to take care of some personal matters."

"What's so personal that she can't discuss it at the family dinner table?" Trevor asked.

"Is something wrong?" Ronnie asked, and Zach wondered if she, too, noticed Kayla's detachment that evening and the hollowed look around her eyes.

"Of course not," Kayla said, but she refused to meet her mother's gaze as she fiddled with the napkin in her lap. "The boys and I have some things we are working out, and I thought it would be best to give them my full attention."

Zach's already piqued curiosity ratcheted up even higher. Did this have anything to do with the way EJ had treated him at dinner last week? Was Kayla being forced to shut down the business she had worked so hard to build because he had unwittingly played with her boys' emotions? He swallowed the lump in his throat as he watched her.

"What are you working out that we can't help with?" her father asked. "You know we'll do whatever you need."

"I know, dad, and I appreciate it. I just need some time to figure out how to handle some things."

Silence filled the room like an unwelcome intruder. Zach felt the tension caused by unanswered questions and familial concern. He wished there was something he could say or do to relieve Kayla of her obvious discomfort, but he knew that anything he said or did would be an invasion in her eyes. He desperately wanted to help and looked toward his sister, hoping she could read his thoughts. As usual, they were in sync, and she cast a knowing glance his way before speaking.

"I'm sure Kayla will let us all help if she needs it," Kate said, reaching over and laying her hand on Kayla's. "I've already assured her that I will update the website to let everyone know we're not taking orders for the time being. When she's ready, we'll start things back up, and everything will run just as smooth as pie."

"Speaking of which," Kayla said, with relief in her voice. "I baked a sweet potato pie and made homemade whipped cream for dessert. EJ, do you want to grab the pie and whipped cream while I get the plates?"

"We'll get it all, Mom," EJ said. "You can sit and take it easy. Come on, Uncle Zach."

Surprised at being included, it took Zach a moment to realize EJ wanted him to go with him into the kitchen. He placed his napkin by his plate and stood without looking at Kayla.

In a marked turnabout from a few nights before, EJ was overly friendly toward Zach as they gathered the pie, whipped cream, and dessert plates in Ronnie's kitchen. The boy chatted about school and soccer, and Zach was cautiously optimistic that whatever animosity had built up between them was now replaced with a mutual sense of concern for Kayla.

"I'm sorry about the other night," EJ said before they went back to the dining room. "I was rude, and I shouldn't have talked to you like that." The young man blushed and looked away.

"It's okay, EJ. I deserved it."

EJ bit his lips and turned back toward Zach, who observed the boy-becoming-a-man with curiosity.

"You do like my mom, don't you? I mean, *like* like her?"

Zach took a deep breath. "It's complicated, EJ. Your mom and me. I think she has some things going on that she needs to figure out before we can begin talking about whether I *like* like her."

EJ nodded. "Yeah, I think so, too." EJ looked Zach directly in the eye. "But don't give up on her. I don't know what's bothering her, but I'm not a kid anymore. There's something going on, and I think she needs you to help her through it."

"I'll keep that in mind," Zach told him. "Now, let's get back in there before Uncle Aaron sends a rescue crew to find us."

Zach plastered on a smile as he followed EJ back into the dining room. He kept his eyes from straying to Kayla as they served dessert, and he averted his gaze as he ate the pie. The least he could do was honor her wishes. Whatever was going on with her, she made it clear that she didn't need or want his help.

Autumn Squash Soup
Origin: Northern Africa

One of my favorite restaurants serves an autumn squash soup that is almost heavenly, but I always thought it was missing something. I played with the recipe until it was prefect. I think that's what I like the best about cooking. All it takes is a tweak here or a pinch there, and you've got a whole new flavor. It's a great metaphor for life. If you don't like the way something tastes, make an adjustment, add something, take something out, but don't just sit back and accept that this is as good as it will ever get. Find a way to make it your own.

From *Around the World in Eighty Meals*
by K.Z. Middleton

CHAPTER FIVE

Zach thought back to the night before as he jogged along the trail in the early morning light. The smell of salt was heavy in the crisp, fall air as the breeze blew in from the nearby Chincoteague Bay that emptied into the Atlantic Ocean. The sun and air felt good on his face, and he sucked in the fresh, clean scent, thankful it wasn't desert sand.

Zach could still picture the grin on EJ's face and the worry in his eyes. Interesting, how kids always seem to know more than adults think they do.

Perceptive little rascals, Zach thought.

So, what was going on with Kayla? And how could he get her to open up to him? She'd made it clear that she didn't want him around and wasn't going to even entertain the notion of confiding in him or resuming their summertime family-like closeness.

Zach had a thought. Perhaps… He stopped jogging and looked up to the sky above the trees surrounding the trail. Yes, he might have an idea that could begin to break the ice. He just had to formulate a plan and put it into action.

As he drove home, he thought about the right way to approach Kayla, but his thoughts were interrupted by a call from his sister. It was too early for a social call, and he wondered what was going on now.

***

Kayla nervously fumbled with her keys as she attempted to start the car. She had managed to get an appointment with Dr. Zink that allowed her to leave as soon as the boys left for school, but the three-and-a-half-hour drive to Baltimore meant that she wouldn't be back when they got home. She had arranged for Kate to be at the house, though it wasn't easy to get Kate to agree without telling her the truth. Kayla promised to tell her everything once she got home.

Kayla nearly jumped through the windshield when the knock on her window startled her out of her thoughts. She looked out and saw Zach standing by the car. Taking a deep breath, she steeled herself for an encounter that she didn't have the time or the desire to deal with. She rolled down the window and shook her head.

"Look, Zach, I don't have time for—"

"Get out," he said as if he was commanding a subordinate.

"Excuse me?" she asked, her blood beginning to boil. Who did he think he was?

"Please," he added softly.

"Zach, I can't do this right now. I need to be somewhere."

"I know. I'm driving."

Exasperated, Kayla shook her head in protest. "No, you're not. I don't know where you got that idea from, but I am perfectly capable of driving myself."

"My sister seems to think otherwise."

"Kate doesn't know what she's talking about. I am fine to drive, and if I don't leave now, I'm going to be late."

"Late to something that is taking you off the island for the entire day. Something that is so important, you won't be here to get the boys after school or make them dinner. It sounds like you're going to be traveling quite the distance."

"Oh, for Heaven's sake. I'm just going shopping. Up to Rehoboth. It's too far to make it back in time to get the boys."

"Not unless you're planning one heckuva shopping spree. And since when do you go all the way up there on a shopping trip alone? Isn't that the kind of thing where you take a girlfriend with you?"

"I couldn't get anyone to go, if you must know. Tammi, Shannon, and Debbie are all working. Marian is busy planning her father's party, and Kate has the baby. Really, Zach, I need to go."

Kayla looked at her watch and began to panic. She didn't need this right now.

"Uh-huh. Late for shopping? If you're so worried about being late, then either move over, or get out and get into my truck. You're wasting time. I'm not leaving."

Kayla slumped in defeat. She supposed she should get used to counting on other people. And the truth was, after today, she would have to come clean to everyone anyway. She just wished it wasn't Zach on whom she was relying at the moment. She grabbed her purse, the file from Debbie's office containing her radiology results and referral, and her phone.

"Fine, but I'm not happy about this."

Zach didn't respond, but as he laid his hand protectively on the small of her back to lead her to his truck, Kayla sensed the tension in his body. He didn't want to do this anymore than she wanted him to. Good. Maybe they wouldn't have to talk to each other on the ride. Oh, gosh, she thought, the seven-hour, round-trip drive.

***

"Mind telling me where we're really going and what time we need to be there?" Zach asked as they neared the highway on the mainland. He was nervous. This was the first time in weeks they would spend more than a few minutes together, and Zach wasn't sure what to say to her.

Kayla bit her lips and closed her eyes. Zach glanced over, and his heart constricted. Whatever she was about to tell him, he sensed, was not going to be good. It made him feel even more on edge.

"Hopkins, noon," she said quietly.

Zach thought he heard wrong and furrowed his brow as he tried to figure out what she had said.

"Say again?"

Taking a deep breath, Kayla looked toward him. "Johns Hopkins," she said a little louder. "The hospital. In Baltimore."

"I know where it is," Zach said calmly. He gripped the wheel and willed his heart to slow down. Her words cut him like a knife. "Why?" he asked, noticing the tremble in his own voice. "What's going on?"

"We'll find out soon," Kayla said. She turned toward the passenger window, and Zach gave her time with her thoughts. He needed her to say more, but he would give her the time to find the words.

After several minutes, she spoke. "Several years ago, my mom had breast cancer, invasive ductal carcinoma, or IDC."

His mouth went dry, and he tried to concentrate on the road as he listened to her speak.

"It's the most common type of breast cancer. Hers wasn't too bad. They removed the cancer, and she had radiation. She's been cured for a few years now."

"I didn't know that," Zach said quietly, still gripping the wheel so tightly that his fingers turned white.

"It was right after Eddie was killed. I was a mess, but it was all over so fast, and she was okay, and we all put it behind us." She turned toward the window again, and Zach noticed her playing with the wedding band she now wore on her right hand. "I always knew there was a chance that I could get it." She turned back toward him. "It's hereditary, you know."

Zach nodded as if he did know and loosened his grip, flexing his fingers a few times to allow the blood to flow back through his hands as he fought the need to pull over the truck and hold her. He already knew what was coming, and he dreaded hearing her say the words.

"How long have you known?" he asked.

Startled by the question, Kayla blinked.

"Since last week."

His heart lurched. Last week, and she already had an appointment at Hopkins? What did that mean?

"Why Hopkins?" he asked, hoping he sounded more curious than worried.

"Debbie, I mean Dr. Swann, wanted me to be seen by the best oncologist in the area. I'm seeing Dr. Zink at Hopkins. Today is a consultation. I've already had a mammogram, an ultrasound, and an MRI."

"And they're conclusive?"

"Well, no. I need a biopsy for that. But it's complicated because of where," her voice caught, and she swallowed. "Because of where it is."

"What do you mean?" he asked, unconcerned about whether she thought he was prying.

"It's in a hard-to-see place, and it appears that it may have," she looked away. "It may have spread from the ducts to the surrounding tissue."

Glancing at Kayla, Zach saw her blink a few times before she reached up and wiped her cheek.

As she moved her hand back toward her lap, Zach reached for her. He grasped her hand and squeezed it.

"It's going to be okay," he tried to assure her. "We'll make it through this."

***

Kayla swallowed and bit back tears. She fought the impulse to pull away from Zach, but his hand felt so sturdy. She could feel his strength flowing into her trembling hand. Rather than fight it, she laid her head back and closed her eyes, enjoying the temporary feeling of peace that his assurances gave her.

When Kayla opened her eyes, they were pulling into the parking garage. Her empty hand felt cold without the warmth of Zach's hand, but she felt rested for the first time in days.

"We're here," Zach said. "And we've got a little bit of time to spare if you're hungry."

"No, thanks. I haven't had much of an appetite lately," Kayla said as she reached into her purse for a breath mint. She smoothed her hair with her hand and readied herself to meet Dr. Zink.

"Okay, we can eat after the appointment. And I do mean 'we.' I'm sure the doctor will tell you that it's important to keep up your strength."

Kayla managed a small smile. "I'm sure you're right," she said as he parked the car.

Twenty minutes later, Kayla thumbed through a magazine as she waited to be called into the exam room. She checked her watch and hoped that the appointment wouldn't take too long. Zach sat beside her, furiously working his fingers on his phone.

"What are you doing?" Kayla asked.

"Texting a buddy in Afghanistan who's getting ready to be discharged from the Marines. Our paths crossed a few times over the years, and we became friends. He's the one who got me going back to church. He's trying to figure out what to do with his life, but I'm no help. I don't know what I'm doing with my own life."

"What's that mean? Don't you like your job?"

Zach shrugged but didn't have the chance to answer.

"Kayla Reynolds?" a nurse called from the doorway across the room.

"I guess that's me," Kayla said, trying to smile.

"Should I wait here?" Zach asked.

"Yes, please," Kayla said, wondering if she was more nervous about the consultation or about Zach being there with her. Definitely more nervous about Zach, she decided. She was petrified about the consultation.

***

Zach jumped up from the chair when Kayla walked into the waiting room. His eyes and throat burned from the odor of medicines, antiseptics, and bleach. Real or imagined, the mingled scents caused him to feel queasy. Or perhaps it was just the look on Kayla's face.

"Well, what did she say?" he asked nervously.

"Hold on," Kayla said. She went to the window and waited to be acknowledged by the woman at the desk.

"Okay, I see that Dr. Zink wants to schedule a biopsy. Is there a day or time that's best for you?"

Zach waited anxiously for Kayla to answer, but she seemed unsure as to what to say.

"Um, Dr. Zink said that I should have someone with me, so I need to find someone—"

"Any day or time is fine," Zach said. "I can have her here whenever you have an opening."

Kayla turned to Zach, but he held up his hand.

"No arguing. Just make the appointment."

"I, uh, I guess I'll take the first opening you have."

"She usually does biopsies on Tuesdays, but she's booked for several weeks. Oh, wait, there's been a cancellation for next Tuesday. 9AM?" the receptionist asked, looking up at Kayla.

Kayla gripped the counter, and Zach noticed her body sag. Another week. He could almost read her thoughts.

"We'll take it," he said.

"But it's so early. What about the boys?"

"Kate and Aaron will help. Or your mom or dad can worry about them." He wasn't taking no for an answer. He looked at the receptionist. "She'll take it."

"Okay," she said, entering the information into the computer. "Here's a reminder. No aspirin for the next seven days. Are you on any type of blood-thinning medication?" she asked, looking at Kayla's chart.

"No, I don't take any medications at all."

Zach heard the catch in her voice and realized how surreal this must be to Kayla—a mother in her thirties with no visible health problems whose life had been turned upside down in a matter of days.

"Okay, please be here at least thirty minutes early. Wear comfortable clothes as you may be sore afterward."

"How long before she has answers?" Zach asked.

"A couple days to a week. Once it goes to the pathologist, it's out of our hands." The woman smiled sympathetically. "But don't worry. We'll take good care of your wife."

Zach saw Kayla wince and wrapped his arm protectively around her waist.

"Thank you," he said as he led her away. "We'll see you next week."

In that moment, Zach pushed aside all thoughts about his past and what affect the truth about his former life might have on Kayla. She was going to need all the help she could get, and Zach wasn't going to back out now.

***

Kayla managed to make it all the way home without crying, but the second she walked into the open arms of her mother, she burst into tears.

"Hush, baby, it's okay," Ronnie said, smoothing Kayla's hair.

"What are you all doing here?" Kayla asked when she looked up and saw her brother and father were with her mother and Kate.

The boys were nowhere to be seen, and she assumed they had been tucked into bed. It was late. Zach had insisted they stop for dinner on the way home, and then a heavy rain began its assault on the coast; and topping it off, there was an accident before the Chesapeake Bay Bridge. Kayla was exhausted.

"Zach texted Kate and told her that he thought we should be here when you got home. What's going on, Kayla?"

"Did he tell you?" Kayla looked at Zach, but he just shrugged.

"No, but he said it was important."

Kayla inhaled and closed her eyes. She could hear the rain, falling in sheets on the roof. "I think we should all sit down."

She moved to the couch, and Ronnie took the seat beside her. Aaron sat in an armchair, and Kate perched on the arm of the chair, Miren's bouncy seat beside her. Trevor lowered himself onto the loveseat, but Zach stood against the wall, never taking his eyes from Kayla.

"I went to see Debbie last week," she began. "I found a, a lump." Ronnie gasped, and Kayla continued. "She did the normal tests and then sent me to Hopkins to see a Dr. Zink, whom she feels is the best in the area."

"And?" Ronnie asked anxiously.

"I have a biopsy next Tuesday."

"I'll go with you," Ronnie said. "You can all stay the night at the house, and your father can get the boys to school that morning. Or we can stay here. Whatever is easiest for you."

Kayla smiled. "Thank you, Mom. I appreciate it."

"What's the prognosis?" Trevor asked.

"We don't know yet," Kayla looked at her dad. "I may or may not lose my breast. Maybe both." There was no embarrassment or unease when she spoke to her father. Their family had been down this road before.

"Kay, I'm so sorry," Kate said.

"Thanks, but it's okay. I've had a lot of time to process this, and, well, whatever happens, I'm ready. I won't go down without a fight." She tried to put on a brave face and hoped they didn't see through her. As she looked around the room, she thought that she had everyone fooled. Until her eyes landed on Zach. He saw right through her, and she shivered at the realization.

***

"How are you doing?" Debbie asked, taking a bite of her Reuben.

She and Kayla met at the Island Deli for lunch in between patients. It was hard for them to squeeze in the time to see each other. Debbie was a well-loved physician, and her schedule was always full. She had two daughters, both older than Kayla's boys, so they rarely saw each other at school or scouting or sporting events, which were the only 'social' events Kayla ever got to attend.

"I'm okay," Kayla said. She sipped a spoonful of autumn squash soup and smiled. She had always enjoyed the soup, but it was never quite right. After some experimenting, Kayla came up with the perfect recipe. She presented her soup to the restaurant's owner, Jane, and they had been serving Kayla's version ever since.

"How was the consultation?"

"It was good. I like Dr. Zink a lot."

"And emotionally, how are you feeling?"

Kayla put down her spoon and wiped her mouth.

"Debbie, I love you, and I appreciate your concern, but we're not at the office. We can talk about other things."

Her friend smiled.

"You're right. Sorry. Force of habit. How are the boys?"

"They're good. Soccer is in full swing, so that keeps them busy."

Debbie stopped chewing and looked at Kayla. She swallowed before taking a sip of her drink.

"You haven't told them, have you?"

"Not yet," Kayla shook her head. "But I did tell the rest of the family."

"That's good to hear. I hoped you would."

"Well, I didn't really have a choice. Zach made me tell them."

Debbie raised her brow. "Zach? Is he still in the picture?"

"What's that supposed to mean?" Kayla took a bite of her dinner roll and sat back.

Surveying her friend, Debbie shrugged. "Oh, I don't know. You spent the whole summer with a ruggedly handsome, single man who seems to adore your kids. He ate dinner with you regularly and went to church with you. He was joining you at your mother's house for dinner every Sunday."

Kayla interrupted, "He's Kate's brother. Of course, he joins us for dinner."

"Joins. So, he still attends?"

"Of course, he still attends. What's your point?"

"You know exactly what my point is. Is there something going on between the two of you? You used to confide in me about all of your love interests."

"When we were in middle and high school," Kayla declared. "We're adults now."

"All the more reason to tell. Love is so much more interesting as an adult." Debbie smiled, and her blue eyes sparkled. "So, tell."

Kayla sighed. "There honestly isn't anything to tell. He's still in the picture, but as a friend."

"Nothing else?"

"Nothing else. I can't even think about more right now."

"Maybe you should," Debbie said, before finishing off her sandwich. "Pretty soon, all of the other single women in town are going to start thinking he's available."

"He's theirs for the taking," Kayla said with a shrug.

"Kayla, I've known you our entire lives. That man is no more available than your father is."

Shabbat Chicken
Origin: Israel

Nobody ever thinks of roasted chicken as anything special, but those of the Jewish religion know that roasted chicken has been a staple of the Shabbat meal for generations. The recipe is easily adapted for each season, allowing fresh vegetables to be used no matter the time of year. My favorite veggies to cook with the chicken are green beans and potatoes. There is just something about that combination that says warmth on a cold night and welcome home to all who enter the house to the fragrance of love, faith, and togetherness.

From *Around the World in Eighty Meals*
by K.Z. Middleton

CHAPTER SIX

"Uncle Zach!" Todd's squeals rang from the kitchen.

Kayla had just finished her accounting for the past two weeks and was on her way to make dinner. She smiled when she walked into the room and saw the grown man and little boy attempting to hide the cookies in their hands.

"Snack time?" she asked with a knowing smile.

"They're supposed to be for dessert, but Todd thought we should check them first to make sure they're edible."

"Oh, is that right?" she said to Zach. "And are they?" she asked Todd.

Todd grinned, his chocolate-stained teeth giving away his crime as much as the cookie in his hand. "Uh-huh. They're really good," he said with a mouthful of half-chewed cookie.

"Okay, no more until after dinner. Now, get in the other room and finish your homework."

Kayla and Zach watched Todd leave the room. As Kayla turned back toward their visitor, she saw him pop the last bite of his cookie into his mouth. He grinned, too, but managed to keep his mouth closed.

"Who are they from this time?"

"Shannon dropped them off at the Coast Guard station. She didn't want to bother you and asked if Aaron would deliver them, but there's a missing fishing boat, so he texted me to come by and pick them up."

"Which you happily did since it gave you another excuse to drop by at dinnertime?" She eyed him skeptically, but she couldn't squelch her smile.

Zach had stopped by every night for the past three nights just before dinner and had stayed for the meal. It felt like summer all over again, only this time, Kayla was much more guarded with her feelings. Summer break was long over, so she had an easy excuse to send him home after dinner. No more cozy nights playing games or watching TV or talking into the late hours of the night. She hoped that she was making it clear that she appreciated his attentiveness but was not interested in anything more. No matter how much she wanted him to stay.

"I hope you don't mind. I just figured you're so used to cooking dinner for a large number that you could use help eating all the food since you're not delivering to families right now."

"And you don't think I know how to cook for just three people?" She walked to the counter and put the cookies in the cookie jar before opening the refrigerator and taking out a package of chicken thighs. "Or are you just checking up on me?"

"Guilty as charged," Zach admitted. "I am your brother-in-law. I owe it to my sister to make sure you're okay."

"Oh, really," she said as she rinsed and patted the chicken. "I talk to Kate several times a day. I think she knows that I'm doing perfectly fine."

Zach took off his jacket and hung it on the rack by the door. He opened the fridge and took out the bag of green beans, holding it up for Kayla to see. She rolled her eyes and nodded.

"Okay, maybe I just wanted to see for myself that you're doing perfectly fine."

Kayla watched as he rinsed the beans and began snapping off the ends. Kate told her that Zach was an amazing cook, and Kayla enjoyed watching him in the kitchen.

"I am, you know. I spent a week worrying, and now I'm resigned to just finding out what's going on and tackling it head-on."

Zach stopped snapping beans and looked at her. "It's okay to be scared, you know. You can lean on us for support. You aren't Wonder Woman."

"I'm not?" She feigned surprise. "How do you know I'm not hiding golden bracelets and a lasso of truth in the closet?"

"I'd like to see that lasso," Zach said in a low voice.

Kayla gasped and blushed, looking away quickly. She hadn't meant to flirt or send off any signals, but she had caught the look in his eyes and knew he was thinking about that lasso and Wonder Woman's famous stars and stripes outfit.

Kayla nervously fetched a casserole dish, coated it with olive oil, and arranged the chicken inside.

"As you can see, dinner's going to be a little late tonight. The boys had soccer practice after school, and I just finished some paperwork. I'm trying to get everything wrapped up before Tuesday, and I don't want to spend the whole weekend working. Anyway, we understand if you can't stay." She avoided looking at him but felt his stare as she checked his progress on the beans.

"I'm sorry, Kayla. I shouldn't have said what I said."

"What?" she asked, feeling the heat in her cheeks while still refusing to look his way.

Zach took hold of her arm and gently turned her toward him.

"I mean it. I'm sorry. For everything. I was a jerk, and when I showed up out of the blue to tell you how I feel, the timing was wrong."

She started to protest, but he put his finger on her lips. They tingled at his touch, and her stomach dropped.

"You've got a lot going on right now, I get it. It's okay. I'm here to help you and give you support. I'm not asking for anything. I'm only here to give. Tell me what you need, and I'll make it happen. No pressure, no strings, just me helping you. Nothing more."

Kayla stared into his eyes, felt his hand on her arm, tasted his skin on her lips. She blinked and nodded.

"Thank you," she whispered. When the unbidden tear escaped from her eye, she held her breath as he gently wiped it away.

"I mean it, Kayla. I'm here for you. Always."

***

EJ cleared his throat from the doorway, and Zach quickly let go of Kayla's arm.

"Are you staying for dinner, Uncle Zach?" EJ asked, looking at him with interest.

"If that's okay with you and your mom." He looked at Kayla who squeezed by him and picked up the beans he had finished snapping.

"I'm okay with it." She turned to her son. "EJ?"

The boy thought about it for a moment. "Sure, that's okay with me." He stared at Zach for another moment before addressing his mom.

"Mom, I have a question for you."

Zach and Kayla exchanged a look before Kayla turned back to EJ.

"Okay, what's up?"

"Can I get a job?"

"What? Of course, not. You're only eleven. You're too young to get a job."

"Please," he pleaded. "There's this guy in town who has a bunch of dogs, and I was petting them after school today, and he said he'd pay me to walk them sometimes."

The hairs on the back of Zach's neck stood as he thought about the little boy whose body had been found on the neighboring island.

"Who is this man?" he asked EJ.

"Some old guy who likes to bring his dogs to the school for the kids to play with. Everyone knows him."

"Well, I don't know him," Kayla said, casting a look toward Zach. "So, the answer is no."

Zach watched EJ as he wrestled with the decision to voice a protest, but in the end, the boy walked away, muttering under his breath, "Thanks a lot."

"I don't like the sound of that," Kayla said.

"I'll call the station tomorrow. They can ask around and see who he is." As of today, Zach was no longer employed by the island police department, but he was willing to offer his help if they needed it. Everyone's top priority was protecting the children on the island.

His thoughts shifted to EJ. He wondered what the boy was thinking. It had to be hard watching your mom interact with another man. He couldn't imagine how hard it had been for the boys to lose their dad at such young ages.

"Have you told them yet?" he asked Kayla.

She shook her head and added the beans to the chicken, placing sliced potatoes around the edge of the baking dish. She sprinkled some seasonings on everything, covered them with foil, and placed them in the preheated oven.

"I don't know how," she said with a sigh as she turned back toward Zach. "Losing their father was so hard. I can't let them think that they might—" Her voice caught in her throat, and she looked away.

"They're not going to lose you, too."

She continued to stare toward the window without acknowledging him. Zach didn't know what to do. He wanted to hold her, but after their encounter a few minutes before, he didn't trust himself to touch her. He wanted what she couldn't give, and he promised not to ask.

"I mean it, Kayla," he said firmly enough for her to look at him. "They're not going to lose you."

"How can you be so certain?" she asked, her voice barely above a whisper.

"Because I have faith that everything will be okay."

Kayla nodded. "From your lips to God's ears."

***

"What are you doing here?" Kayla asked Zach as he stepped into the kitchen early Tuesday morning. She glanced outside, but there was no sign of her mother's car. Zach quickly closed the door to the morning air as Kayla wrapped her arms around her chest and shivered. The weather had turned colder overnight, and the temperatures were quite low that late-September morning.

"Kate's sick," Zach said. He shook his head and held up his hand, obviously sensing her alarm. "No, nothing serious. She has another cough and sore throat."

"Zach, is Kate okay? Really?"

"Yeah, she's okay. I just worry about her. I hate that she's been sick so much, and fall has barely begun. I'm concerned about how she will do this winter. I know Dr. Sprance says her heart is fine now, but she was so sick last year, I can't help but worry."

"Oh, phew. You had me worried. We'll have to hope for the best and say extra prayers that she stays well. Anyway, you haven't really answered me. What are you doing here?" She peeked at the clock over the stove. She needed to get moving. Where was her mother? They were going to be late for the appointment.

"Your mom's with Miren. Aaron has some kind of important meeting today that he couldn't get out of. He tried with no luck. I offered to take Miren, but Ronnie said she was starting to cough, too, and she was worried that I might not know what to do if she got sick. Don't worry about the boys. Your dad will get them up and take them to school. Ronnie said they stayed over there last night."

"They did. Mom wanted me to stay, too, but I, well, I guess I just needed some time alone to get my thoughts together."

"Understandable. Are you ready to go?"

"Of course, that's why... You're here to take me back to Hopkins," Kayla said. She closed her eyes and reminded herself that Miren was a baby and that she was a grown woman. Kayla knew that her mother made the right decision, but she had been so grateful at the thought of having her mom with her for the biopsy. She took a breath and tried to offer Zach a smile.

"Looks like you're stuck with me again." Zach said apologetically, and Kayla felt bad for not being more grateful.

"I guess we'd better get going, then," she said. Kayla turned to get her warm coat from the closet but stopped and looked back at Zach. "Thank you," she said. "It really does mean a lot to me that you're going."

"It's the least I can do. I told you I would be here for you, and I meant it. Of course, I understand if you'd rather called Shannon or Tammi or one of your other friends. I know that this is a personal matter, and you may not want me there."

Kayla smiled. He really was a good man, despite the way he acted a few weeks back. She shook her head.

"They all have work. I can't ask them to suddenly drop everything and leave, and Anne is already getting the boys after school. But," she hesitated, "aren't you supposed to be at work?"

Zach blinked without answering, and Kayla wondered what was going on. She narrowed her eyes at him as she slipped on her jacket.

"Come on. I'll tell you my news in the truck."

Realizing they were already late, Kayla hastily zipped her jacket. She grabbed her purse off the hook in the kitchen and followed Zach out the door.

***

Kayla watched Zach as he maneuvered the truck out of the driveway and down the narrow, island road. In just a short time, he and Kate had become such integral parts of her life and the island itself that it seemed hard to believe they hadn't lived there forever. She studied the man beside her.

Zach was well over six-feet tall. He maintained his military buzz, and was always dressed in clean, crisp jeans or khakis and an ironed shirt. His steely green eyes reminded her of the color of the Chincoteague Bay during winter, as if they were covered with a thin layer of ice but teeming with life underneath. His chin was hard, and he wore a scar under his right eye that she often wondered about. A childhood accident? A wound from his time in Iraq or Afghanistan? He didn't talk much about either. In fact, he rarely talked about himself at all. Almost everything she knew about him, she had learned from Kate. As children, they grew up living near jungles and on isolated islands all around the world while their father, a renowned anthropologist, studied indigenous peoples and wrote his one and only book, which was critically acclaimed the world over.

Kate and Zach were best friends, unbreakable confidants, and ardent allies. But while Kate lived out her adult youth as a sometimes wild and reckless party girl, before seeking refuge and stability on Chincoteague, Zach had graduated from West Point and served his country for thirteen years. Kayla had no idea what he had done in the Army, but she knew he had ghosts from his life in the military that still haunted him. She wished she knew more, but she didn't think it was her place to ask.

"You're staring," Zach said, never taking his eyes off the road.

Kayla felt the heat rise into her cheeks and looked away. She played with the wedding band on her right hand until she had the courage to face him again.

"So, tell me this news of yours. You evaded my question about work, so I'm assuming one thing has to do with the other. I didn't see you around all weekend, and you missed dinner at my mom's yesterday, so you must have something in the works."

Zach nodded, glancing her way for a moment and then returning his eyes to the road.

"I've got this friend, Nick, who's leaving the Marines next month. He's a decent guy even if he is a jarhead."

Kayla vaguely recalled hearing Zach mention a friend who was being discharged and trying to figure out what to do with the rest of his life. She wondered what that had to do with Zach.

"Uh-huh," she answered in a tone meant to let him know she was listening and waiting for more.

"Nick's had it rough, in and out of foster homes since he was a kid, a less-than-stellar academic career, et cetera. The military saved his life. You know the kind."

"I do," Kayla said as she watched him. His eyes stayed on the road, but his fingers lifted from the steering wheel in an almost mesmerizing way, making small gestures as he talked.

"Anyway, Nick never really had a real home, and he's got nowhere else to go, so I told him he could move in with me until he figures out what he wants to do."

"Okay," Kayla elongated the word. "That's very kind of you, but what does it have to do with your job?"

"Nothing really, I guess." He glanced her way. "I quit. Gave my notice a couple weeks ago. Oh, speaking of which, I did call and have them check out that guy with the dogs. Seems he's just a lonely widower who likes kids and dogs. He's been on the island forever. Brent something. I'm sure you'd know him if you saw him. Everyone else knew who he was."

"Yes, I think I do. Thanks for checking. Now what about your job? Why did you quit? Do you have any other offers lined up?"

Zach shrugged. "No, but I'm not too concerned. I've got a decent amount saved. I've spent my whole life taking commands from someone higher up. Even when I was giving commands, I was still following them from Uncle Sam. It feels good to make my own decision and not have to answer to someone."

Kayla let her silence speak for her. She turned to gaze out the windshield, pondering what it must be like to have to answer to no one and have enough money to just up and quit a steady job. She was just about at the end of Eddie's insurance money when she quit her job at the local bank and opened Second Helpings. It was a scary time, and she still wasn't sure she made the right decision. She hadn't bought a new outfit in years, and her car had almost two-hundred-thousand miles on it. Her health insurance nearly broke them each month. She shook her head just thinking about what this latest crisis might end up costing her. She prayed that her insurance would prove to be as good as it seemed.

"You don't approve," Zach said after a few moments.

"It's not my place to approve or disapprove," Kayla tried to sound nonchalant, but inside, she was swirling with questions. How would he make an income? How could he pay his rent-to-own deal on the house? What about his car payment? How would he take care of the boys, if she...

Kayla suddenly sat up.

"What's wrong?" Zach asked, averting his eyes from the road to look at her before swiveling his head back to the highway.

"Nothing," she said as her mind began racing. For the first time, Kayla realized that a part of her had been watching Zach lately, sizing him up, looking for signs that he would make a good father. Not because she planned on dating him. But because she needed a plan B. Her parents weren't getting any younger, and Aaron had his hands full taking care of Kate and Miren. Though she hadn't done so consciously, from deep inside, she now admitted to herself that she would want Zach to care for her boys if something happened to her.

After Eddie was killed, Kayla contacted an attorney and had a will drawn up. She was a single parent with two small children. She needed to know that they would be taken care of. She appointed Aaron as their guardian. But now that he was no longer unattached and had a baby and a wife with her own medical problems, Kayla had been searching for the right person to raise her children. When had she begun to see Zach as that person? She barely knew him as far as his fathering skills went. Sure, he was great with the boys and with Miren, but still.

What was I thinking?

"Kayla, are you okay?"

Kayla realized they were sitting on the side of the road. Zach was watching her intently, his icy green eyes filled with concern.

"I'm sorry, Zach. I had a moment of panic. I guess I was just putting myself in your shoes." She forced a smile.

"Kayla, I hope you're not worried about how you will be able to manage without a job. You know that

your family, and that includes me, will take care of you
and the boys."

Kayla nodded.

"I know, but thanks. I'm okay. Every now and then,
it just hits me that I've got so much to deal with right
now." And that was the truth. Except that 'every now
and then' was every waking moment when she wasn't
the least bit distracted. "You can get back on the road.
I'll be fine."

Zach tenderly took her hand and held it in his. Kayla
felt her own hand begin to tremble with fear. Fear of the
biopsy, fear of the diagnosis, fear of the future, and fear
of her feelings for this man who seemed to be on her
mind almost as much as the lump in her breast.

"Are you sure?" he gently asked.

She nodded and bit her lips together. "Yes," she said
weakly. "I'm sure. And I don't want to be late. You've
been making good time."

After a moment, Zach released her hand and reached
for the gearshift. Before putting the truck in drive, he
looked back at Kayla. She offered a smile and patted his
arm.

"I'm good. Tell me about your plans for when Nick
arrives and what you were up to all weekend."

Kayla listened to Zach talk as they continued on
their way to Baltimore. The cadence of his voice was
comforting, reassuring, and admittedly sexy. Kayla let
his prattle lull her into a soothing trance as the fields and
trees along the highway gradually succumbed to houses
and small businesses and then to strip malls, office
buildings, and big box chain stores and finally to inner
city high-rises. In what seemed like no time at all, they

were at Johns Hopkins, and Kayla steeled herself for what was to come. But, as she walked through the doors of the hospital, her eyes welled up with tears, and all the resolve she had mustered melted away like a cherry-flavored snow cone on a hot summer day.

Feijoada
Origin: Brazil

Of all the ethnic foods that my sister and I ate growing up,
feijoada was, and still is, one of my favorites. An
indigenous woman in a small Brazilian village taught my
mother to make the dish. I remember the first night we
had it in our hut. I was part excited and part anxious
because I loved the dish when I ate in other homes, and I
was afraid that my mother wouldn't be able to make it the
same way. I remember getting into trouble that night
because I tried to lick my bowl clean. I love making
feijoada because it reminds me that the simple things in
life are often the things we should cherish the most.

From *Around the World in Eighty Meals*
by K.Z. Middleton

CHAPTER SEVEN

The next several days dragged like a child's last week of school before summer vacation. The chilly days turned colder as the October winds whipped around the island, intensifying the waves off the shore and moaning through the eaves of the roof at night. Zach battled the wind as he ran along the trail. The tall pine trees sheltered him from the cold gusts of air but not from his thoughts about the woman who lived next door.

He couldn't imagine how Kayla felt. If he could barely stand the wait, then how was she able to push through each day? And do so with a smile? He was left both bewildered and amazed by her determination, strength, and ability to stay positive. Oh, he had seen her shadow through the kitchen window at night as she paced the floor. He saw the lines under her eyes and the moments she let her guard down when she thought nobody was looking. He knew that she was scared to death and most likely spent the past several nights crying herself to sleep. But every day, she put on a happy face, made her boys breakfast, packed their lunches, did their laundry, cooked their dinner, helped them with homework, and drove them to soccer and Boy Scouts and whatever else they had going on. She was a paragon of strength and dignity, and when he looked at her, he was reminded of a verse in Proverbs, 'She is clothed with strength and dignity, and she laughs without fear of the future.'

But Zach knew that, while she smiled and laughed, she was afraid; and he longed to know how he could alleviate her fears. As he ended his run, he bent over and took deep breaths, trying to figure out how to help Kayla if no news came today. Making it through the weekend would be torture for her, for both of them, but it was Kayla who mattered. Standing up and taking one last deep breath of the salty air, Zach began to devise a plan to help Kayla stay positive for the next few days.

There was a buzz of conversation inside the grocery store, and while Zach wondered what was going on, he minded his own business. As he passed a group of women, their conversation piqued his curiosity, and he kept his ears open for more information.

"He didn't show up for school this morning," one woman told another.

"My kids have always walked to school, but not anymore," a mother was telling the store's cashier.

"These things are happening too close to home," a young woman in the produce aisle said to someone on the other end of the phone.

Zach's stomach churned as he followed the thread of conversation. Another missing boy. He now strained to hear every word as he made his way up and down the aisles. Henry. That was the name he heard more than once. He breathed a sigh of relief, feeling guilty as he thanked God that it wasn't EJ or Todd and offering up a prayer for the missing boy. Knowing she was awaiting news from the doctor, Zach wondered how the island gossip was going to affect the single mom who already had enough to worry about.

After paying for his groceries, Zach headed home, checking his phone constantly as if he could will it to ring and bring him some news about Kayla. When he pulled into his driveway, he saw Ronnie's SUV in the driveway next door. Was this a casual visit? A mother checking in on her daughter? Or a roundup of the troops to face the music?

Hesitating before reaching into the truck for the bags, Zach reluctantly carried his groceries into the house, attempting to see if he could detect some kind of aura being given off by the house next door. Was there something in the air—a sound, a smell, a taste? Anything that could send him a clue as to what was going on? Would he be able to hear a cry if he opened a window and kept as quiet as a mouse? Would the cry be of sorrow or joy? The not knowing was killing him, and he again thought of Kayla and what she must be going through.

Ignoring the constant pull toward her, Zach put away the food and went upstairs to shower. Once dressed, he went back to the kitchen and began to prepare his mother's recipe for feijoada, a traditional Brazilian dish. He sautéed the beef and added it to black beans, okra, and banana in a large pot and set it on the stove to cook for the afternoon. If he couldn't telepathically get Kayla to call or come over to tell him if there was news, he was going to let his mother's tasty and hearty stew entice her and the boys into spending the evening with him. Keeping them busy tonight and all weekend was the only way he could think of to help and one way to ensure that Kayla's boys were kept in sight and out of harm's way.

Zach watched through the window as Trevor exited the house next door and opened the door to the shed where Kayla kept the lawn mower. Zach watched Trevor start the mower and wondered if he should offer to help. He looked at his meal preparations and decided against it, but he would offer to cut Kayla's grass in the future.

He hoped that Kayla would take him up on dinner. If she said no, at least he'd have food prepared for Nick's arrival the next day. The thought caused Zach to hesitate as he sprinkled some seasonings into the pot. While he knew that he had to level with Kayla about his past, he had allowed himself to put the inevitable on the back burner while she dealt with her medical crisis. Now that Nick was on his way, things were going to change. It was one thing for Aaron and Kate to know about his past, but now a complete outsider was joining their small island family. Zach prayed that Nick wouldn't let anything slip before he had a chance to tell Kayla himself.

***

"He does realize that I can cut my own grass, right?" Kayla asked her mother. She stood at the window, watching Trevor cut the small patch of lawn in her front yard. "And it's barely grown since the weather changed."

"Let your father be. He wants to help you in whatever way he can."

Kayla sighed. "I know, and I appreciate his help, but he's been here almost every day this week. I'm starting to think he's going to announce that he's moving in."

"He just might," Ronnie said with a grin. "You're his little girl, and he's worried about you. Let him help. Try to come up with a list of things you'd like done around the house. That way, he's doing the things you really need and want done."

"I can do that," Kayla said, sitting on the couch next to her mother. There were things that her father could do—check the chimney before it got too cold, hang a second shelf in her office, change the oil in her car. He liked doing those kinds of things, and Kayla could ask him to do them rather than pay someone else to.

Her phone vibrated. Kayla picked it up and smiled as she read the text.

"Who's that?" Ronnie asked casually.

Kayla felt heat rush into her cheeks as she hastily typed a response and put the phone back on the cushion beside her.

"Just a dinner invitation. For the boys and me," she hurriedly added.

"From Zach?" Ronnie asked, and Kayla wondered what made it so obvious that it was him.

"Yes, from Zach," Kayla said pulling her legs up onto the couch and curling them under her. She picked up her tea cup and blew on her tea before taking a sip. "He's been a real rock for the boys this week. They know that something's going on, but he's been great at distracting them and keeping things light. It's so nice of him to try to shelter them like that. Anyway," Kayla waved dismissively as she changed the subject. "What are you and Dad doing this weekend? Are you participating in the art sale?"

Ronnie cocked her head to the side as she surveyed her daughter. Kayla looked away, knowing she hadn't fooled her mother in the slightest.

"Yes, and then going to the oyster festival. What's Zach making for dinner?"

"He didn't say," Kayla said with a shrug. "Probably steaks on the grill. You know how men are."

"Uh-huh," Ronnie responded. Kayla knew she wasn't going to get off that easily. "Zach's becoming a regular here, isn't he?" Ronnie took a sip of her tea and raised her eyebrow, daring Kayla to change the subject.

"What do you mean?" Kayla asked, trying to sound as if she had no idea where this was going.

"Zach. What's going on between the two of you?"

"Absolutely nothing," Kayla said without hesitation or defiance. She spoke the truth, so she didn't need to worry about being cryptic or giving away any secrets. "We are friends. He has been very good to us, very attentive to our needs. It's been nice to be able to rely on him with no strings attached."

"And is this arrangement long-term?"

Kayla put her cup down on the table and leaned back on the couch, folding her arms across her chest.

"There's no 'arrangement.' We're friends who are lucky enough to be able to count on each other without any expectations."

Just then, Kayla's phone buzzed. As had been the case recently, her stomach clenched at the sound. Lifting the device to check the screen, she felt her mouth go dry. Her eyes met her mother's gaze, and both women sat frozen as the buzzing continued. Coming to her senses, Kayla shakily slid her finger across the screen and then tapped the speaker button.

"Hello," she said, her voice catching with sudden fear.

"Yes, is this Kayla Reynolds?" the faceless voice asked.

"Yes, it is," Kayla said, her breath quickening.

"This is Marcie, from Dr. Zink's office. We have the results of your biopsy. When can you come in?"

Kayla swallowed. "When do you have an opening?"

"We have an opening for three on Monday. We have a few other times available during the week, but Dr. Zink doesn't like to waste any time when dealing with biopsies."

Kayla looked up at her mother, who nodded and leaned over to take hold of her daughter's empty hand.

"Monday at three sounds good. I'll be there."

"Okay, Dr. Zink will see you then."

After thanking Marcie, Kayla said goodbye and disconnected the call.

"Well, I guess we won't know anything until Monday," she said, falling back onto the couch and closing her eyes. "How on earth will I make it through the weekend?"

Ronnie patted Kayla's thigh. "The same way we women have always made it through life's toughest times. You will spend quality time with your boys and hold your head up, knowing you can do anything with the love of your family and God on your side."

"How do you do it?" Kayla asked, shaking her head.

"Do what?" Ronnie sat back against the couch.

"Take everything in stride. Not panic, not break down."

Ronnie laughed. "Oh, I've had my share of panics and breakdowns. In time, you learn that you can curl up in a ball and let your fear dictate your every move, or you can lift your chin, put on a smile, and tell God, 'This one's yours. You take care of this problem while I continue living my life.' And you know what?"

Kayla waited for her mother to finish.

"He always does. You do what you need to do and let Him do the rest."

"What if it doesn't turn out the way we want it to?"

"Then what have you gained by worrying about it? Bad things are going to happen. Things sometimes go the way we prayed they wouldn't. But you have the choice to assume the worst and stop living, or live the best life you can regardless of the outcome."

Kayla glanced out the window, taking in the house next door and the short distance that separated them.

"But what if the decisions you make directly impact the lives of others? What if I try to live my life, without worrying about dying, and I end up hurting someone else in the process? What if my actions cause someone else pain? What if I die, and he has to suffer because I let him think everything was going to be okay?"

Ronnie took a deep breath and said quietly, "We're all going to die, Kayla. The question isn't, what if you die while trying to live. The question is, are you going to live until you die?"

Wiping a tear from her cheek, Kayla offered her mother a feeble smile. "Mom, you're such an optimist." She shook her head and reached for her mother's hand. "But I guess it has served you well."

"It's not optimism. It's faith. And you'll find that your own faith will get you through this just like mine did. And like me, if you have faith, in God, in yourself, and in others," Ronnie glanced out the window toward Zach's house, "you will come out of this just fine. No matter what the outcome."

In spite of her pep talk, Kayla could see the tears her mother was holding back. But she was right. Kayla wanted desperately to live. Whether that meant living a full life or a few months, she was going to find a way to make them count.

***

"Dinner was excellent," Kayla said as she and Zach finished loading the dishwasher. The boys were settled on Zach's couch watching a movie. The kitchen, where Kayla shared many cups of tea and coffee with Kate, felt warm and comfortable. She leaned against the counter and watched Zach wipe down the sink and stovetop.

"I loved the stew. What did you say it was called?"

"Feijoada."

Kayla repeated the word a couple times, trying to perfect it. "It's not easy to say." She laughed and felt herself blush.

"It's not quite the same as what we used to eat in Brazil, but it's close. My mom's a great cook and can tweak any recipe," he said. "She can make anything from Australian lamb burgers to kapenta and sadza, my personal favorite." He flashed her a boyish smile.

"What on earth is that?"

"Kapenta is a Nigerian dish made with small freshwater fish, and sadza is maize porridge. You eat it with your hands; and the salty taste of the fish, which is cooked with tomatoes, onions, ground nut powder, and fresh greens, goes perfectly with the porridge. Oh, man. I can almost taste it now." He rolled his eyes into the back of his head and licked his lips. "I've tried to replicate it, but nothing beats Mom's."

Kayla grinned. "It must have been amazing to experience all those different cultures. You and Kate had quite the childhood."

"I guess so," Zach said. "We didn't know anything else, so I think we took a lot of it for granted." He threw the sponge in the sink and leaned back on the counter, his arms crossed in front of him. "We played whatever games the other kids played and lived life like they did. It never occurred to us that kids in the States were playing with video games and watching TV. Heck, I didn't know what a video game or a TV was until I was ten."

"You didn't miss much," Kayla told him, glancing at her boys in the next room. "I wish my boys watched less TV and learned more about foreign cuisine and games."

A hush fell over the room as Kayla gazed at EJ and Todd. She still had so much left to teach them.

"They're going to be okay," Zach said quietly.

Kayla looked at him and smiled. "I know. No matter what happens, they're going to be okay. They have a great support system."

"So do you," he said, reaching out and gently laying his hands on her shoulders, caressing her tense muscles. "You can lean on us, you know. Me, Kate, Aaron, your parents. Even my parents would come up in a heartbeat if you needed them."

Kayla enjoyed the pressure of his hands as they gently massaged her shoulders.

"They would. They're really great people. Maybe I'll have to recover some place warm and move into their spare bedroom in Miami Beach."

Zach's hands went still, and Kayla felt him tense.

"That's the first time I've heard you say that," he said.

"Say what?"

"Recover. Do you know something? Did you get news from the doctor?"

She closed her eyes and shook her head. She had managed to avoid the subject all evening, but she knew that eventually, he'd ask. "No, but the results are in. I have an appointment on Monday."

She looked at him, and his hands gripped her a little tighter.

"I'm scared," she whispered.

Zach didn't answer with words. Instead, he ran his arms down her back as he pulled her into an embrace. She closed her eyes and let him hold her, taking in his scent. The fragrance of the unnamed aftershave she had come to associate with him was mixed with the smell of stew and spices, and she could still smell the laundry detergent on his shirt. She fought the urge to inhale so deeply that his scent would become a permanent part of her being. He rubbed his hands up and down her back while lightly kissing the top of her head, causing her to wonder if she would lose her hair. She supposed that was jumping the gun a bit.

"What can I do for you?" Zach whispered into her hair. "How can I make this better?"

"Pray," she said, pulling back to look into his eyes. "Pray that, no matter what happens on Monday, we will get through this and that those boys won't have to lose both their father and their mother." The words caught in her throat.

"I will," Zach promised. "If nothing else, I will make sure they don't grow up without a parent."

The meaning of his words was made clear by the look in his eyes, and Kayla's heart momentarily skipped a beat. She was too overcome with emotion to respond.

Sensing her loss for words and fearing their evening together was about to go bad, Zach reached for her hand. "Movie time?"

"Sounds good," she answered wistfully and let him lead her into the living room. She tried not think about how right it felt to be there with Zach and the boys, just like a normal family with a long future ahead of them.

***

"Are you sure this isn't too much trouble?" Kayla whispered as they tread the soft dirt between the houses.

Zach smiled as he looked down at the sleeping boy in his arms. "I wouldn't have offered if was a problem. It's not like I have far to go."

EJ led the way and held the door open for his mother and Zach. Todd snuggled closer to Zach's chest as the cold night wind rushed past them on their way up the stairs to the house on stilts. All of the houses on the island were built high off the ground to withstand hurricanes and flooding, but Zach took the dozen or so steps with ease. Todd was nothing compared to the ammo and other gear Zach was used to carrying.

"His room is in the back," Kayla said quietly as she led the way down the hall. Zach knew this, as he'd been in the little boy's room many times over the summer, helping him gather toys for the beach or find a lost pair of shoes, but he didn't say so to Kayla. He just enjoyed the feeling of carrying the small child to his room and tucking him beneath the Star Wars themed sheets.

Zach lightly kissed Todd on the forehead and watched a small, sleepy smile curl on the little boy's mouth. He almost hated to turn and leave the room.

"Good night, EJ," he said, passing by the older boy's room on his way back down the hall.

"Good night, Uncle Zach," EJ said. "I had a good time at your house tonight."

"You're welcome any time," Zach answered, a warm and welcome feeling taking hold in his gut. What he wouldn't give to be able to do this every night—have dinner with Kayla and her boys, watch a movie together, and tuck the kids in bed. He'd give even more to not have to say goodbye at the door and head to the lonely house next door. His thoughts drifted back to the missing boy, and his gut wrenched. Kayla hadn't mentioned anything, and Zach assumed her friends, who were all undoubtedly texting each other about Henry's disappearance, had decided to spare Kayla from more bad news. Or perhaps the boy had been found safe and sound.

"Thanks for everything," Kayla said, interrupting his thoughts as they neared the door. "It means a lot to know that we can count on you."

"You're welcome. Kayla, I-" Before Zach could finish his thought, Kayla leaned up and kissed him on the cheek, and when she paused, her face barely touching his, Zach's reflexes kicked in.

He turned his head just enough for his lips to touch hers in a light kiss. Resisting the urge to pull her to him, he drew back slightly and looked into her eyes, unsure how she would respond. Neither said a word, both seemingly spellbound by the moment, unwilling or unable to move as if the glow of the moonlight through the window held them together with an invisible rope. Zach could feel the quickening of his heart and the bobbing of his Adam's apple as he swallowed.

"Good night, Zach," Kayla whispered and slowly backed away.

The void in the air around him suddenly made him feel as if he was being swept into a black hole. He longed to reach for her, to beg her to let him be more than a friend, to promise her forever... He stopped himself. For Kayla, forever might be twenty years or twenty days. The uncertainty was akin to a sudden punch to the gut. He couldn't do that to her, force her to face that reality. Not when her appointment was still more than forty-eight hours away. And not when he had never had a chance to tell her who he really was. He stepped onto the front porch.

"Good night, Kayla. Sleep tight," he said as he turned to walk away.

He didn't look back, but he was down the steps and well on his way back to his own house when he finally heard the click of the door latch. Smiling to himself, he thought, *So, that's what it's like to steal a kiss and walk away into the moonlight.*

It was a feeling he rather enjoyed.

Fried Oysters
Origin: New England

Though oysters have been eaten throughout the
Mediterranean and along the Atlantic Coast for thousands
of years, the deep-fried oyster is a relatively new invention.
It is said that Aphrodite was a fan of raw oysters, but I
prefer mine fried to a crisp. As a child, I knew, just by
opening the front door, that oyster season was upon us.
My father makes the best fried oysters I've ever eaten, and
I find myself comparing all other recipes to his. So, you
may argue that there's no better way to eat an oyster than
by pulling it right from the shell and letting it slide down
your throat, but I will always choose my daddy's fried
delicacies.

From *Around the World in Eighty Meals*
by K.Z. Middleton

CHAPTER EIGHT

Zach held Todd tightly, trying not to wake the sleeping child, and wondered how he could sleep through all the noise. A bomb exploded nearby, and Zach nearly lost his footing, but he held steady, cradling the little boy to his chest. Todd was so still. He must have been in a very deep sleep. But when Zach looked down at the child, he recoiled in fear.

Todd's little body was covered with blood. Zach cried out for help, but there was nobody around. He looked for his battalion, but the streets were deserted. Where had they gone? He had to save Todd, he had to save...

But it was not Todd. The little boy had olive skin, and he was older than Todd in spite of his small size.

"I'm so sorry," Zach said over and over as he gently laid the boy, who was not breathing, on the ground. Another explosion ripped through the crumbling city, and Zach felt a piece of rubble imbed itself into his face, just below his eye. He screamed in pain and looked around again for his men. Seeing the caravan loaded up and ready to leave the city, he yelled for them to stop. Voices called to him, and he struggled to see them through the dust and smoke and the blood that gushed down his face. He took one last look at the boy before he ran for the truck, jumping into the back just in time to high-tail it out of harm's way.

When he looked back at the scene, he was certain he saw Kayla, dust circling her as she stood reaching for him. He called her name as he sprang up, sweat running down his face and back in spite of the chill in the air.

Zach threw off the covers and headed to the bathroom. It was the first nightmare he'd had in weeks, but it had been one of the worst ones yet. He could still feel the child in his arms even though he'd never actually lived through anything quite like what he went through in the dream. The little boy had been a figment of his imagination, the whole scenario a combination of things he'd witnessed but not lived personally. He'd seen cities destroyed by bombs, dead or dying children, guys almost get left behind, and civilians begging to be taken with them as they drove back to their base. Those were scenes that he could never forget, but he never imagined that Kayla or her boys would be at the heart of them.

He brushed his teeth and splashed cold water on his face. He fingered the scar under his eye where a piece of rock had become embedded after an explosion a man on his team had accidentally triggered. He feared that the injury might end his career, but once he was examined and stitched up, the medic assured him that his eye had not been harmed. Now, Zach wondered if losing his eye and his job as a sniper would have left him better off. He reached for a towel and wiped his face. No use asking *what if.*

He figured he might as well get his day started. Nick would be there by nine, and Zach wanted to help him feel welcome and comfortable. Of course, that wouldn't take much. Like a soldier, a Marine learned to make himself comfortable anywhere there was a place to lay his head. But Zach had other plans for the day as well.

He wanted to introduce Nick to Kayla and the boys and then take everyone to the oyster festival at the park. Kayla had agreed to help him usher Nick around the island. Though he hadn't told her so, Zach hoped to keep her so busy all weekend that she wouldn't have time to dwell on Monday's impending news. He also hoped that Nick kept his mouth shut about Zach's past. Sometimes that boy's mouth worked faster than his brain.

***

Kayla was in shock as she read the news in the online version of the local paper.

"This good?" Trevor asked. He held the shelf in place for Kayla to see.

"What?" she looked up in a moment of confusion. "Oh, yes, fine." She returned her attention to the screen.

"Everything okay?"

"No, not at all," she told her father with a sigh. "Did you hear there's another missing boy?"

"Yeah, we heard yesterday before we came over."

"So, Mom's visit and your cutting my grass was just a ruse to keep me away from the internet and the news reports?"

"Kayla, honey, your mom and I always have the best of intentions for you. Nothing we do is merely a ruse."

"I know. I'm sorry." She turned back to the screen.

"Kayla," her father lowered the shelf and waited for her to look at him. "The boy disappeared from Stockton. He wasn't here or on Assateague. I'm sure it's unrelated to the other, uh, incident."

"I wish I could believe that," Kayla said, putting her face in her hands. "All I can think of is it's another missing boy close to Todd's age."

"But not here, honey." Trevor said with conviction, though not quite enough to quell Kayla's fears or her sadness.

Kayla shook her head. "Not here, but still too close. Stockton is only a half hour away."

Trevor took a deep breath and nodded. "I understand, honey. Hopefully they find him alive and well."

"I hope so, Dad," Kayla said as her phone buzzed. She swallowed as she read the text from Anne.

"What's wrong now?" her dad asked.

"The missing boy is Justine and Hank's nephew." She looked up at her dad. "This really is hitting too close for comfort. I wonder if Aaron has talked to Hank." Hank was one of Aaron's closest friends.

"I'm sure Aaron will reach out to him," her father said.

"I'm sure you're right," Kayla said, returning to the computer.

According to the article, Henry's mother had sent Henry and his older sister, Gloria, to school that morning just as she normally did. She watched them round the corner and went back inside to get ready for work. Gloria, twelve, met up with some friends and lost track of Henry. When he wasn't with them, once the group reached the school, Gloria assumed he had run off to find his own friends on the schoolyard. Once classes began, he was nowhere to be found.

Kayla couldn't believe this was happening. She looked up from her screen when her phone began to buzz with an incoming call.

"Hi, Anne," she said when she answered. "How's Justine?"

"She's a mess," Anne said. As usual, Anne had her finger on the pulse of the island. She was the strong one of the group, the one all of the others went to for help. She'd been a rock for Kayla after Eddie's death and Kayla's move back to the island, and she was there for Kate when she was on bed-rest with Miren. Everyone knew they could count on Anne.

"I'm putting together a meal calendar for Hank, Justine, and the kids," Anne told her. "Hank's helping with the search, and Justine is fielding calls from people who want to help the family. Hank's sister isn't up to taking their calls, as I'm sure you understand." Kayla did understand. She had been there herself. Anne continued, "I don't want her to worry about having to cook meals for herself and the kids. I know that things are up in the air for you, but the gals and I decided you'd be upset if we didn't ask you to help. Would you be willing to perhaps buy a gift card from one of the local restaurants or have a pizza delivered one night this week?"

"Anne, I will make a meal. It's a no-brainer." She watched her father level the shelf and mark the holes for the screws as she listened to Anne.

"No, Kay, don't. Nobody expects you to cook. I hate to even ask, but we knew you'd want to be involved."

"Of course, I do! I'm not dead."

The line was silent for a beat before Anne spoke, "Of course not, I just mean—"

"Anne, enough. What night do you need me to take? I'm sure the boys will want to help, and it will give me something to focus on. In fact, I'll take tonight or tomorrow if that helps."

"You know, that might work out perfectly. I was going to make them dinner tomorrow night, but I have nobody for Monday. You know what a busy night that is, and you have your appointment that day." Kayla smiled as Anne prattled on, talking out loud as she thought everything through. "Yes, that should work. Lizzie and I can take care of Monday while Paul and Ben are at Scouts." Kayla pictured the happy foursome and wondered for the millionth time what life would be like if Eddie were still alive.

"It's settled then," Kayla said. "I will take care of Sunday, and you do Monday. And Anne, thanks for including me."

"Oh, honey, you will always be included. No matter what. Call me on Monday, okay?"

"I will," Kayla promised before saying goodbye.

Standing from her desk, Kayla stretched.

"Want some coffee?"

"No, thanks," Trevor answered, concentrating on his work.

Kayla reached for her coffee mug. Todd had made it for her at the local clay bakery for her birthday, and she smiled as she looked at the lopsided writing,

Mommy, I love you. Love, Todd.

Hearts and flowers dotted the mug, all in her favorite colors of pink and purple. It was one of the best presents she'd ever received.

As she refilled her cup, something caught her eye through the window. She looked up as a small, beat-up car pulled into Zach's driveway. Curiosity got the better of her, and she continued to watch as the newly-discharged Marine stepped from the car. He was shorter than Zach, with a shaved head and a toned body. He looked very young as he stretched and took in the view of the water on the other side of the marsh. She watched as the kitchen door opened and Zach stepped onto the deck. She couldn't hear what they said, but she imagined they greeted each other in that macho, man-to-man way that Aaron and Zach used with each other, using words best left said in tents and bunks, not quite fit for civilian ears.

When Zach reached the yard, he and Nick hugged, not an awkward man-hug but a sincere, tight embrace, the kind that let a person know he was truly welcome. Zach pointed toward his house, the water, and then her house, obviously giving Nick the lay of the land. Kayla ducked behind the curtain, not wanting them to know that she was spying but unwilling to stop watching them just yet.

"Mommy, what are you looking at?"

Kayla jumped at the sound of Todd's voice. Hot coffee sloshed from the mug, and she quickly put the cup down and ran cold water over her hand to wash away the coffee and soothe her reddening skin.

"I heard a car and looked to see who it was. Uncle Zach's friend, Nick, just arrived."

Todd eagerly padded over to the door and peered out through the screen.

"What time are we going to the oyster festival?" he asked without taking his gaze from their neighbor and his new housemate.

"As soon as Zach calls," Kayla said, her eyes back on Zach and Nick as well.

"Is Grandpa going, too?"

"Yes, honey, but he's going with Grandma."

"Okay. I'm going to go get dressed and tell EJ to get ready, too."

"You do that," Kayla said, distractedly, as she watched Nick pull a single camouflaged duffle bag from the back seat of his car and a guitar case.

How interesting, Kayla thought.

The former Marine followed Zach up the steps to the house. Zach held the door for Nick to go in. Before following him into the house, Zach turned back to face Kayla's house. Looking right toward the kitchen window, he smiled and waved, then he turned and went inside. Kayla felt her face heat up as she stepped back from the window. How did he do that? His sixth sense and keen eyesight were amazing.

I'll have to suggest he start thinking about what kind of career would make use of those skills. Unbelievable.

Kayla shook her head and smiled as she went to get ready for the day.

***

Dozens of tents filled the park, and people lined up thirty or forty deep to get their helping of the local seafood. The Oyster Festival was one of the fire department's biggest fundraisers, and people from near and far came to the island to partake of the offerings.

"You slip your knife inside like this, twist it a little, and pull apart the shell." Zach explained.

Nick, held his knife in one hand and the oyster shell in the other. He was bewildered.

"How the f—"

Zach's reflex was lightning fast as he dropped the knife and reached over to hit Nick upside the head.

"The kids," Zach admonished him. Todd giggled, and EJ rolled his eyes.

"I'm sorry, man, but how the *heck* do you snap it open like that? And where did you learn to do it?"

"Kayla's father taught me. It's not that hard once you get the hang of it."

"How about you open them, and I'll just eat 'em?"

"It doesn't work that way with seafood," Zach laughed. "If you want to eat, you need to learn to shuck."

Nick grudgingly watched Zach demonstrate the method again while marveling at how effortlessly the boys shucked their own oysters.

"Shouldn't we be cooking these?" Nick asked as he watched them all drop the oysters into their mouths, imagining the feel of the slimy mollusks sliding down their throats.

"You don't have to," Zach said. "They're tastiest just like this." Zach held a pearl-colored oyster in the air, tilted his head back, and dropped it into his mouth. Todd laughed and followed suit.

EJ laughed. "Don't listen to him. He's messing with you. These are cooked. They're steamed."

Kayla appeared with a plate that looked much more to Nick's liking.

"Eating them right from the shell is just uncivilized," she said to Zach. "*This* is the way to eat oysters."

"Fried?" Nick asked.

"Yep, my favorite. I'd rather have them fried than any other way. Want to try one?" she asked Nick.

His mouth watered as he reached for one of the golden-brown delicacies.

"Holy—" Nick caught himself in time, backing out of Zach's reach. "Man, this is good," he said instead as he chewed. "I'm getting me some of those. Want another beer, Zach?"

Zach nodded, and Nick stood and headed to one of the lines.

When he returned, Nick was introduced to the group's newcomers—Kayla's brother, Aaron, and his wife, Kate. He offered his seat to Kate, who held a baby, but she declined, saying they were getting in line and would see them later.

Over the course of the day, Nick met too many people to name and tried a smorgasbord of oysters—raw, fried, on the half shell, and steamed. He also tasted shrimp, clam fritters, and clam chowder. Some things he had tried before, and others were completely new. One thing he knew for sure, he would never go hungry on this island.

***

The boys ran down the spiral staircase of the Assateague Lighthouse while Kayla, Zach, and Nick followed behind at a slower pace.

"They're full of energy," Nick remarked.

"You have no idea," Kayla said under her breath. She sensed Zach's gaze and looked behind her to see him smiling, his scar blending into the crease above his right cheek as his eyes danced with amusement.

"They can definitely keep you on your toes," Zach said. "If you're around next summer, you can go to the beach with us and try to keep up with those boys as they ride the waves on their boogie boards. Before you know it, EJ will have all the girls begging for rides on his surfboard."

Kayla abruptly stopped on the step as her heart lurched in her chest. Not wanting to spoil the day, she took a deep breath and forced unwanted thoughts back into the recesses of her mind. She was not going to let uncertainty about her future ruin their day.

Zach must have realized what had happened because, as they exited the lighthouse, he tenderly took her elbow, causing her to look up at him.

"He will, you know," Zach said gently. "And you'll be there to see it."

Biting her lips together, Kayla nodded.

From your lips to God's ears, she thought.

Zach let go of her arm as Nick turned around and smiled at them.

"Thanks for showing me around today. This seems like a great place to live."

"Kayla can tell you. She's lived here almost her entire life."

"Really? No desire to branch out and see the world?" Nick asked.

Kayla glanced quickly at Zach and then back at Nick. She guessed that Zach hadn't told his friend much about Kayla's past.

"We moved here when my dad was in the Coast Guard and just stayed. Aaron and I were six at the time. I went to college at Yale and then lived in Baltimore for a few years before my husband, uh, died." She thought it best to leave it at that. The rest could be found online easily enough. Kate had managed to learn the entire sordid story within days of being on the island.

"Yale." Nick whistled. "Wow. Never went to college myself. I learned from the school of hard knocks. But, to be honest, I wouldn't mind getting my degree someday. I always wondered what it would be like to own my own business." He smiled as he watched EJ and Todd playing their own game of tag, oblivious to the tourists visiting the lighthouse.

"Kayla can tell you about that, too," Zach offered. "She owns her own business."

"Impressive," Nick said, eyeing Kayla in a way that almost made her feel uncomfortable. That was, until Zach protectively put his arm around her shoulders.

"She's impressive, all right," Zach said, squeezing her against him.

Unwilling to be a piece in this macho game, Kayla loosened herself from Zach's grip and stepped toward the boys.

"Come on guys, enough running around. You're going to get us kicked out of here."

Obeying without further ado, Todd and EJ stopped running and looked at their mother.

"Can we walk down to the beach?" EJ asked.

"The water's going to be cold," Kayla reminded him.

"That's okay," he answered. "I won't go in. I just want to see how high the waves are today."

Kayla looked at Zach.

"Okay by me. Nick?" he asked.

"Sure, I'm game for a walk to the beach."

The three adults followed the boys down the sandy road.

"So, Kayla," Nick asked. "What's this business of yours?"

"Well, to tell you the truth, I'm kind of taking a hiatus for a while. But I cook dinners for families who don't have time to cook for themselves."

"It's hugely popular," Zach said. "You wouldn't believe how many meals she prepares over the course of a week."

"Then why stop?" Nick asked before he paused to watch a bald eagle fly overhead. "Majestic, isn't he?"

Kayla and Zach looked up. They were silent as they watched the bird circle overhead before disappearing into the trees.

"So," Nick asked again when they resumed walking, "why the hiatus if things are so successful?"

Zach reached for Kayla's hand and squeezed it. Though she knew she should let go, Kayla held onto his hand, soaking up the strength and reassurance it exuded.

"I've got some personal issues to tend to," she said, trying to sound nonchalant while keeping it vague.

"I can understand that," Nick said as they reached the end of the road, the open Atlantic stretching out before them. "I've spent my whole life trying to tend to personal issues, or avoid them, depending upon how you look at it."

He looked back at Zach and Kayla, his gaze pausing for a moment on their clasped hands before looking back out at the water. They stood in silence as Todd and EJ estimated the size of the surfs that crested before them. Looking out at the enormous waves and the vast ocean, Kayla felt small and vulnerable. She closed her eyes and prayed that, somehow, the three of them would find the answers they were seeking and the happiness that seemed to be eluding them all.

"Mom, can we go get ice cream?" Todd called from the edge of the shore.

Leave it to Todd to remind me that sometimes happiness can be found in something as simple as a bowl of ice cream.

"Sure," Kayla called back. She looked at Zach. "To the Creamery?"

"Sounds like a perfect plan," he grinned.

***

Kayla was surprised when Zach and Nick squeezed into the pew beside her and the boys the following morning. She assumed they would attend the early Mass and found herself happy to see them both. She smiled at the two men, pleased that both seemed so comfortable inside the little church.

"This must be Nick," Father said after Mass, shaking his hand. "Welcome. I've heard a lot about you from Zach."

Kayla looked at Zach and wondered when he'd told the priest about Nick. If he felt her gaze on him, he didn't acknowledge it. She knew the two men were friends, but she now wondered how close they were. Zach kept things pretty close to the vest. Did he talk to the priest about the things he kept hidden from everyone else?

"Thanks, Father. Nice homily," Nick said.

"Thank you. I hope you enjoy your stay here."

They said goodbye and stepped to the side so that Nick could be reintroduced to the rest of the family. They had only met briefly at the oyster festival.

Trevor shook hands with Nick. "I hope you enjoyed the festival," he said.

"Very much, sir," Nick said. "Thank you."

"You'll both be heading to the house for Sunday dinner, won't you?" Ronnie looked at Zach and Nick.

"Nick? Up to you," Zach said as Kayla attempted to stifle the warmth that spread through her as she gazed at Zach. Something was changing between them, and it both intrigued and frightened her at the same time. She hadn't bargained for this. Even over the summer, when things seemed to be progressing toward a possible relationship, she hadn't allowed herself to believe it was possible. And since finding the lump, her whole landscape had shifted.

She couldn't be falling for Zach. Not now. That was the last thing she needed. Or was it just what she needed? She wished she knew.

***

When Kayla offered to do the dishes after dinner, Zach announced he would help her. By an unspoken agreement, everyone else settled back down and let the two of them take on the task. As he carried a stack of dishes into the kitchen, he heard Trevor and Aaron peppering Nick with questions. He's a Marine, Zach thought. He should be able to handle a couple Sailors giving him the third degree.

"Are you ready for tomorrow?" Zach asked. It was the first chance he'd had to be alone with Kayla all weekend.

She sighed and shrugged her shoulders. "As ready as I can be," she said, not taking her eyes off the dishes as she rinsed them in the sink.

Zach opened the dishwasher and began loading it as Kayla handed him dishes, glasses, and utensils.

"Your mom's taking you, right?"

"She is. I'm glad she'll be there. She'll know what the doctor is talking about and what questions to ask."

"Hey, I thought you'd want to know. That guy with the dogs, Brent Phelps, he has a solid alibi for when Henry disappeared."

"Thanks for letting me know. I'm glad to hear it. I always liked him."

Zach watched Kayla wash a pot.

"Is there anything I can do to help? For tomorrow, I mean?" Zach asked, desperately wanting to do something.

"I don't think so, but thanks for asking."

Kayla gave him a crooked smile, and his heart melted as he recognized the fear and uncertainty in her eyes. All he wanted to do was wrap his arms around her and tell her that everything was going to be okay.

"How about I make dinner for you and the boys Tuesday night?"

"Thanks, Zach. I'll take you up on that. The boys will be staying here with Dad tomorrow night, so I'm sure that will mean pizza or Chinese carry-out. A nice dinner on Tuesday will be something to look forward to."

Her genuine smile caused a roller coaster effect in Zach's gut. He reached for her soapy hand and looked into her eyes.

"I promised I'd be here, Kayla, and I'm not going anywhere. No matter what. It's time you realize that."

"We agreed on no strings," Kayla pleaded as she shook her head and tried to pull her hand away. Zach held it tighter.

"We did, and I'm not going back on that. But you're not going to go through this without me by your side, strings or no strings. And once this is behind us, we can talk about how tight those strings are going to be because I'm not losing you. Period."

Though she tried to hide it, Zach saw the spark in her eyes. She felt it as much as he did. She could hide behind her diagnosis for as long as she wanted, but he would be there now, and in the future, whatever it might hold. He pushed aside thoughts of the conversation they still needed to have about his past. He would cross that bridge when they came to it.

Chicken Pot Pie
Origin: Greece

If there's anything I love more than feeding my family a rich, hearty meal, it's making a meal that allows me to lose myself in the process. That's how I feel when I'm working with dough. Whether I'm making pâte brisée (a rich pastry dough) for blackberry pie or for chicken pot pie, I love the feel of the dough beneath my hands. It's as if I'm kneading my heart and soul into it with every push, every stretch, every press. Kneading, rolling, and filling dough is simply food for the soul, and it brings me back to the basics of food, family, love, and thanksgiving for all that we have.

From *Around the World in Eighty Meals*
by K.Z. Middleton

CHAPTER NINE

As soon as they got home, Kayla instructed the boys to do their homework, and she went right to work in the kitchen. She stirred the pot pie filling and started putting together the dough. She lost herself in the task, making her signature dish without a recipe and without having to think about the ingredients or the steps. Kayla was on autopilot, and she loved it. She reveled in the feeling of the smooth pie crust as she kneaded it beneath her palms. She stirred the thick filling again, tasted it, added more seasoning, and then tasted it again. It was perfect, and she allowed herself to take pride in her work.

This was what she missed, what kept her grounded. She loved Second Helpings and didn't want to have to give it up, but she didn't love the hectic pace at which she had to cook the meals. By providing dinner for sometimes as many as five or six families each night, she had lost the passion for cooking. She had forgotten how it felt to let the seasonings slowly run through her fingers as she dropped them into the pan, to knead dough until it was smooth and shiny, to place a beautifully prepared dish on the table and watch everyone enjoy their meal. She thought that she could have all of that and share it with others. Now, she saw that all she was doing was hurrying through the process in order to have everything ready for pick-up. She was cooking her beloved recipes but without the love.

Using her palms, Kayla slowly rolled the dough into two perfect balls, setting one aside, and flattening the other onto the counter. She was in a trance, unable to see anything beyond the pastry as she rolled it out to the perfect size for the round baking dish.

"Did you not get enough to eat at your mother's?" Zach asked, his voice soft and low.

Kayla's trance was broken. She slowly looked up at him, feeling as if she was awaking from a dream. A dream where she was doing her favorite thing, with Zach lazily watching her as he leaned against the doorjamb, a look of pure love and admiration on his face. She blushed, realizing that she was not dreaming, and that that was exactly how Zach was looking at her.

"I'm sorry," she said, hoping the catch in her voice didn't give away the rapidity of her pulse. "I didn't know you were there."

"I could tell. You looked… peaceful." He pushed away from his stance against the wall and walked toward the countertop where she rolled the dough. He spread his hands apart and placed them on the hard surface, surveying her work.

"I was remembering how much I love to cook, especially when there's a special reason."

He cocked his head to the side. "And the special reason?"

"It's for Justine and the kids. Hank is helping with the search, and Justine is taking calls from those who want to help, so Anne organized a meal calendar. She asked if I would donate a gift card or have a pizza delivered." Kayla shook her head and smiled. "She should have known better than that."

"She should have. You'd never send someone a pizza."

Kayla looked up and saw the humor in his expression. He was teasing her, and it sure felt better than him feeling sorry for her. So often these days, she felt like everyone was looking at her with pity or trepidation. She much preferred being teased.

"How's Nick settling in?" she asked as she rolled the dough over the thick, marble rolling pin and lifted it to the baking dish. She gently set it down over the dish and unwrapped the dough so that it fit perfectly inside the hollow of the dish.

Zach watched her with appreciation, and it made Kayla feel good. She was in her element, and she knew it.

"So far, so good. He's checking the listings in the paper, circling potential jobs, and coming up with his plan of attack."

Kayla turned to stir the filling and watched Zach, from the corner of her eye, break a small piece of dough off from the second ball and pop it in his mouth.

"I saw that," she said without turning around.

"Man, I forgot that all moms have eyes in the back of their heads."

"We do," she said as she returned to the island. She pressed the dough onto the counter, sprinkled flour over it, and began to roll it out. "So, what brings you over, other than to steal a piece of pie crust? You can't be hungry after Mom's Sunday spread."

"You'd be surprised," he said, moving behind her to enjoy a giant inhalation of the pie filling.

"Don't touch that," Kayla commanded as Zach picked up the spoon.

"How did you—?"

"Eyes in the back of my head," she reminded him. "You didn't answer me." She finished rolling out the top of the pot pie before returning to the stove and turning off the flame under the filling.

Zach watched as she poured the filling into the pie shell and proceeded to cover the top with the dough, using the same maneuver she used to lay the bottom crust in the dish.

"I wanted to make sure you don't need anything before tomorrow."

"You asked me at Mom's if I was ready." She crimped the edges of the crust and poked three holes in the top of the pie.

"That's not the same," he said, opening the oven for her.

After placing the pie in the oven, Kayla noted the time and began cleaning up her cooking tools.

"I suppose it's not," she said, turning toward him and resting her back against the kitchen sink. "I'm good. The boys need to pack for Dad's, but otherwise, there's not really anything to do."

"And you're still holding off on telling them what's going on?"

"Until I have a diagnosis, there's really nothing to tell."

"So, the boys have to pack. What about you?" Kayla felt a chill run down her back as he looked at her with such intensity that she felt naked.

"I'm okay," she faltered. "There's not much for me to do."

"How about that dinner?" He gestured toward the oven. "Can I take it to Justine's for you?"

Kayla looked at the oven and thought for a moment before shaking her head. "I want to take it and let them know that I'm thinking of them. But…" She hesitated and lowered her voice. "Maybe you could go with me? Under the circumstances, I'm not sure I want to go alone. The boys want to go with me. They've met Henry and are close to Justine's kids. I'm afraid it might be difficult. I don't even want to imagine what those kids are going through." She shuddered and glanced toward the den where the boys did their homework.

"Of course, we'll all go together."

"Perfect," Kayla said. "The pot pie will be ready in about forty-five minutes. Should we meet at the truck, or would you prefer we take my car?"

"The truck is fine. I'll go tell Nick what's up."

Kayla watched him go and let out a breath. As much as she hated to admit it, having Zach in her life felt a lot better than not having him around at all. While she was reticent to put her complete trust in him, she found herself wanting to lean on him. Still, he was holding something back, and she needed assurance that they could count on him to be there when it matters. With her impending diagnosis and Henry's disappearance, she realized all the more that you never know what the future will hold or if there will be a future at all.

***

"It's been over twenty-four hours," Justine said. She was sitting on the couch next to Hank, their hands clasped. Kayla sat beside her. Zach was perched on the edge of an overstuffed chair, wishing he could say or do something to help.

"You know what they say, that once a child has been missing for twenty-four hours, the likelihood of finding him is almost non-existent." Justine's voice broke as she spoke. She blew her nose with a shredded tissue.

Hank shook his head. "It's like he just disappeared."

"I know everyone is doing all they can to find him," Kayla assured Justine, wrapping her arm around her friend and squeezing her tightly. "I'm sure they'll find him," Kayla said, ignoring the warning look that Zach gave her.

"Did you hear what happened to that little boy they found on Assateague?" Justine broke down and sobbed. She looked at Hank and continued through her tears. "What if he has Henry?"

"We're not going to think like that, Justine," Hank said firmly but with tenderness. "There is no reason to believe that the two are related."

Zach watched the scene, and his heart ached. He leaned back and looked toward the playroom where the boys were sitting with Hank and Justine's kids. The mood didn't seem to be any lighter in there. Zach was at a loss as to what to say. Though no official report had been released about what was done to Ryan Graham before his death, he had seen the report. The island was rampant with rumors, each one more horrific than the next, and none were far off the mark.

"How can someone do those things to a child? To anyone?" Justine cried. "How can someone have such little regard for human life? Anybody who can just pick up a weapon and kill another person doesn't deserve to live."

Zach felt as if he'd been punched. He looked down at his clasped hands, unable to face the grieving mother.

"Justine, honey, come on," Hank pleaded. "Don't let the kids hear you talking like that. We need to keep up hope for Eileen." Hank's voice cracked. "She needs us to be strong."

"Hank's right," Kayla said. "Your family needs you all to be strong. Henry might have just wandered off. We don't know that anyone, that he's…"

Zach looked up and saw the pleading look in her eyes. "They're right, Justine. Hopefully we'll hear something soon." He hoped he said the right thing and that his voice didn't betray his own feelings of guilt.

Justine nodded before turning toward Kayla. "I'm sorry to be like this. I've had to be strong all day, and it's just…it's really getting to me right now. Thank you for coming over and for bringing dinner. We do appreciate it."

"Of course," Kayla said. "You just let me know if you need anything." She hugged Justine and stood. Zach stood as well, taking his cue from Kayla. Justine grabbed Kayla's hand and held it tight.

"I heard about your, your—"

"My appointment," Kayla said quietly, glancing into the next room.

"Yes. I'm so sorry."

"There's nothing for you to be sorry about. I'm going to get through whatever this is, and so are you."

Zach admired Kayla's brave front.

Justine nodded again and let go of Kayla's hand. "Thank you," she said softly.

Zach stood and walked to the playroom doorway, motioning to the boys that it was time to leave.

"Call me if you need anything," Kayla said to Hank, who offered his thanks before pulling his wife closer to him.

Zach turned away from them, feeling like a voyeur, and ushered the boys to the door. He held it open for EJ, Todd, and Kayla before closing it behind them. Todd reached for Zach's hand, and Zach sensed the boy's fear. Putting his free arm around Kayla's shoulders, he led them all to the truck and opened the passenger side door. He patiently waited for the boys to climb into the back and for Kayla to climb into the front before closing the door and walking to the other side of the truck. He took one last look at the house before opening his own door and climbing inside. Drops of rain began to dot the windshield.

"I feel terrible," Kayla said, looking straight through the front window. "I know all too well what they're going through. The waiting is unbearable. To not know where he is or what's happened. And then to know that some soulless excuse for a human could just shoot another person with no regard for his life or his loved ones…"

Ryan Graham hadn't been shot. Zach knew that his was a far more painful, slower death; but he also knew that Kayla was thinking about Eddie, not Ryan. She turned to look at him, her eyes glistening with tears as she mentally relived the death of her husband.

"It's sick, the things that people do to one another. I'll never understand it."

Zach felt as though he might be sick. His hands clenched the steering wheel, and his stomach churned. He swallowed down the bile that rose into his throat. If she expected a response, he was unable to give one. He just stared ahead as he drove, finally acknowledging to himself that Kayla would never accept him for whom he was.

***

Kayla took a little extra time to tuck the boys into bed that night. Todd didn't have much to say, so Kayla did something she hadn't done in a long time. After checking to make sure he had packed everything he needed for his sleepover with Grandpa, she pulled a book from his shelf and asked if he wanted her to read it to him.

Todd was reading the *39 Clues* series and was more than happy to have Kayla read aloud from the latest volume. They snuggled together on the bed and read two of the short chapters. After, as they talked about the kids in the book and the latest mystery they were solving, Todd became quiet.

"Mommy," he said softly, "do you think Timmy's cousin is okay?"

"I hope so, Todd. Do you want to say a special prayer for him tonight?"

The little boy nodded and climbed out of bed to kneel on the floor. Kayla joined him, closing her eyes as Todd said his normal bedtime prayers and then listened as he prayed for his friend.

"Dear God, please let Henry be okay. Please bring him back to his family. Amen."

Kayla started to get up, but Todd continued. "And please, God, help my mommy with whatever is bothering her. Please take care of her, too."

Overwhelmed with emotion, Kayla silently helped Todd climb back into bed and pulled his Star Wars comforter snug against his chin.

"I love you, Mommy," he said when she bent to kiss him.

"I love you, too, Todd. I promise, everything is going to be okay."

She said a silent prayer that she was telling the truth. After turning off Todd's light and closing his door, she peeked into EJ's room.

"Ready for tomorrow?"

"Yeah, but I still don't understand why we have to stay at Grandpa's again. Why won't you be home?"

"I will be home, EJ, but it will be late." Kayla walked to his bedside.

"But why? We know something is wrong. Please tell me where you're going. Please don't be like Dad." As soon as the words left his mouth, EJ looked away, his cheeks turning pink in the glow of his lamp.

"Like Dad?" Kayla asked, her heart skipping a beat as she sat on the bed.

EJ swallowed before turning back to face her.

"Yeah, he went to work one day and never came back. Timmy's cousin went to school, and then he didn't come back. Where are you going? How do we know you'll come back?"

Kayla had never stopped to consider what the boys might be thinking. It didn't occur to her that they might associate her going to Baltimore with Eddie's disappearance and death. Was Henry's disappearance the catalyst that brought on these fears, or had they been worried for the past few weeks, just as she had? Oh, what had she done to her precious boys?

Kayla reached for EJ's hand. Trembling, she took a deep breath and tried to come up with the right words that would make him both understand and not be afraid.

"EJ, can you remember, right after Daddy died, when Grandma was sick?"

"You mean when she couldn't pick up Todd and had to have help to do everything?"

"Yes. Do you remember why she was sick?"

"Yes, it was because she had cancer." His eyes grew wide as he sat up in bed. "Is Grandma sick again? Is that why the two of you are going somewhere tomorrow and won't be back until late? Is she going to be okay?"

Kayla closed her eyes and inhaled through her nose, slowly releasing the air through her lips.

"No, EJ, Grandma isn't sick." She squeezed his hand and looked him in the eye. "I am," she said quietly.

Alarm spread across EJ's face, and Kayla watched her young man turn back into a little boy before regaining his composure and clutching both of her hands.

"But you're going to be okay, right?" His voice wasn't that of a frightened boy. It was that of a pre-teen trying to be grown up but looking for assurance.

"I don't know what will happen, EJ," Kayla said honestly. "I plan to be all right. We're not even sure yet that there's anything to worry about. I might or might not have cancer. We find out tomorrow. If it's not, I might still have to have surgery to prevent me from getting cancer. If I do have it, well, we'll have to wait and see what the doctor says is the next step."

"Why didn't you tell us?" he pleaded.

"I didn't want to say anything until I knew for sure. I didn't want you to worry."

EJ nodded and squeezed their joined hands as tightly as he could. "I have been worried. You haven't been yourself. Todd feels it, too. And everyone stops talking whenever we enter the room. We knew something was going on. You should have just told us. We can help take care of you."

Kayla smiled. "Thank you, sweetheart. You're right. I should have known that you were big enough to handle it and help out. But let's not tell Todd just yet. He's still a little boy. I need you to look out for him. We don't know what happened to Henry, and your brother is sad and scared. He needs his big brother to be brave. After I see the doctor tomorrow, and we know what to expect, I promise, no more secrets."

EJ thought it over for a moment and then nodded. "Okay, Mom. I'll look out for Todd. And when you know what's going on, we can tell him together."

Kayla hugged her son. It seemed that each time she looked at him lately, she saw less and less of her little boy and more and more of the man he was becoming. She felt proud and knew that Eddie would have felt the same.

"Goodnight, EJ. I love you."

"I love you, too, Mom."

Kayla switched off the lamp and closed the bedroom door behind her.

Rather than going to her room, she walked through the house. She picked up a stray Lego in the living room, checked that the doors were locked, and stood in front of the refrigerator, surveying the many papers held to the door with magnets shaped like the alphabet and ones with local business numbers. She smiled as she looked at the photo of Kate, Aaron, and Miren on Miren's three-month birthday and the one of EJ and Todd playing on the beach. She recalled how she had helped EJ study for that science test, now proudly displayed with a big red A+ written at the top.

On the way to her bedroom, Kayla stopped in the boys' bathroom to straighten up the towels and put the cap on the toothpaste. She picked up the plaster mold of Todd's tiny hand, a Mother's Day present he had made in kindergarten. She lovingly caressed the little soap dish, running her finger along the curves of his palm. The room still held the humidity leftover from EJ's shower, and it smelled of soap and shampoo and little boy.

Turning off the light, she walked to the master
bedroom at the end of the hall. Beside her bed was a
photo of her family, taken six years earlier. Eddie
beamed as though he didn't have a care in the world.
Two-year old Todd grinned from ear to ear, and five-
year-old EJ smiled in spite of his missing front teeth.
Kayla wore her hair longer then, and several rings
gleamed from her fingers. She wondered whatever
happened to them. It had been so long since she worried
about jewelry or dressing up. They had been hoping to
conceive another child that year, but Eddie began
working later, talking less, and making excuses for his
absence, both physical and mental. How simple life
seemed on that day, just a happy little family posing for
a photo. Would she and the boys ever find that kind of
happiness again, or was it always just an illusion, not
existing then and not possible in the future?

Not wanting her thoughts to go there, Kayla pushed
the memories and the doubts aside. She just had to get
through tomorrow. After that, she could begin thinking
about the future and what it would hold. For tonight, she
would pray for Justine and Hank and for their children
and the rest of their family; she would pray for her own
children; and she would pray for the strength to make it
through whatever was to come for all of them.

Girls' Night Out Margaritas
Origin: Mexico

Nothing says a Girls' Night Out like a good Margarita! My own mother introduced them to me when I was in my thirties. I had just gone through a horrific experience and returned to my hometown to start over again. My mother told me that alcohol can't fix your problems, and prayer is the only sure remedy for whatever ails you, but that a night out with friends and a pitcher of Margaritas always helps! Of course, I found out right away that it wasn't the drinks that made the difference; it was the friends we shared them with.

From *Around the World in Eighty Meals*
by K.Z. Middleton

CHAPTER TEN

Zach watched Nick check one of the six fishing lines they had standing along the beach. So far, they had no bites, but that was normal. Surf fishing took a lot of time and patience. It seemed that Zach and Nick had enormous amounts of both.

Opening the beach chairs he brought with them, Zach made himself comfortable near the rods. The cold October water rushed in and out as the sun rose higher in the morning sky. The temperature was expected to reach the low 70s, and the morning was perfect for sitting on the beach, watching the lines disappear into the water.

"High tide was just about two hours ago," Nick said. "We should get a bite soon."

"Patience you must have, my young Padawan."

Nick laughed. "So, now I'm Luke and you're my master?"

"Master, I am, young Jedi," Zach replied.

"Oh, great Yoda, what wisdom do you have to impart on this Jedi-in-training?" Nick took a seat in the second chair and opened the cooler. "Hey, there's only water in here. Where's the beer?"

"It's only a little after nine," Zach said, looking at his friend.

"It's five o'clock somewhere," Nick said, opening a bottle of water and downing the entire thing with one gulp.

"I guess it is," Zach agreed. "But this isn't the Marines, and you'll learn real fast that civilian life is a whole lot different from life on a base."

"I'm ready for civilian life if it means bagging me a woman like yours."

Zach turned toward the younger man. "What's that supposed to mean?" he growled.

"Hey, take it easy. I get it. She's off limits. But tell me something, oh great Yoda. Are you and Kayla friends, dating, or just sleeping together?"

Zach felt his pulse quicken and his jaw tense. "If you're going to live in my house," he said through clenched teeth, "then you will respect my privacy, and you will respect Kayla. Is that understood?"

Nick took off his baseball cap, scratched the top of his head, and put the cap back on. "Yes, sir. I'm sorry man. I didn't mean to offend you . . . oh, great master" he said trying to recover the levity from moments before. "But seriously, I'm guessing she's pretty special." Nick looked at Zach, but Zach just gazed out over the horizon. He didn't want to talk about Kayla.

"So, are there any other single women on the island? It doesn't seem like the ideal pick up place."

Zach took his time answering. "Nick, you're right. This isn't a pick-up place. If you want that, then you'll have to drive up to Ocean City where there are plenty of bars and nightclubs. You might find a girl who's willing to take you home for the night. You might even find one worth dating for a while, but then what? At the end of the week, vacation's over, and she goes back home. Or at the end of the year, her semester at the university is over for the summer, or she graduates, and she's gone. Where does that leave you? Prowling the bars looking for another girl to take you home that night. At some point, you have to stop prowling and start looking hard for someone who's going to be willing to stick around and accept you for who you are, flaws and all."

"That's not an issue for me. I have no flaws." Nick raised his brow and grinned at Zach.

"Yep," Zach sighed. "I can see that. You're the perfect man."

"Well, I am a Marine. I can see how you, an old washed up Army guy, can't appreciate my perfection, but trust me, I am too good for just one girl, especially one who's going to 'stick around.' No, sir, ain't nobody got time for that." He put his arms behind his head and leaned back in the chair with his eyes closed and cap low on his brow, stretching out his legs in the sand.

"How old are you, Nick?"

"Twenty-Seven. Still in my prime. I've got a long time before I need to start thinking about settling down, if I even want that."

"You don't want a good woman to come home to at night? A family? Kids?"

"With a white picket fence and a minivan in the driveway? Hell, no, I don't want that." He winced and looked over at Zach. "I'd rather be my own man, make my own rules and decisions. I don't need some broad telling me what to do."

"Agreed," Zach said. "But not every woman is 'some broad.'"

"Then why are you living alone when you have a built-in family next door? I see the way you look at her. What gives?"

"I told you, it's none of your business."

"When I came down this morning, you were watching her house like you expected Public Enemy Number One to walk out of there and right into the crosshairs of your rifle scope. You were intense, man. She's got you all tied up in knots, but you don't even act like a couple. I can't figure you out."

"Are you going to mind your own business, or are you going to continue pestering me until I show you how a soldier deals with a jarhead who won't shut up?"

"Whatever, man. I'm just sayin' that if you call that settling down with a good woman, there's something one of us doesn't understand."

Zach watched the gulls dive in and out of the waves. There were fish out there, but so far, their fishing lines were still.

"Her husband was murdered," he said quietly. "Shot."

"And?"

"Don't you think that complicates things considering my past?"

"She doesn't seem to see it as a problem."

For the next few minutes, the only sounds to be heard were the crashing of the waves and the call of the gulls. Zach wrestled with how much to say. Talking to Father

Darryl always helped. Perhaps talking to Nick might help as well. They had done and seen similar things.

"She doesn't know."

"I see," Nick said. "And you're afraid to tell her."

Zach let his silence speak for him.

"Look, Zach," Nick said, turning toward his friend. "I'm no expert when it comes to women, especially decent women worth hanging onto, but if you really want to be with her as much as I think you do, then you should tell her. She will either take it well or send you packing. One thing's for certain; if you don't level with her, and you continue to let it come between the two of you, you'll spend the rest of your life wondering what might have been."

Zach let his friend's words sink in for a bit before saying anything.

"You know, Nick, you aren't as stupid or as big a jerk as you like people to think you are."

Nick laughed. "Don't let that get around, you hear?"

***

"Kayla Reynolds," the nurse called from the doorway.

Kayla took a deep breath and looked at her mother and sister-in-law. "Well, I guess this is it."

"It's all going to be fine, Kayla," Ronnie assured her.

"I pray you're right," she said as she stood. "Let's go get this over with."

The three women gathered their coats and purses and followed the nurse down the hall. Though painted a cheery yellow, with photographs of flowers, beaches, and sunrises along the walls, the hallway seemed more like a narrow, prison walkway to Kayla. She felt like Sean Penn advancing toward death row, with Susan Sarandon by her side, as someone called out, 'Dead man walking.' A shudder went through her, and she tried to shake that image from her mind.

They were led into an office rather than an exam room, and after only a few minutes, Dr. Zink walked in. She washed her hands in a small sink in the corner and then shook their hands, introducing herself to Ronnie and Kate.

"We have the results back from your biopsy, Kayla." She double-checked her laptop. "I'm afraid they're not good."

Kayla was glad to be seated because she was sure she felt the ground open under her. She was dizzy and felt nauseous.

"Is it cancer?" Ronnie asked.

"I'm afraid so," Dr. Zink answered. "And, as we suspected, it has spread to the ducts."

"No!" Kayla exclaimed. "No! This is not happening." She stood and paced in front of the desk before she stopped and slammed her fist down on the polished oak. "My husband is dead. Do you hear me? He's dead. And I have two little boys at home. They can't lose me, too. Is that understood? I cannot leave them."

"Kayla, I'm not planning on losing you," Dr. Zink said calmly. "I'm planning on helping you beat this disease so that you and your boys can live long, happy lives together."

Taking a breath, Kayla closed her eyes and willed herself to calm down. Her mother and Kate were silent, no doubt allowing her to vent as needed. She shook her head and inhaled again before sitting down.

"Okay, Doctor, what's next?"

"We'll do surgery to remove the cancer. We'll need to talk about whether or not we do a mastectomy. We'll need to know what recourses we have available to us during surgery."

"Do you think I'll need one?" Kayla asked.

"With your family history and considering how advanced your cancer was even after years of screenings, it's something we want to consider, especially if the cancer has gone into the lymph nodes under the arm. We won't know if that's the case until after we biopsy the tissue, so we might not even know that day if you're going to need more surgery. But Kayla, removing a breast doesn't always mean that the cancer won't return. It's not cut and dry."

"I thought removal was always the safest way to go."

"Not anymore. Research shows that it's about fifty-fifty either way."

"What do you recommend?"

"I recommend that you read the brochures I'm going to give you and think about what you'd want to do. If, once we're inside, I don't see an option, I will make the decision for you. If I think we can save the breast, and that's what you want to do, I'll reconstruct as best I can. Either way, you will need follow-up treatments."

"Will I need radiation or chemo?"

"In your case, I think chemotherapy is our best option, but again, we need to get in there and see exactly what we're facing. Now, let's talk about the exact procedure."

Kayla listened and nodded, making mental notes here and there, as Dr. Zink threw around words like lumpectomy, breast-conservation, sentinel lymph node biopsy versus axillary lymph node dissection, and treatments with medication such as anthracyclines.

Two hours later, flanked by her mother and best friend, Kayla exited the elevator to the parking garage pretty exhausted after undergoing several more tests and another chest x-ray. Ronnie and Kate looped their arms through hers as if she needed their support just to make it to the car. Once inside the garage, she shrugged them off.

"I can walk just fine on my own, thank you very much." She took another step and then turned around to face them. "I can walk, I can drive, I can cook, and I can take care of my boys. And by God, I'm going to keep doing those things until I'm too sick to do them, and then I'm going to work my butt off to get my strength back up so that I can do them again. I've never been a quitter or someone who lives in fear. If I can make it through losing Eddie, I can make it through anything."

"That's my girl," Ronnie said, linking her arm back through Kayla's.

"We're right here to help you win the battle," Kate said, taking the other arm.

"All for one, and one for all," Kayla shouted, feeling somewhat silly but desperately needing to feel in control. She ignored the strange looks from passersby in the parking garage and smiled as an older man winked at her.

"Dinner's on me," Ronnie said. "And I'm not taking no for an answer. You'll need to keep up your strength, and we might as well begin with a good, totally-bad-for-us dinner, and a pitcher of strong margaritas."

Though she had no appetite, Kayla didn't want to tell her mother no. And she could use a good, strong drink. Or three.

***

Aaron picked up EJ and Todd from school on Tuesday and took them home. Kayla, Ronnie, Trevor, and Kate were waiting inside the house when Aaron's truck pulled into the drive. Kayla was nervous about talking to the boys, but she knew they had a good support system surrounding them.

"Mommy!" Todd yelled as he flew through the door and flung himself into her arms. "I missed you."

"I missed you, too, sweetie."

When EJ walked in, his eyes met hers, and Kayla tried to offer him a reassuring smile. She saw the flash of understanding in his eyes and the slight slump of his shoulders before he straightened himself up and allowed her to envelop him in her open arms.

"It's bad news, isn't it?" He whispered into her shoulder. She was struck by how tall he was and wondered why she hadn't noticed before.

Pressing her lips tightly together, she pulled back and took his hand. Taking Todd's hand, she led them both to the sofa.

"Boys, I need you to sit down. I have something to tell you."

"Is it about Timmy's cousin?" Todd asked. "It's been days since he got lost, and nobody has found him."

Her heart missed a beat, but she regained her composure, asking forgiveness from above for forcing the little boy's disappearance from her mind for the time being.

"No, honey, it's not about Henry. It's about us."

She looked at EJ, but he avoided her gaze. She saw the tears he held back and knew that he was trying to be strong for her and for his younger brother.

Kayla took a seat on the coffee table so that she could face them both.

"Boys, I have something to tell you, and it may sound scary at first, but we're going to be okay. The three of us are going to get through this."

Todd furrowed his brow in confusion. "What is it, Mommy? Another bad storm like the one last year when we had to stay at Grandma and Grandpa's for a week?"

Kayla smiled, "No, honey, not a storm." Though she could relate to the analogy. It certainly felt like a violent storm was ripping through her life, leaving destruction in its wake. "Todd, do you know what cancer is?"

"Kind of," the little boy said slowly. "Benny's granddad had cancer and went to Heaven like Daddy did."

Not the best scenario to follow, Kayla thought. She tried to think of a way to approach the topic without frightening him.

"But Laurie Stewart's dad had cancer, and he got better," EJ reminded him. "And so did Grandma, when you were a baby."

God bless you, my sweet son, Kayla thought, nodding at EJ.

"You did?" Todd looked around his mother and focused on Ronnie.

"I did, and I'm still here," she said with a smile.

"Todd," Kayla said, trying to recapture his attention. "I had to go to the doctor yesterday. A doctor who was far away from here. That's why you stayed with Grandpa last night."

"Why did you have to go to the doctor, Mommy? Are you sick?"

"Well, baby, that's what I'm trying to tell you. I am sick. I have something called breast cancer."

"Isn't your breast your booby, where your baby milk is, like Aunt Kate?"

Everyone laughed, and the mood lightened for just a moment.

"It is," Kayla told him. "Very good. Breasts contain milk for babies. But they also have tissue in them just like many other parts of your body. And sometimes, that tissue gets sick and starts making all the other tissue around it sick. Just like when someone in your class has a cold and then after a few days, everyone in the class has a cold."

"Oh, I get it," Todd said, but Kayla could see by his frown that he still didn't quite understand. "Does your breast tissue have a cold?"

Kayla smiled. God, she loved that kid. "Kind of, honey. But tissue in your body doesn't get a cold, it gets cancer."

Todd's eyes widened as understanding dawned on him. "Mommy, is your breast sick? Is it going to get better?"

"Yes, it's sick, and the doctor says I have a good chance of getting better." She looked at EJ. "But I have to have surgery first. That's what they do with breast cancer. The doctor will cut me open and cut out the sick tissue. But the thing with cancer is that sometimes, even when you think it's all better, it comes back. So, the doctors give you lots and lots of medicine to try to make sure it doesn't come back. And that medicine is going to make me feel sicker even though I need it to get better. It's going to make me weak, and it might make my hair fall out. But if that happens, when I'm all finished with the medicine, my hair will grow back. And then I'll be all better."

"Okay, Mommy," Todd said, holding back tears.

She knew she was telling him too much, making promises she didn't know if she could keep, rushing to the end before they even knew for sure what the next step would be after the surgery. There was so much they wouldn't know until she was lying on the operating table. But she couldn't just leave it at that and make him think there was no hope. She needed him, all of them, to believe that she would get better. She needed to believe it herself.

***

Zach was washing dinner dishes but not from the dinner he promised. He had texted Kayla early Monday to wish her luck and back out of their Tuesday night dinner plans. He knew by her short reply she was upset, but he couldn't face her after Sunday night. He knew now that he could never tell her the truth about his past. His phone was on the counter beside the sink in case someone thought to call him with news. He continuously peered through the dark at the lights in her house. He watched the faint shadows and movement and was desperate to know what was being said. It had been hours, and he didn't know how much longer he could stand the wait. When his phone buzzed, Zach practically dropped it into the sink as he fumbled to answer it.

"Kate, hey, what's going on?" He asked urgently.

"Zach, can I come over?"

"You bet. Hurry up."

He wiped his hands with a nearby dish towel, then tossed the towel onto the counter. He stood by the door and watched as his sister walked quickly down the steps of Kayla's house, using her phone as a flashlight, and hurried toward the light on his back deck. He held the door open for her, and she melted into his arms.

"Zach, I'm sorry I didn't call sooner," she said, looking up into his eyes. "I didn't feel it was my place to tell anyone before the boys knew."

"Dr. Swann's suspicions were confirmed." He stated the obvious. The fear in her eyes and the way she held him, as if she needed his strength to stay standing, gave her away.

"Yes. It's definitely cancer. In the breast tissue and the milk ducts."

"What's the prognosis?" he asked, leading her to the kitchen table, pulling out a chair, and easing her down onto the seat.

"We don't know. She has to have surgery."

"When?" he asked, sitting down beside her.

When Kate told Zach the date of the surgery, he thought she'd made a mistake, or that he'd heard her wrong.

"What? But that's," he abruptly stood and went to the calendar hanging on the wall. He began to count the days.

"Thirty-two days from now," Kate said.

Zach turned back to her, a range of emotions rippling through him, everything from fear to outrage.

"I know," she said before he could find his voice. "It seems like a long time. Ronnie says that's normal."

"Normal? It's normal to make her wait an entire month? What the...?" He shook his head. "Why? Can't they go in sooner? Won't it get worse if she waits?"

"Dr. Zink says that it doesn't move that fast. She said that waiting a month is fine and that Kayla has nothing to worry about as far as that goes."

"Easy for her to say." Zach threw up his hands and began pacing across the floor. "What about Kayla? She has to wait a month before they even do the surgery? And then what? Will they do radiation?"

"Because of the dense tissue, the cancer possibly spreading to other breast tissue or lymph nodes, and her family history, they'll most likely do chemo. That is, depending upon the outcome of the surgery. Her doctor hopes to save her breast, but since there's concern about a recurrence, that might not be possible. There are many factors. Worst case scenario is that they open her up and realize they can't do anything at all." Kate choked on her words, and Zach sat back down beside her. He wrapped his arms around her and held her while she cried.

"I better get back over there. The boys have school tomorrow, and Aaron will have to go to work. They've probably finished the dinner dishes by now."

"What about Kayla? Is someone staying with her tonight?"

Kate shook her head. "She said she'll be fine. Instead of stopping for dinner on the way home last night, Mom ordered a pizza and stopped and bought everything to make Margaritas. I shouldn't have had that second one, to be honest." She rolled her eyes. "We were up half the night last night. It was all I could do to hold my head up today. Hopefully we'll all sleep well tonight."

Kate got up to leave, but Zach stood and grabbed her arm.

"Listen, Kate, tell Kayla I'm sorry. Please. Let her know I'll be praying for her."

Kate cocked her head and looked at her brother. "Why can't you tell her yourself? She said you backed out on dinner tonight. That hurt her. She needs you, Zach. Go see her."

Zach shook his head. "I don't think so. I think she's better off not seeing me. Trust me, it's for the best."

"Zach, what are you talking about? For the best? For whom?"

"For everyone. In fact, once Nick's on his feet, I'm thinking of heading to Florida. I'm sure Mom and Dad would appreciate having me nearby. They aren't getting any younger."

"Well, they sure don't act like they're getting any older. They're on a cruise in the Mediterranean. So much for Dad's beliefs about the way we're destroying the earth and taking land away from the native people who rightfully own it. Between his new-found obsession with golf and Mom's sudden fondness for cruise ships, they're leaving their carbon footprints all over the globe."

"All the more reason. I can take care of the house and the yard when they're away."

"Zach, what's gotten into you? You love it here. You wanted to make a home here. And whether you want to admit it or not, you love Kayla. I know you do. I know you better than anyone in the world, and I've seen the way you look at her, the way you act around her. You've been in love with her since the day you met."

"I'm no good for her, Kate. Just let it be. My leaving would be the best thing that could happen to her."

"You're an idiot," Kate yelled at her brother, pushing him away as hard as she could. "You're the most selfish jerk I've ever met. I don't even recognize you. You scared, selfish son of a..." Her eyes blazed with fury as she shook her fist at him. "She loves you, and she needs you. More than she's ever needed anyone. And you're going to run out on her? I can't believe what I'm hearing. My big brother, who I always thought hung the moon, is nothing but a coward. Some big, tough soldier you are. Well, you know where you can go,

Zachary Daniel Middleton. Don't bother coming to say goodbye when you leave. I'll be with Kayla. Picking up the pieces to her broken heart."

Kate threw open the door and stormed out of the house, letting the screen door slam behind her.

"Family squabble?" Nick said from the doorway to the living room.

"Go f—"

"Tsk, tsk, tsk. Watch that language, Captain Middleton."

"What do you want?" Zach roared. "Don't you know better than to stick your nose where it's not wanted?"

"Perhaps if you all didn't invite the entire neighborhood to come see the show with all that shouting, I would have stayed in my room like a good little boy. So, what's this I hear about you moving to Florida?"

"Don't worry. I won't leave you high and dry," Zach said sardonically.

"I'm not worried. Not about me anyway. You, on the other hand…"

"What about me?" Zach opened the refrigerator, swiped a beer, and reached for the magnetic bottle opener hanging on the door. He wrenched the cap lose with such force, it flew off the bottle and into the air. Taking a long swig, he watched as everyone started to leave the house next door.

"You talk a big game, sport, but your sister's right. You're nothing but a coward."

The bottle stopped in mid-air. Zach turned around to face the man he had invited to share his home and wanted to deck him.

"It's true, man. From what I can see, you've got a great woman in your life, who's as crazy about you as you are about her. After just two afternoons together, I could see it as plain as day. And you're so hung up on the past, you won't even consider trying to have a future. You're afraid to take a chance in life, but meanwhile, she's fighting for hers. And what are you going to do? Leave her when she needs you the most. What the hell is wrong with you? If I had a woman like that, all that crap I said at the beach would be out the window. I'd do anything to make her mine."

"You don't know what you're talking about," Zach said, trying to keep his temper in check.

"No, Zach, you're the one who doesn't know what he's talking about. I just hope you figure it out soon." He nodded toward Kayla's house. "That woman deserves someone who's going to love her, stick by her, and help her get through the toughest fight of her life. I just hope you come to your senses before it's too late."

Nick turned and walked away, leaving Zach to his thoughts. He emptied the bottle and threw it through the doorway into the living room, letting it smash against the fireplace, sending shards of glass around the room. Sitting at the table, he buried his face in his hands and wept.

Prize-Worthy Pumpkin Bread
Origin: Germany

When I need to relax, I bake. My obsession with baking began when I was in middle school. Every time I had a big test coming up, I found that baking helped me calm my mind so that I could study more effectively. Perhaps it was the aroma of chocolate or lemon or spices that wafted from the oven as I sat at the table and went over my notes. Whatever it was, I have always had the urge to bake whenever I have something weighing on my mind, and my meditative formula of choice is a pumpkin bread recipe my mother discovered years ago. I have never tasted any other as good as this.

From *Around the World in Eighty Meals*
by K.Z. Middleton

<u>CHAPTER ELEVEN</u>

Kate's phone rang Friday morning. Her first thought was of Kayla. Was something wrong? Or was it Zach? Had he finally come to his senses, or was he calling to say goodbye?

"Hold on, baby, Mommy has to see who this is." Kate put down Miren's spoon of applesauce and picked up her phone. She shook her head and sent the call to voicemail. Before she finished dipping the spoon into the bowl for another helping, the phone rang again. Sighing, she answered the call.

"Hey, Megan, what's up?"

"Kate, are you home?"

"Yes, I'm feeding the baby. You sound weird. Are you okay?"

"I don't know. Can we talk?"

Kate looked at Miren. She hated to be on the phone while she was feeding or playing with her little girl. She wanted Miren to know that she would always have her undivided attention. But there was something in Megan's voice that worried her.

"Sure, mind if I put you on speaker? It's just Miren and me here."

"Um, how about I just come in?"

Kate looked around. "Come in? Where are you?"

"Sitting in your driveway. I rented a car. I needed to get away."

Kate stood and rushed to the front door. Sure enough, when she opened the door, she saw an unfamiliar car in the driveway. Megan was sitting in the front seat.

"Yes, come in," Kate said quickly, waving from the front door. She disconnected the call and ran back to the kitchen to check on Miren.

"Kate?" Megan called from the doorway.

"Come back here," Kate called.

Megan appeared in the kitchen doorway as Kate wiped a bit of applesauce from Miren's chin.

"So, this is Miren," Megan said with a smile. "Hey, cutie. I've heard a lot about you."

Kate didn't know what to say. It was surreal seeing Megan in her kitchen. Their friendship, the time they worked together, and the partying they did seemed like the life of a different person. Kate could hardly remember those days, before she came to the island, before she met Aaron and Kayla, before she became a bona-fide writer and upstanding member of the community. The old her, 'Katherine,' would be mortified to know that stunning, confident, male-magnet Megan was standing there looking at Kate, unshowered with oatmeal and pureed peaches in her hair. Kate resisted the urge to apologize for her appearance.

"Megan, what are you doing here?" she asked, and then it hit her. Kate reached for Megan's hand. "Did Brad, or anyone, do something to you or hurt you?"

Megan burst into tears.

"Kate, it was awful. He called me into his office for a meeting. And then he, he…"

Kate's grip on Megan's hand tightened. "He backed me up against a wall, held my hands above my head, and kissed me. When I refused to kiss him back, he let go and told me that I had better learn how to cooperate, or I was going to be selling ads for the rest of my life and never write a word for that magazine or any other. I felt so gross, Kate. Nobody has ever treated me like that. I couldn't stand the thought of going to work this morning, so I, I left."

"And you came here," Kate said sympathetically. She released her hold on Megan, and now looked at her friend with compassion.

"Yes," Megan admitted. "I just kept thinking about you and how you were so brave when you left and made a new start, and I thought, if Kate can do it, so can I. But I didn't know how or where to start. After it happened, I said I was sick and left work. Then I went home and got into bed. I couldn't eat, and I never slept. Then I got up this morning and packed, took a bus to the nearest rent-a-car place, and here I am."

"How did you find me?"

"Snapchat. I told my phone to take me to your location."

"Wait, you can do that?" Kate asked grabbing her phone.

"Yeah, anyone can find you. But I deactivated that on my phone as soon as I decided to leave."

"Can you do that to mine?" Kate asked, chills running down her spine. After being stalked and nearly killed, the last thing she wanted was for others to be able to locate her so easily.

"Yeah, hand me your phone." After a few taps on the screen, Megan handed the phone back to Kate. "There you go. Nobody can see where you are now."

"Phew." Kate blew out her breath. "Thank God." She put down the spoon and wiped Miren's face with the edge of the bib before turning back to Megan. "So, what are you going to do now?"

Megan sat back and sighed. "I have no idea."

Kate smiled. "That sounds familiar."

"I know it would be too much for me to stay here. I won't do that to you guys. You're practically newlyweds. But is there somewhere I can stay? Until I figure out what I'm going to do next?"

"You want to stay *here*? In Chincoteague?"

"Yeah. Why not? It worked for you."

Kate looked at Megan. She was young and gorgeous. She was smart, though she tried to hide it. Heaven only knows why. She had luxurious black hair that fell halfway down her back and always looked perfect. Her dark brown eyes were like pools of chocolate, and her skin appeared sun-kissed all year long. She looked like she belonged on an island. But didn't she have a responsibility to tell someone about Brad?

"I'm not sure where you can stay, but I can check. My friend, Shannon, works at the local library. I can ask her to look at the bulletin board and see if anyone has posted anything for rent. But Megan, I think you should go back. At the very least, call Sydney in HR. Tell her what happened."

"I can't, Kate. What if I have to face him? What if they insist we meet or something? I can't do that. It would be humiliating. And what if he's like Mark and turns psycho or something? What if he makes sure I can't work for any media outlet ever again? He knows how much I want to write meaningful stories that touch people's lives. This job was supposed to be a stepping stone for me, not a means of getting stepped on."

Megan looked utterly defeated, and Kate understood. Though the jobs they had in advertising ended up being on the road to nowhere, they both started with high hopes that it would lead to something big in journalism.

Kate sighed. "Look, I really think you need to let someone know what happened, but I understand that you need to get to that place on your own. I'll help you find a place to stay, but I'm not going to stop encouraging you to call Sydney. She will be on your side. You know that."

"Kate, I'm not blind. I see what others see when they look at me. Most women think I'm a threat to their relationships. They'll say I asked for it. But I didn't." She looked at Kate defiantly. "I've never been successful at finding girlfriends I could trust. Except you. And I'm afraid that Sydney's just like all the rest. She'll say it was my fault, that I led him on, or I deserved it in some way. Well, no thanks. I'm not going through all that."

"I think you're wrong about Sydney. And what if there are others?" Kate asked. "What if you're not the first woman he's done this to? What if you're not the last, and you could have stopped it?"

Megan rolled her lips inward and thought about that. "I don't know," she said quietly. She looked at Kate, her eyes full of uncertainty.

"Just think about it," Kate said, patting her arm.

"Okay, I will. And Kate, thank you."

"You're welcome, Megan. I'm sorry this happened to you."

"Me, too," Megan said sadly.

Kate hoped she would be all right. Megan had a strong personality. If she could be a victim to Brad, then anyone is vulnerable to his advances.

***

"So, she just showed up on your doorstep?" Kayla asked, shaking her head in disbelief.

"She did. Can you imagine? She just packed up and left without a word to anyone. How crazy is that?"

Kayla just looked at Kate. "Did you just hear yourself?"

Kate paused for a moment, raising a brow as she looked at her sister-in-law. "What?"

"Didn't you do exactly the same thing?" Kayla took a loaf of pumpkin bread from the oven and placed it on a cooling rack before reaching for a second one.

"It was different for me," Kate said, walking to the counter and inhaling the spicy scents of pumpkin, cinnamon, and ginger that rose above the loaves.

"How so?" Kayla asked with her hands on her hips. Then her expression softened. "Oh, Kate, did that guy do something to her?"

"He did, but I don't feel like it's my place to say anything. Megan isn't ready to face it, so I don't think I should talk about it to anybody else. Hopefully she's going to tell someone. I'd hate for him to do the same thing to someone else."

Kayla looked stricken. "Was it, did he, how bad was it?"

"Not the worst-case scenario but bad enough. Sexual harassment, for sure."

"Poor girl. Well, I agree. I do hope she finds the courage to tell someone. It might be the only way she can find closure."

"You know," Kate said. "I can't imagine what I would do if some guy like Brad started harassing Miren. What will this world be like when she's out there?"

Kate looked lovingly at her daughter and shifted the baby to her other hip.

"Let's pray that women are a lot farther along in this crusade by the time she's out there," Kayla said, taking her niece from Kate and bouncing her up and down as she made faces at the little girl. "Where's Megan now?"

"At the library. Shannon has some leads on rentals and possible short-term jobs. I offered to go with her, but she said she was okay and didn't want to completely disrupt my day. We're going to meet after lunch, so I can drive her around to see the rental options. She wants my opinion on them. Then we have to find a way to get her rental car to wherever it needs to go."

"Sounds like a solid start." Kayla loosened Miren's hold on a lock of hair, grimacing as the baby's sticky fingers pulled out several strands with her strong grip.

"So, what's on your agenda for today?" Kate asked.

"Baking. I'm baking all of my favorite things and freezing them in case I'm not up to doing it later."

"Okay. I guess that makes sense."

"What else am I supposed to do?" Kayla asked, snuggling Miren close enough to her face to inhale the comforting aroma of baby shampoo mixed with scented powder.

"How about go back to cooking for others? Start the business back up. You've got a month. You could be working and bringing some satisfaction to yourself and others. It would certainly keep you busy."

Kayla shook her head. "I don't know, Kate. I've been thinking about it, and I'm not loving the job as much as I thought I would."

"Why not?"

"It doesn't *feel* right. I thought I would enjoy cooking meals for others so that their loads would be lighter and their days a bit easier. But all it does is make my days more complicated. I'm running to the store all the time, and I feel like the boys get the short end of the stick. There are nights when we have to rush through our dinners because it's so late by the time I get the other dinners out. And we don't always love what we eat because we end up eating whatever the orders are that night. I don't have time to make different meals just for us. It's just not what I thought it would be."

Kayla handed Miren back to Kate and checked on the bread. It was still too warm to package, but she wanted to get another batch done and needed the loaf pans. She proceeded to pour the sugar into the mixing bowl and added the eggs and canola oil.

Kate put Miren in her bouncy seat and settled into her chair as Kayla turned on the mixer and moved on to the next step in her recipe. Kayla didn't mind the audience. It felt natural to chat as she measured the dry ingredients.

"So, what can we do to fix the problem? Can you make the meals ahead of time? Get them done over the weekend?"

Kayla frowned, holding a measuring cup of flour in the air over the mixer. "That means I'd have to take time away from the boys on Saturdays or skip Sunday dinner at Mom's. And some of the foods are better when they're freshly made."

"Can we adjust the menu so that the meals are quicker to prepare or can be frozen and cooked that evening?"

"Maybe," Kayla said as she began adding more ingredients to the batter. "I'll have to think about it."

"Just let me know how to help," Kate said. "I'll do anything you need."

Kayla turned to Kate and smiled. "What did I do before you came here?"

"I have no idea," Kate said. "I've been asking myself the same thing."

Kayla rolled her eyes and laughed.

"So," Kayla said nonchalantly. "Have you talked to Zach?"

"Not since Tuesday. You?"

Kayla bit her lips and shook her head.

"Kay, I'm not sure what to say about my brother. He's going through something that I can't help him with. I wish I could say more or that I could do something to help, but he has to figure this out on his own."

"I know," Kayla said. "It's a lot to process. Just when we were starting to get back to where we were before the last time he disappeared on us, I end up with the big C." She let out a little puff of air and gently shook her head. "I'm just surprised. I mean, he's known for weeks that this might happen." She stopped what she was doing and looked at Kate. "He made promises to me. He said he wasn't going anywhere. He said he'd be there for me throughout this whole thing and that when it was confirmed…anyway, maybe I'm wrong. Maybe I misunderstood. He never actually said we'd have a future together, just that we'd see where things stood."

Kate looked torn, and Kayla knew that she was privy to more than she could say.

"Please, Kate, please level with me. What is going on? I'm so tired of the roller coaster. Please tell me if I should cut my losses and forget about him? I can't take much more of his indecision. I need to expend my energies on other things."

"Kay, I—" Kate looked away and then turned back toward Kayla. "Do you have any idea what happened? Why Zach pulled back this time? Was it something that was said or something that happened?"

"Not that I can think of. He came over on Sunday, after we got home from Mom's. I was cooking dinner for

Justine and Hank, and he said he'd go with me and the boys to deliver it. Oh, Kate, it was awful. Justine was such a mess. The whole house just seemed to drip with despair. She's so worried that the same thing that happened to that little Graham boy is happening to her nephew. When we left, she was just sitting there crying, and Hank was trying to hold it together. On the way home, I told Zach that I couldn't understand how someone could do such a thing, with no regard for human life. Whoever did this is a monster."

"Kayla, what exactly did you say to Zach?"

"What do you mean?" Kayla noticed a shift in Kate's posture. Her eyes were wide with alarm. "Kate, what are you thinking?"

"Kayla, listen to me. I need to know what you said to Zach. Exactly what words did you use?"

"I, I don't know exactly. I think I said that it must have been a soulless excuse for a human who would shoot someone with no regard for them or their families. Or something like that. I was projecting, I guess. We don't know exactly what happened to Ryan Graham. The police have been very tight-lipped about it. We've only heard rumors. But sitting there with Justine brought back all of the hurt and anger about Eddie. I guess I was just laying it all out there."

Kate took a deep breath and nodded slowly. "Okay. What did Zach say?"

"He didn't say anything. As a matter of fact, he was quiet the whole ride home. He didn't even ask to come in or tell the boys goodnight. He just told me goodnight and went inside. I was so preoccupied that I didn't even think anything about it at the time. All I could think of was that poor little boy and my doctor's appointment the next day. And then he texted me on Monday morning to say good luck, and he cancelled making dinner for us on Tuesday. I have no idea why." Kayla's heart ached as she sank into the chair next to Kate. "It's my past, isn't it? It's too much baggage. He probably thinks I'll never get over losing Eddie, that I can never love another man. I've scared him off, haven't I?"

Kate pressed her lips together until they turned white while Kayla waited for a reply. Closing her eyes, Kate took a long, deep inhale. Opening her eyes, she reached over to take Kayla's hand and squeezed it.

"Kayla, you told me that you love Zach, but do you truly love him? I mean, are you in love with him?"

"Kate, I do. I know I haven't shown it, and I've only told you how I feel. But my diagnosis has made me realize that I can't take life for granted. When Zach started coming back around, I was angry. Then I was confused. I thought it would be selfish to start something when I had no idea what my prognosis would be and if I'd be around for the long haul. But, Kate, I'm beginning to realize that life truly is short. I never thought I'd have a chance at love again, and now, I feel like I'd be a fool not to try. What if I'm not going to make it? Shouldn't I try to make the most of life while I can? And what if Zach's support is just what I need to pull me through? Oh, Kate, that does sound selfish. Am I wrong? Say something. Please, tell me what to do," Kayla implored.

"First, relax and take a breath. No, you're not being selfish. You deserve to be happy, and so does Zach, no matter how long or short the time might be. But Kayla, I need to know, and this is important, would you love him no matter what? Do you love him unconditionally? No matter his faults? No matter his past?"

"Kate," Kayla grabbed Kate's hands and held them as tightly as she could. "I love him. There is nothing he could say or do to change that."

"Then, Kayla, you need to tell him that. But you need to promise me something first."

"Anything."

"You need to promise me that you won't forget you said that. You will love him no matter what."

Kayla released Kate's hands and sat back and looked at her sister-in-law. Kate's brow was creased, and she rolled her lips together several times. There was concern written all over her face.

"Kate, what aren't you telling me?"

"No, you just said unconditionally. You said nothing would change that. Right?"

"Kate?"

"Go. Talk to him. He needs you as much as you need him. But, I mean it Kayla, don't do it if you can't keep that promise. I won't let my brother suffer any more than he already has."

Kayla slowly nodded. What had she just promised? And why was Kate so worried that it was a promise she might not be able to keep?

***

"What's this?" Trevor asked from the doorway to Kayla's office.

Kayla looked up from her computer and smiled. Her father held a glass of water that had a string running up the inside and looping over the edge.

"Todd's latest science experiment. He's growing salt crystals."

Trevor held the glass close to his eyes and peered inside. "I don't see anything."

"It takes a few days." Kayla shook her head. "That kid has become a mad scientist. Ever since Mr. Palmer, arrived, science is all Todd cares about. I never know what he's going to come home wanting to do next."

Trevor laughed. "There are worse things he could be into." He turned back to the kitchen and put the glass down on the counter.

"Very true." Kayla chuckled as she thought about her son and his new enthusiasm for his favorite subject and favorite teacher. She was so happy that Todd looked forward to school every day. That was one battle she was grateful to not have to fight.

"Hey, how are you doing?" Trevor asked, returning to the doorway.

"I'm okay, Dad. Thanks for asking." She smiled, but she knew that her father was not fooled.

"Want to talk about it?" He walked into the room and sat on the large armchair in the corner.

"About the cancer? Not really," she said, leaning back in her chair.

"About Zach," her father said matter-of-factly.

Kayla couldn't suppress her surprise.

"Zach? What about him?"

"Do I need to have a talk with him? Find out why he stopped coming around? Maybe rough him up a little?" He grinned, but Kayla knew he was serious about wanting to help.

"Dad, I love you, and you've always been my hero, but Zach is twice your size. I wouldn't advise 'roughing him up.'" She loved that her father was such a wonderful dad.

"I could take him," Trevor said, "but I won't if you don't want me to."

Kayla was pretty sure her father knew he couldn't beat up Zach, but she sensed that he was serious about finding out what was going on with her neighbor. She held her hands out in front of her.

"Dad, I don't know what's going on with Zach, but I've got a lot going on in my own life right now. I don't really have time to worry about what's on his mind." She tried to sound nonchalant even though she wished like crazy that she knew what was going on in Zach's mind.

Trevor watched her for several seconds before nodding and rising from the chair.

"If you change your mind…"

"Thanks, Dad. I'll keep that in mind." She smiled as she watched him leave. She loved Zach, more than she'd loved Eddie. But there would never be a man she loved more than her father.

***

Zach and Nick got out of the truck as Kate's SUV pulled up to the curb outside the little bungalow. They waited for her to open the door and climb out.

"Sis, what are you doing here?"

"Hey, Zach," Kate said without fondness or enthusiasm. "What are you doing here?"

"Nick heard that this place is for rent. How about you?" It was then that Zach realized Kate wasn't alone. He reached his hand out to Megan when she walked around to the driver's side of the vehicle. "Hi, I'm Zach, Kate's brother."

"Hi, I'm Megan. Nice to meet you." She offered a slight smile.

The girl was stunning, and Zach had to force himself to look away.

"Megan and I worked together at the magazine. She's taking some time off for herself. We're here so that *she* can look at the bungalow."

"Oh. Well, that's awkward," Zach said. The four were silent until Zach blew out his breath and shook his head, shifting his gaze from his sister to Megan. Whatever decision was made about the house was not his. He'd let Megan and Nick work that out.

"So, are you here for long?" Zach asked Megan, thinking again that she might be one of the most beautiful women he'd ever seen. Exotic was an even better description.

"I'm not sure," Megan said uneasily. "I'm kind of pulling a Kate."

Zach was confused and looked to Kate for an explanation.

"Megan left the big city to, ah, to find herself. I guess you could say she took a page from my book, no pun intended."

"Pun?" Nick asked, looking from Kate to Megan and back to Kate.

"She's writing a book about how she found herself," Megan supplied.

"Cool," Nick said before skirting around Zach to offer his hand to the newcomer. "I'm Nick. Sounds like you and I have something in common, Megan."

"We do?" Megan said, shaking his hand. She smiled at Nick, but Zach saw no warmth behind it. She seemed hesitant, guarded even.

"What do you two have in common?" Zach asked Nick, forcing himself to turn away from Megan.

Nick shot Zach a look and turned back to her. "I'm starting over, too. I just got out of the Marine Corps." The two made casual conversation as they walked toward the front door of the rental.

"So," Kate began, "have you talked to Kayla?"

Zach stopped and looked at his sister. "Why are you doing this? I told you it's not going to happen."

"Because I thought maybe you had come to your senses." Kate's eyes blazed with anger, and Zach noticed the familiar twitch in her jaw that told him she was close to losing it. Again. "She's sick, for Heaven's sake. Maybe dying." Her voice cracked. "And you're really going to turn your back on her?"

"Look, I'm no good for Kayla. She'll have a better chance at recovery if I'm not around." Zach started to walk toward the cottage, but Kate took a hold of his sleeve.

"Is that what you really think? That she'd be better off without you?"

"Yes, it is," Zach said through clenched teeth. He'd had enough of this conversation. He had no intention of changing his mind. He'd rather she remember him as a jerk than as a killer.

"She's in love with you, you know," Kate said quietly, and Zach's heart leaped in his chest. He stiffened, and Kate's grip tightened. "She's head over heels in love with you and thinks she did something wrong, something to turn you off. She thinks you're jealous of her dead husband or can't handle her being sick or some other ridiculous notion. Her heart is broken, and you don't even care. For thirty-two years, you've been my hero, but now I can barely look at you. Go home to Mom and Dad. Be lonely and miserable for the rest of your life. You deserve it."

Kate spun toward her SUV and said to her brother. "Tell Megan I'll wait outside." Without waiting for a response, Kate got into her car and slammed the door.

Zach stood on the sidewalk and looked at his sister through the window. She refused to look back at him, and eventually, he turned toward the bungalow. He knew better than to push her, but he was aching to know if Kate's words were true. Had Kayla admitted that she was in love with him? Did she really think that he would turn his back on her just because she's sick? What kind of man did she think he was?

In spite of the cold wind that blew on that mid-October day, Zach felt sweat rolling down his back. Of course, Kayla believed that. Why wouldn't she? He hadn't given her any reason for staying away. He hadn't told her outright how he felt. She probably had no idea what to think. He promised her he would stand by her no matter what. He told her he would never leave her. Yet here he was, not only avoiding her, but planning on leaving town altogether. Her words came back to him again, *You're a sorry excuse for a man.*

Zach quickly walked up the steps and into the cottage. His heart was racing, and he felt nauseous.

"Nick," he called, following the voices down the hall. The smell of fresh paint filled Zach's nostrils as he briskly walked toward the back of the little house.

"Hey, what's up?" Nick stuck his head out of one of the rooms.

"I've got to go. I'm sorry. Kate's outside. Can you manage—"

Nick cut him off. "Go, man. It's all good."

Zach turned as Nick called after him. "And for what it's worth, she'd be a fool not to see past your past."

Zach heard Nick chuckle at his own words before Megan asked, "Wait, what's going on? What am I missing?"

Zach didn't wait to hear Nick's answer. Nick would have to find his own way back. Hopefully Kate wouldn't mind taking him home. Zach had too much at stake to stay and babysit two capable adults or to face off against his sister.

He sprinted to his truck, started the engine, and threw it into drive. He heard the gravel fly up from under the tires as he pulled onto the street, leaving his seething sister in a cloud of dust. He had no idea what he was going to say to Kayla. He spent the entire short ride praying that the Holy Spirit would do the talking for him.

Hearty Tomato and Chicken Strew
Origin: West Africa

There are many recipes that my family learned to make
from the Indigenous peoples that my father wrote about.
This is one of my favorite recipes because it simply says,
home. Throughout the villages of West Africa, there can
always be found, a simmering pot of stew on the stove. I
remember walking through our village, stopping outside of
house after house just to inhale the aroma of stew. When
the world seems to be falling apart, I find comfort by
filling the house with the fragrance of tomato and chicken
stew and sharing it with others, just like the women of
those West African villages do.

From *Around the World in Eighty Meals*
by K.Z. Middleton

CHAPTER TWELVE

Kayla's heart was torn in two as she read the text. Her legs felt weak, and she wasn't sure she could stand. She reached for something to hold on to. Pictures ran through her mind—lazy summer days on the beach, laughter around the table, riding bikes to the park, having picnics, flying kites, and going out on her father's boat. She groped for smiles, happiness, and bliss; but the harsh reality of the message would not go away.

"Are you okay?" Tammi asked, rushing from the entrance to the post office when she saw Kayla leaning against the light post.

"Are any of us?" Kayla looked to Tammi for assurance. She held up her phone so that Tammi could read it.

Tammi nodded. "Rob just called me. He's in shock. All of the nearby police departments are. They've never had to deal with anything like this before."

"Neither have the rest of us," Kayla said, bile filling her throat. She turned to Tammi. "What's going on? Why is this happening?"

"I don't know," Tammi replied, wrapping her arms around her friend. "I just don't know."

Kayla saw the anguish in Tammi's eyes and knew it mirrored her own. She looked down the street as if there was someone or something that could provide answers. The little boy's body had been found. It would be taken for an autopsy, a funeral would be planned, and the sweet little boy would be laid to rest. But where was the rest for his family? For his friends? For all of them in the area? Why was this happening?

"Justine and Hank are going to need us to be strong," Kayla said, wondering how any of them could find that kind of strength.

Tammi nodded, "Yes, somehow we must find a way to support them. But honestly," she said to Kayla, "I have no idea where to start or what to do."

Kayla understood. That made two of them.

***

Zach's heart sunk when he saw the empty driveway. He tried to imagine where Kayla could be. He reached for his phone and called Aaron, hoping he would answer. Zach was certain that Kate would not.

"No time to talk, Zach. I'm on my way to the station to meet with Paul."

Aaron's voice was strained, and the hairs stood on Zach's neck as a cold chill shot through him.

"What's happened?"

"They found the missing boy, my friend's nephew. His body was dumped behind the grocery store in Stockton sometime last night."

"Same signs of struggle and torture as the Graham boy?"

"Looks that way. The police are questioning anyone who might have seen or heard something during the night. All of the local agencies, the Feds, even my guys, are meeting to see what we can do."

"Let Paul know I'm available, too. Whatever he needs."

There was a pause on the other end.

"I thought you were clearing out, heading south," Aaron said after a moment.

Zach swallowed. He knew his sister would have told Aaron what he said and was grateful that the man, who had become his closest friend, still respected him enough to answer the phone.

"I can't go," Zach said. "My life is here. For now. Unless I'm told otherwise."

"By whom? Kayla? Why would she do that?"

"You know as well as I do," Zach said.

"I also know my sister. And you're missing something, Zach. She doesn't judge. She's open and honest and accepting. Maybe you should try that, too."

"I'm going to try."

"Do better than try. I wasn't crazy about the two of you at first, but you're a good man, Zach. We all know it, including Kayla. Give her a chance."

"I hope she'll give me one."

"You'll never know unless you try. Gotta go. Good luck."

Zach let the phone disconnect on its own. He had no idea where Kayla would be in the middle of the day if she wasn't at home, but he knew she had to come back at some point.

He left the truck in his driveway, made his way across the yard, and sat on the steps to her house. Whenever Kayla got home, he'd be here waiting.

***

Kayla's heart began to pound as she pulled into the drive. It had been almost a week since she'd seen Zach, five days since her diagnosis, and three days since she told the family. He had gone completely AWOL again, yet there he sat, looking as guilty as a schoolboy.

Todd barely waited until the car came to a stop before he threw open the door and ran toward his idol.

"Uncle Zach, where have you been?" he asked, throwing his arms around Zach.

"I've been busy, buddy. I'm sorry about that. It won't happen again."

Kayla shook her head as she slammed her car door. *Famous last words*, she thought.

"Are you okay with this, Mom?" EJ asked quietly as they came around the front of the car. EJ carried a cardboard box from the island's pizza place.

"I have bigger problems than Zach, EJ. Let's just go inside. There's something I need to tell you boys."

"More bad news?" EJ asked, his eyes boring into her.

"I'm afraid so," she said. "But we're all going to be okay. I promise."

EJ nodded and headed toward the house. He stopped halfway up the steps to nod at Zach but didn't speak to him.

"So, I guess you heard," Kayla said, letting her shoulders hang in despair.

"I did, and I'm so sorry. I should have been there."

She shook her head. "I just don't know how his family is going to get through it."

Zach opened his mouth as if to speak but closed it again, a perplexed looked on his face. Kayla realized they were referring to two different things.

"You were talking about me." She swallowed and blinked. "I'm okay. Right now, I have to talk to the boys. They found Hank's nephew. He's dead," she said quietly, finding it hard to say the words.

Kayla tried to go past Zach, but he reached for her arm and held it, forcing her to turn toward him.

"I heard. Aaron told me. Let me help you. I know you must be angry with me, and we really need to talk, but we can do that later. Please, let me help you do this one thing. Then, if you wish, I will go."

Kayla sighed and thought, *as if your leaving was my decision.*

She looked toward the house and then back at Zach. The truth was, she didn't want to tell them alone.

"Okay, come in. I guess we could all use the support right now."

***

Todd cried himself to sleep that night. EJ put up a good front, but even Zach could tell that the boy was upset and afraid. It didn't seem fair that one family should have to deal with so much at one time. And he hadn't helped things. He could feel the tension when he and Kayla walked into the house together. She was on edge, and EJ was wary of him. Not that Zach blamed either of them. It was his own doing.

Once both boys were tucked into bed, he and Kayla went to the kitchen to finish cleaning up from dinner.

"I've never known you to not have the desire to cook," Zach said, bending the pizza carton so that it fit into the trash can.

"Take-out pizza is a rare treat around here, and now I've had it twice in one week." She laughed without humor. "You know, sometimes I think the boys like that better than my cooking."

"They're young. They'll come around," he smiled.

"I figured it would help. I didn't feel like standing in the kitchen while they sat in the other room and watched TV, and I thought it would help lighten the mood. I guess that was wishful thinking." Kayla went to the back door and stared out at the marsh and the water beyond it.

Zach went to her and put his hands on her shoulders. He felt her stiffen at first, but then she relaxed and leaned back onto him as if she needed him to hold her up. His hands slipped down to her arms and he rubbed them up and down her sleeves.

"I don't know what I'd do if—" She stopped and shook her head. Zach felt her shaking as she began to cry.

Turning her around, her put his arms around her and held her. Her tears soaked through his button-down, but it didn't matter. He inhaled the smell of her—the strawberry-scented shampoo, the fabric softener she added to her laundry, the faint smell of tomato and garlic. How could he have ever thought of walking away? This was where he belonged. He knew it with every fiber of his being.

The timing was all wrong. He knew that, too. But he couldn't help himself. Leaning back just a bit, he pulled his right arm around and raised his fingers to her chin. Tilting her head toward his face, he leaned down and kissed her. He was tentative at first, not knowing what her reaction would be. But when she didn't pull away, he pressed his lips a little harder against hers. Slowly, she lifted her arms to his neck and gave in to his kiss.

After a moment, he pulled back, and his eyes searched hers. They were soft and tender, full of emotion. Was it sorrow, pain, or fear? No, he didn't see any of those. What he saw was trust and maybe even love. Was Kate right? What had he done to deserve Kayla's love? Nothing as far as he could see. Still staring into her eyes, he tried to find the words to tell her how he felt, but they were drowned out by the other words in his head. Killer, murderer, monster. He closed his eyes and dropped his hands to her waist.

"We need to talk," Zach said. "There are things I need to tell you."

Kayla was quiet as he took her hand and led her into the living room. He sat on the couch and pulled her down next to him.

"First, I'm sorry. I seem to be saying that too often lately, but I am. I've been trying to figure out how to tell you, what to say to you, but the truth is, I've always known what I need to say. I just haven't wanted to say it."

Kayla looked hurt and confused. "You don't know how to say it?"

Zach looked into her hazel eyes, which at the moment were a deep, greenish brown. He loved the way they changed, depending upon what she was wearing, or the lighting, or even her mood. He didn't know what she was thinking at the moment, but he had a pretty good guess. If she thought he didn't know how to tell her he loved her, then he knew of a hundred ways she was wrong. He could think of a dozen ways to actually say the words and even more ways to show her how he felt. He tried to smile.

"What I need to tell you has to do with the past. My past. And I'm not sure that tonight, with all that happened today, is the best time to say it. But there doesn't seem like there will ever be a good time."

"Zach." Kayla laid her fingers on his lips. "Before you say anything, I need to tell you something."

Zach sat up and looked at her. Man, she was beautiful. Sure, she had gone through a lot for her age, and it was beginning to show; but if given the chance, he would kiss every line on her face and wrap his fingers around those few strands of grey hair. She had lost weight, and her clothes were beginning to hang loose on her frame, but she fit perfectly into the mold of his body. Next to somebody like Kate or Megan, Kayla would probably go unnoticed, but her eyes sparkled like gems, and her smile could light up a room.

"What is it?" he asked, praying she wasn't going to tell him to leave.

"That kiss was the first time I've kissed anyone other than my husband since I was twenty-one years old, and it was nice. More than nice." She blushed and turned away. Zach waited patiently for her to continue. "But it's all I can give physically. I'm not, never have been, like that. And I have the boys to think of."

"Kayla, I know that. I would never—"

"Please hear me out. I don't know what the future holds for me, and I don't want you to feel obligated to take care of me or stay with me, especially if, well, if I'm not always the woman I am now." She looked away, and he understood what she was trying to tell him. She turned back to him and licked her lips before continuing. "I'm not sure when, or if, I'll be able to give more. I don't know what will happen to me or my body. And I know you aren't looking for a commitment." She hesitated. "But the kiss, it was nice." She bit her lips and blinked slowly as she looked at him.

Zach resisted the urge to wrap his arms around her and crush her with the strength of his love. He so wanted to hold her, kiss her, make her feel no pain, no worry. He gently put his hands around her neck so that his fingers tangled into the ends of her hair.

"You're beautiful, do you know that?"

Again, she blushed, but he held her tight so that she couldn't look away.

"And to be blunt, Kayla, I don't care what you have or don't have physically. That's not what makes you a woman. It's the person inside that matters to me, not what's on the outside. And I'm not asking for anything physical right now. I just want to be here for you." He saw the tear form in her eye and wished he didn't have to continue, but he had no choice.

"But Kayla, there are things you don't know about me. Things that might change the way you see me. If, after what I have to say, you can't look at me the same again, I'll understand. I will walk away and never bother you for the rest of your life if that's what makes you happy. I've tried to leave more than once, but you're like a magnet I can't resist."

She smiled slightly, and his heart constricted.

"But if you're willing to accept me for who I am, for my flaws, my insecurities, and my past, I promise you that I will never leave your side. Ever."

"Zach, I don't think there's anything you could say to me that would make me love you any less." She gasped, and her eyes widened. She hadn't intended to profess her feelings, but he wasn't going to let her take it back.

"Kayla, I have never loved anyone the way I love you." He saw the relief in her eyes and felt her body release the weight of the unknown. "But I can't change the things I've done, and loving me and being able to accept and live with my past are two very different things."

"Zach, you make it sound like you did horrible things. I can't imagine that. You're too good a person."

"Kayla, stop." He pulled away from her and stood. "I try to be a good person. I've always tried. But my actions were not always within my own control. When I was in the Middle East, I did things…"

"Zach," Kayla took his hands. "You were at war. Of course, you did things you wouldn't have done otherwise. I understand and accept that. Aaron's in the military. My dad was in the military. I get it."

"You don't get it," Zach lashed out, pulling his hands from hers. Kayla glanced toward the bedrooms, and Zach ran his hands along his short hair, trying to calm himself down. He took a deep breath and focused on a spot on the wall, unable to face her. "I wasn't just a soldier. I didn't just fight alongside other soldiers. I was special, part of an elite force, doing things other soldiers didn't do."

He inhaled deeply and let out a long breath of air. He rubbed his hand up and down his face as he tried to muster the strength to say the words. Finally, knowing he had to see her reaction when the truth came out, he settled his gaze on her face and steeled himself.

"I was a trained killer, a sniper." He said the next few words slowly and evenly, enunciating every syllable. "I shot people for a living."

***

For the third time in a week, the floor fell out from beneath her. Kayla saw the doctor as she gave her the bad news. She saw the text about little Henry. She heard Zach's words but didn't want to accept them.

I shot people for a living.

She reached for the nearest thing that would give her support and then recoiled as her hand landed on Zach's chest. She covered her mouth, certain she was going to be sick. Other scenes ran through her mind.

Mrs. Reynolds? I'm sorry to have to tell you that your husband...

Boys, daddy isn't coming home...

Do you love him unconditionally? No matter his faults? No matter his past?

"Kayla, are you—"

She shut out the rest of his words. Her chest felt like it was on fire. There was a ringing in her ears. The room began to spin, and everything went black.

***

Zach paced back and forth in the hallway. He could hear the muffled voices coming through the door, but they were speaking in hushed tones such that he couldn't make out the words.

"What's going on?" EJ asked, rubbing his eyes and trying to stifle a yawn.

"Everything's okay, no worries. Go on back to bed" Zach guided EJ back into his room and tucked him into his bed.

"Is Mom okay?" he asked, breaking into another yawn.

"She's fine. She, uh, fell, but she's okay," Zach lied, not wanting to tell the boy that his mother had fainted, and it was all Zach's fault. "Your grandma is in there making sure she didn't hurt herself."

"Okay, Uncle Zach. Goodnight." The sleepy boy rolled over and, in no time, began to breathe peacefully. Zach backed out of the room and closed the door just as

Ronnie opened the door to Kayla's room and stepped into the hall.

Zach couldn't read the look on her face. He felt like a teenager being called to the principal's office. Would she lower the boom on him?

"Let's talk," Ronnie said, brushing by him to go to the living room.

Zach hadn't felt this nervous since his first day at West Point.

"Is Kayla okay?" he asked. He barely recognized his own voice. It was filled with worry and tinged with regret.

"She's fine," Ronnie answered as she lowered herself into the arm chair. Zach took the couch and leaned forward on his knees, his face in his hands. He waited for Ronnie to speak before looking at her.

"Zach, I'm not blind. I've been around a long time, and I can read people pretty well. I've known for almost a year that you are in love with Kayla. And I've known for almost as long that she's in love with you." She took a deep breath as Zach anticipated her next words.

"You've been around our family enough to know that we look out for each other and that we rely on God to show us the way."

Zach nodded, and Ronnie continued.

"I've been waiting patiently for God to lead you two to each other. I didn't know how or when it would happen, but I had confidence that it would. I believe we are at that place and time now. But, Zach, Kayla is going to need some time to process everything. This week has dealt her one blow after another, and she feels like she's in the driver's seat of an eighteen-wheeler going downhill without brakes. Between the diagnosis, this little boy's death and his killer on the loose, and your news," the raised brow and frown let him know that she knew exactly what he had told Kayla, "I'm afraid she's in a state of shock."

"You don't seem surprised," Zach said. "About my past, I mean. Did Aaron tell you?" Ronnie shook her head.

"Zach, you forget who Kayla's father is. He knew from the moment he met you that you were no ordinary soldier. If you had been Navy, he would have pegged you for a SEAL. He suspected Green Beret or something along those lines. So, he did some research and learned the truth. You can find anything on the Internet these days."

Zach nodded. "And you never told Kayla? And you're both still okay with me, with us?" He was shocked that they had known all this time yet still treated him like he was their own and kept his secret.

Ronnie laid her hand on Zach's arm. "That wasn't our call, Zach. It still isn't. I'm not going to tell you we were thrilled, but you were only doing what you were ordered to do in the line of duty. You've got a lot of baggage, a lot of things you're going to need to work through, that you've been working through, I assume." Zach nodded, and Ronnie continued. "But Kayla loves you, and you love her. Trevor and I have no doubt that you will take care of her and the boys. But for now, Kayla needs some time."

"I understand, Ronnie. I feel terrible that this all happened like it did. I never wanted to hurt Kayla.

That's why it took me so long to tell her, why I kept backing off. I was so afraid that it would be more than she could handle."

"Oh, believe me, Kayla can handle a lot. She's one of the strongest women I've ever known, daughter or not."

"You'll hear no argument from me," Zach said closing his fingers into a two-handed fist and resting it beneath his chin. He wasn't sure what he was expected to say.

"She will come around, but it's going to take some time."

Zach nodded. "What should I do in the meantime?"

"Pray," Ronnie told him. "Pray for Kayla, for her health and well-being. Pray that she's able to make the decision that is best for her, for all of you. Pray for her boys. Pray for Henry and his family. Pray that they find this madman before he takes someone else's child. Just pray. And ask God to show you what is expected of you now and in the future."

Zach looked down at the floor between his feet. Ronnie's words weren't quite what he'd expected to hear. Praying was all good and well. He did it all the time. But how was that supposed to help him now? Her advice gave him no place to go, no hope or promise, not even doubt or worry. It just left him confused.

"I'll stay here tonight. You can go home," Ronnie said as she stood. "Thanks for calling me."

That was it. He had been dismissed.

"You're welcome," Zach responded though he felt like he should say more. "Ronnie, I—"

"Go home, Zach. Go to bed. We've all got a lot on our minds. Things will be better tomorrow."

Zach hoped she was right, but in truth, he was more than a little concerned about what tomorrow would bring.

Métis Baked Pudding
Origin: Canada

Growing up amongst Indigenous peoples, you learn to never let anything go to waste. Any time there was leftover bread, we made baked pudding using a recipe we learned from the Métis peoples in Canada. It's the perfect ending to a meal on a chilly fall or winter night. It doesn't take a large helping to make your insides feel warm and cozy, yet still, you will find yourself going back for more. Eating it will always remind me of home, no matter where home is. Sharing it with others makes me feel like I'm welcoming them into my family.

From *Around the World in Eighty Meals*
by K.Z. Middleton

CHAPTER THIRTEEN

"So, your brother is kind of an intense guy," Megan said as Kate drove her to the car rental place on Saturday.

"Sometimes. I'm really sorry about that whole scene. Zach and I have not been seeing eye-to-eye lately, and I couldn't stand the thought of being in that little cottage with him. I'm really glad you liked it though."

"I did, but so did Nick. He says it's fine if I take it. I assured him that it's temporary, but he said to take all the time I need."

"That's nice of him," Kate said, thinking he might not be so bad after all. So far, she wasn't sure how she felt about her brother's housemate. "Does that mean you're thinking about going back and letting someone know what happened?"

"I don't know," Megan said. At least she was being honest, Kate thought. "I know that it's the right thing to do, but if I go back, how big a can of worms will I be opening? Maybe I'm the only one he's done this to. After all, he's only been a supervisor since about a month before you left. It's barely been a year."

Kate inhaled and blew out her breath as she thought about that. "A year is long enough for him to try his little routine on several women. Is that young girl still there? If I were Brad, that's about the age I'd go after."

"Young girl?"

"The one who started right before I left—Lacy or Lucy or something like that."

"Jaycee, no she left a couple months after Brad was promoted. She just up and left like I…Kate?" Megan asked worriedly. "Do you think he went after her? She was so quiet and innocent. That would have freaked her out even more than it did me."

"It's possible," Kate said. "You have no idea why she left?"

"None. But maybe I could ask around…"

"Maybe you should," Kate agreed.

***

"Take it easy, man. You're going to punch a hole right through that bag," Nick warned as Zach laid another hit on the punching bag.

The gym was crowded, as it always was on Saturday mornings, but Zach saw only the bag and heard only the voices that haunted him all through the night. He had followed Ronnie's advice and prayed. He'd prayed all night long. He'd prayed as he dressed. He prayed in the car while Nick babbled on and on about his dinner at Kate and Aaron's. The only time he wasn't praying was when he took all his frustration out on the leather pouch in front of him.

Taking a breath, he stepped back from the bag and tried to flex his fingers inside his gloves. Deciding he'd had enough of a workout, Zach began taking off his safety gear.

"I'm ready to go," he said to Nick. "You coming or staying?"

"I'm right behind you. I finished about thirty minutes ago."

Zach glanced at the clock on the wall and winced. He'd been at it for over an hour, punching the daylights out of the bag. He was going to regret that later. He could already feel his muscles starting to ache. He rolled his shoulders and stretched his arms a few times.

Once in the truck, Nick looked at Zach. "What's gotten into you? You barely said a word all morning, and you almost rendered that punching bag unusable."

"I've got a lot on my mind," Zach said.

"I heard about the kid they found. Aaron told us at dinner last night. I'm sorry, Zach. He said Kayla and the boys were taking it pretty hard. Did they know him?"

At the sound of her name, Zach felt a sharp pain in his chest.

"Not really, but his aunt and uncle live here on the island. Kayla and the boys are friends with them."

"Megan said she had a cousin who was murdered in D.C. That's gotta be rough. I thought all the families I've been a part of were messed up, but she's got a brother in a gang and another who died in jail. Her grandmother raised them. I'm not sure why. It's really impressive that she's gotten as far as she has in life. She went to college on a scholarship and graduated with a degree in communication. Now she's starting a whole new chapter in her life. Kate helped her get a job at the local paper, so she's going to be putting her degree to use."

Zach glanced over at Nick. "You learned a lot about her in one evening."

"She's easy to talk to. And easy to listen to, I guess. Funny, though, she talks a lot about her family and her life growing up in DC, but she won't talk about her career or why she's here."

"Leave her alone, Nick. Don't mess with her. Kate told me that you should stay away from her. She said Megan's fragile. I'm not sure what that's all about."

"Yeah, there's definitely something going on there. Kate didn't seem thrilled when Aaron invited me to stay for dinner. We ran into him back at your place. He was checking on his sister. I thought about turning down his invitation, but Megan said she wanted me to go, so I went with them back to their house. I guess we hit it off pretty good."

"Be careful, Nick," Zach warned, once Nick stopped talking long enough for Zach to speak. "You've got a lot to figure out before you jump into a relationship."

"Who said anything about a relationship?"

Zach let it go, but he vowed to keep an eye on Nick. That boy could sometimes be his own worst enemy, and Zach got the impression that Megan was keeping secrets. One of them was going to end up hurt.

When they pulled up to the house, Zach saw Kayla's SUV in the driveway. He was surprised that the boys' soccer games were over already. He wondered if the games were cancelled due to the news about Henry. He put the truck in park and sat behind the wheel, watching the house as if he was on a stake-out.

"Mind if I go inside and take a shower?" Nick asked.

"Go ahead. I'll get one when you're done."

"Thanks. And by the way," Nick added after he'd opened the passenger door. "Megan really liked the cottage. I'm going to let her have it and keep looking. I hope that's okay with you."

Zach never took his eyes off of Kayla's house. "I told you, Nick, you're welcome to stay as long as needed."

"Thanks, man. I appreciate it."

Zach nodded but continued to stare. What was Kayla doing right now? How were the boys holding up? After a few moments, Zach climbed out of the truck and headed up the steps to his house, but he gave one last look across the yard before opening the door. Then he said another prayer.

***

Anne, Shannon, Marian, Kate, Tammi, and Kayla gathered around Kayla's kitchen table on Saturday afternoon.

"What are you proposing?" Anne asked with a frown. "That we start some kind of neighborhood watch like they have in the suburbs?"

"Something like that," Kate said. "We need to look out for one another and for our families."

"Like I was saying," Kayla continued with the plan she was laying out. "I'm worried about the boys and who's going to watch out for them after my surgery. I might not be able to keep my eye on them like I ordinarily would. And you're all busy moms. Think about how easy it is to lose track of a child for a few minutes or more."

"So, we all join forces watching out for each other's kids?" Shannon asked.

"Exactly," Kayla said. "We make sure that no child is ever alone even if he's just running to the bathroom during soccer practice. The coach can't watch every kid and perform his coaching duties every second he's with them. I say, we put together a schedule of our kids' activities and then take turns choosing who will cover what. And I mean everything from school events to sports practices and games to hanging out with friends."

"Well, there won't be much hanging out with friends for my crew," Marian said. "I wanted kids for so long, and I'm not taking any chances. I'm not letting them go anywhere without me. I'm not even letting them ride the bus to school. I'm driving them to and from school."

"You can't suffocate them," Anne said. "Besides, do you really think it's necessary? I mean, the first boy was a tourist, and he disappeared from Assateague. Justine's nephew was from Stockton. What makes you think our kids are in danger?"

"It's too close for comfort," Shannon said. "Those boys both disappeared from Maryland, yes, but Assateague juts right up against us, and Stockton is a half hour away. Who knows where this guy will strike next."

"I agree with Shannon, but I don't want my kids to feel trapped," Tammi said. "And I don't want them frightened. Can't we watch them from afar?"

"How would that work?" Shannon asked.

"I guess we can make it work," Anne said. "Though a little bit of fear never hurt anybody, and I'm still not convinced the guy stuck around here or that the killings were related."

"It's true," Kate said. "A little fear can go a long way when it comes to protecting yourself. And we don't know where the guy is or what he will do next."

Kayla's thoughts turned to Zach. Fear. Was that what she was feeling toward him? No, she wasn't the least bit afraid of him. She would trust him with her life. But life was exactly the problem. Did he value life? When he held a gun, did he turn into a different person? While he was large and strong and had a certain look about him that could make your blood run cold in the right circumstances, she still couldn't see him as a ruthless killer. But then again, she had never seen Eddie's boss as a ruthless killer either. She'd never liked the guy and sure as heck hadn't trusted him, but she would never have thought he could raise a gun to Eddie.

And then it dawned on her. The police told her that *Eddie* was the one with the gun. They never found out where or how he got it, but he was the one who went after Moore. So, perhaps it was true that you never really knew someone. She wondered, did she really know Zach?

"Kayla? Did you hear me?" Shannon asked, bringing Kayla back into focus.

"I'm sorry. I spaced," Kayla admitted. "What did I miss?"

"I think I've got a way to do this," said Tammi, always calm and clear-headed in any crisis. She proceeded to tell them her proposal. Then the women laid out ideas, hashed plans, and came up with workable strategies to keep their children safe while not disrupting everyone's lives.

"Are you sure you're okay with all of this?" Anne asked Kate. "You don't even have a child in school yet."

"I love all of your kids as much as I love Miren," Kate told the other moms. "I'm in this with you."

"So is Debbie," Kayla added. "She wanted me to tell you all that she's in. And her girls can help, too. They can both drive now."

They firmed up the details and agreed to touch base throughout the week to see how things were going. Kayla felt somewhat relieved by the time they left, but she still had a lot on her mind.

"Mind if I ask how you're feeling?" Kate asked once everyone was gone. "And I don't mean health-wise."

Kayla looked at her sister-in-law for a few moments, confused and wondering how she could have known, and then Kayla realized the obvious.

"Zach called you."

"He texted me this morning," Kate clarified. "He feels terrible about the way it all happened. But my concern isn't with Zach. It's with you. Are you okay?"

"I'm not sure how to describe what I'm feeling. I don't know, myself. I keep trying to reconcile the man that Zach says he is with the man I've come to know. It just doesn't make sense."

"Kay," Kate laid her hand gently on Kayla's arm. "For what it's worth, the Zach you know is the Zach I know, the brother I've loved, trusted, and respected my entire life. The other Zach, he's part of a world that we will never be a part of. The things he did are so foreign to the person he truly is and the life he longs to have that I don't think we will ever see that side of him. He isn't the monster he thinks he is, and I think you know that as well as I do."

Kayla knew that every word Kate said was true. But still…

"You know the night Miren was born?" Kayla asked

"You mean the night Zach shot Mark." Kate said matter-of-factly.

"Yes. I never questioned Zach's precision. Aaron told me that Mark had you in his arms. He was hiding behind you. But Zach was able to shoot him without hesitation. There was never a doubt in Aaron's mind that Zach would be able to hit Mark without endangering you or the baby. And I never asked how. I never stopped to think about it at all. I knew Zach had military training, but it never occurred to me that his skills went beyond those of a normal soldier trained for combat." She shook her head. "Why didn't I see it then?"

"Kayla, why would you? Zach's my brother, my best friend since birth, and I didn't know."

"He didn't tell you?" Kayla looked at Kate in surprise.

"No, it was Aaron who figured it out. I had to pry it out of Zach. He was trying so hard to leave that life behind, but he didn't want to keep it from you. He knew he was risking everything by telling you, but that's how much he loves you, how much he wants to be honest with you. He wants no secrets between you even if it means he loses you. He wanted to shield you from the truth, to protect you, but he knew he couldn't."

Kayla swallowed as she let Kate's words sink in.

"I'm not sure what to say to him."

"Just tell him how you feel. All of it, the good and the bad. Lay it all out there. Then work through it together."

"You sound like my mother," Kayla said with a smile.

"That is the kindest thing you could ever say to me." Kate smiled back at Kayla, and for the first time all week, Kayla thought, perhaps, there was a light at the end of the tunnel.

That evening, after the boys went to bed, Kayla googled, *Zach Middleton, Army sniper.*

She was shocked by what she found. How had nobody else on the island come across this? Right there, on a popular online encyclopedia site, Zach's name appeared in a list with the likes of Rob Furlong and Chris Kyle. The Pentagon had confirmed one-hundred-forty-three kills, credited to Zach. He was hailed as one of the greatest heroes of the Iraq and Afghanistan Wars. One of his kills saved an entire school from a man with a rocket launcher.

She sat back and stared at the screen. The man who called himself a killer was admired by those around him as a life-saver. He actually had a bounty on his head. His own life was in danger every time he stepped off a plane or exited a helicopter in the Middle East. Yet he gave his all to his country and asked for nothing in return.

Kayla slowly closed the laptop. She rose from her chair and turned off the light. Gazing across the yard, she wondered what he was doing at that moment. Lying in bed that night, the words on the screen glowed in her mind. She had been such a fool, and she prayed that she would be able to make things right.

***

The air was crisp and clean Sunday morning after a cold overnight rain. Geese honked as they flew over the parking lot on Assateague. Zach looked at his phone, surprised to receive the text from Ronnie. He and Nick had gone to the early Mass before going for a run on the beach, so they didn't see Ronnie or the rest of the family at church. He thought it best to give everyone a wide berth until they all figured out where he stood with them.

We missed you at Mass this morning. We hope you and Nick will be joining us for dinner. We plan to eat at 5 as usual.

What does this mean? Zach wondered as he read the text. He hesitated before responding.

"What's up?" Nick asked as he tied his shoe.

"Ronnie wants us to go to the family dinner at five." He looked at his friend. "Are you up for it?"

"The question is, are you up for it?"

Zach thought about it. He hadn't seen Kayla since Friday night, and he missed her terribly. He now realized that each time they were apart, he was drawn to her even more.

"Yeah, I'm up for it. I'm going to take it as a sign that she's okay being around me. Ronnie wouldn't have asked if she didn't run it by Kayla first."

"You sure about that, man? Women can be tricky sometimes."

"Like you're an expert on women," Zach said, playfully punching Nick before opening the door to the truck.

"Hey, I'll have you know that I *am* an expert on women," Nick called over the hood.

Zach laughed. "Yeah, sure you are, Nick. Sure, you are."

Zach turned on the radio for the short drive back to the house. Ed Sheeran's *Thinking Out Loud* filled the airwaves, and Zach pondered his words. People did fall in love in mysterious ways, and whatever God's plan was for Zach and Kayla, Zach prayed that his mistakes weren't too large for them to overcome.

The lyrics perfectly summed up how Zach was feeling. He just hoped that, in spite of his past, Kayla would understand and love him anyway.

***

The butterflies in Kayla's stomach seemed to be caught in a tornado as they tumbled round and round. She was nervous about seeing Zach, and she was even more nervous to talk to him alone. Of course, that precluded her marshalling the courage to speak to him at all.

When he walked into the house, the butterflies came to a standstill. Everything came to a standstill, including the beating of her heart. He was freshly shaved and wearing jeans and a button-down shirt that matched the green color of his eyes exactly. When their gaze met, her fears vanished, and all of her lingering doubts and misgivings melted away. She needed him like fish need the ocean, like the beach needs the sand. He was the moon in her night sky and she never wanted to be in darkness ever again.

She could barely get through dinner with him sitting across the table from her. Each time their eyes met, she felt a jolt and wondered if everybody at the table detected the waves of electricity that passed between them. He felt it, she knew. She could tell by the ever-so-subtle rosiness in his cheeks when she realized he was watching her as she ran her tongue across her lips. She saw it in his eyes as he joined the conversation yet never took his gaze from her. She felt it when their fingers accidentally brushed as they both reached for the iced tea pitcher.

When everyone was almost finished their dinner, Ronnie stood to clear the table. Kayla motioned to Zach with her head, beckoning him to follow her. Neither said a word as they slipped out of the room and headed toward the front door.

"It's cold outside," Zach said when she opened the door. "Where's your jacket?"

Still unable to speak to him, she pointed to the closet. He retrieved both his brown bomber jacket and her off-white North Face. They slipped them on as they walked onto the porch, but still, she shivered, and wondered if it was caused by the chill in the air or the current between them. They sat side-by-side on the porch swing, and he used his foot to gently set the swing in motion.

***

Zach knew that Kayla had something on her mind, so he waited patiently for her to speak. After what seemed like an eternity, she took a deep breath and began.

"Zach, I've done a lot of thinking and a lot of praying over the past couple days."

She paused, and her words hung in the air. Zach thought she couldn't have prayed half as much as he had recently.

"About a year ago, I met someone," she said, and his heart took a nose-dive. This was so unexpected that he didn't know how to respond, which was fine because his throat was suddenly too dry to speak. Who? Where? How had he not known? What was all her talk the other night about not having kissed anyone else but her husband?

"I knew I was in trouble from the moment he stepped into my house. EJ and Todd were taken in by him immediately. They had him in trapped in the living room, pulling out toy after toy. They practically fought each other for his attention, EJ talking about a television show, and Todd trying to show off his Legos. He had no idea what kind of tsunami had hit him, but he took it in stride. I can remember it like it was yesterday." She grinned up at him.

Zach remembered it, too. He relaxed as he recalled the scene at Kayla's house the first time she invited his entire family over for dinner. When Kayla called them in to eat, the boys each took one of his hands, both talking non-stop. His head had been spinning.

"I was as mesmerized by him as the boys were. He kept us captivated throughout the meal with his stories about his Army buddies and the practical jokes they played on one another. And then after dinner, he volunteered to help me with the dishes."

"It was the only way I could think of to be alone with you," Zach said, recovering his voice. He reached for her hand with a slight hesitation before taking it into his. He held his breath until he was sure she wasn't going to pull away. "I was drawn to you from the moment I saw you."

"When everything happened with Kate," she continued, "I saw how much you loved her and the depths to which you would go to care for her. You gave up your whole career for her."

"Well, not exactly," Zach interrupted. "I was already planning on getting out and making a new start. Kate just presented me with the perfect reason to get out earlier than expected, and luckily for us both, the Army agreed."

"And then you were there, next door, every day and every night. I didn't know how long you'd stick around, so I played it safe. I tried not to give you too much indication that I, well, that I had feelings for you."

He wanted to tell her that he had been doing the same thing, but she didn't give him a chance.

"And when Kate was better, you stayed. She and Aaron got married, and she and Miren moved in with him. Then you bought the house next door to mine. I thought that maybe you would ask me out or give me some sign that you had feelings for me, but it was always about the boys."

"You're wrong, it was never about just the boys." He turned toward her, wanting to tell her the truth, but she put up her hand.

"My story," she interrupted with a smile, and he let her go on. "I thought that you were just being nice, trying to fill the void left when Aaron needed to be with his own family. Then you stopped coming around, and I was hurt."

He had hurt her. He knew that already, but the words plunged into his heart like a dagger.

"I never meant to hurt you. I was trying to prevent you from being hurt," he was quick to say. But again, she stopped him from saying more by laying her fingers on his lips. He resisted the urge to taste them.

"I know. That's the thing that keeps coming back to me. You and Aaron are so much alike. Kate and I have said so from the beginning. You're saviors. It's what you do. You protect people. You protected Kate. You protected the boys on the beach all summer better than any lifeguard. You protected me."

She gazed at Zach, taking both of his hands into her own and holding them as tightly as she could.

"That's the man you are, Zach. That's the man you have always been. When you look in the mirror, you see a killer. But when the rest of us look at you, we see a protector. A man who would do anything to protect his country, his family, my family. It's what you do, not who you are. You are a hero—Kate's, Todd and EJ's, and mine."

Zach's heart swelled at her words.

"Does this mean that you'll give it a chance, give us a chance?"

"Zach, I want to give it more than a chance. I want to give it everything. But I need to know that you understand that I don't know what the future will hold. If something happens to me, I need the boys—"

"The boys will be fine. I will see to it. I love them, Kayla, as much as you do. As much as if they were of my own flesh and blood. And I do love you. And I truly believe that everything is going to be okay."

When Kayla's smile widened, Zach's insides melted. He was putty in her hands.

"I love you, too, Zach. I have for so very long. I just didn't know how to admit it to you or to myself for that matter."

"We're going to make this work, Kayla. I'm going to be with you every step of the way through your surgery and recovery, because there will be a recovery. And once we get through the next few months, the future will be ours."

Zach didn't care how sappy that sounded. He felt as if he could walk on water. Kayla loved him. Even better, she trusted him and wanted a future with him. And though it was what he prayed for, it was still more than he ever could have hoped for.

Guitar music suddenly flowed from inside the house, as if a sign, playing the same Ed Sheeran song that caught Zach's attention in the truck earlier. It was the perfect accompaniment to the beating of Zach's heart at this moment. He let go of Kayla's hands and slipped his arms around her waist, pulling her close to him. When his lips met Kayla's, he knew that he was finally home.

***

Holding hands, with grins that radiated like the sun, Zach and Kayla walked inside the house and met the questioning looks of their family. At once, Nick stopped playing his guitar, and everyone broke into smiles.

"Well, it's about time," Ronnie said as she went to Kayla and hugged her. "I trust you'll take good care of her," she said to Zach over Kayla's shoulder.

Kayla blushed. "Mom, it's not like we're getting married," she whispered into her mother's ear.

When Ronnie pulled back from the hug, she looked at Kayla, her knowing eyes twinkling. "For now," Ronnie said, and Kayla felt a warm glow coursing throughout her being. She looked back at Zach, and he winked at her. She couldn't remember the last time she was this happy. Even cancer couldn't take away her joy.

"Hey, man," Nick said to Zach, shaking his hands. "I'm happy for you. And you," he said, turning to Kayla, "are missing out on something great. I can't believe you'd choose him over me."

Everyone laughed, and Kayla decided she liked having Nick around. It was nice to have someone who knew how to lighten the mood and not take everyone and everything so seriously.

"Okay, enough," Kayla said. "What's for dessert?"

"You're in for a treat," Kate said as she rose and headed toward the kitchen. "Zach brought bread pudding. I put it in the oven after dinner, and it should be just about perfect."

"Bread pudding, huh?" Kayla asked, smiling at Zach.

He shrugged. "Just an old recipe I learned as a kid."

"You never cease to amaze me," Kayla told him.

"Then you're in luck, or I'm in trouble, because I plan on spending the rest of my life trying to amaze you."

Potato Perogies
Origin: Poland

My mother, Sicilian by blood, was always eager to try new recipes. She could copy her mother-in-law's Irish recipes just as well as she could recreate the Polish recipes handed down by my father's maternal grandmother. I remember how visits to my great-grandmother's home always included a meal of perogies with some kind of spicy side dish. It's hard to pace yourself once you begin eating them, but they sure do provide a delicious, satisfying meal.

From *Around the World in Eighty Meals*
by K.Z. Middleton

CHAPTER FOURTEEN

"Mom, did you see that? Did you see me score, Zach?" Todd asked excitedly as he ran up to Kayla and Zach after his game.

"We did. Good job." Zach gave Todd a high-five.

"Can I go to Ben's house? He got the new Star Wars video game. And Mr. Palmer taught us how to do a cool science experiment at school, and we wanna try at home."

An uneasiness crept up Kayla's spine. She knew Todd would be more than safe at Anne and Paul's house, but there was something that made her feel uneasy. She couldn't quite put her finger on it.

"I guess so," she said hesitantly.

"Thanks, Mom. I'll call you when it's time to pick me up." Todd was gone before Kayla could ask if he had permission from Anne and Paul, but as she watched, she saw both boys, as well as Tammi's son, Ethan, being herded into Anne's van. Kayla waved to her friend and then looked around for EJ.

"You okay?" Zach asked.

"Yeah, I'm fine," she said, craning her neck to look toward the other field. "Did EJ say anything to you after his game?"

"No, he was still with his team when I headed over this way. Do you want me to go find him?"

"We can both go. I'm sure he's fine…"

Zach took Kayla's hand and squeezed it reassuringly. They were all on edge when it came to the kids these days. Over the past week, Henry's autopsy had come back. While the Maryland and Virginia State Police were both remaining very close-lipped about the details, they did release a joint statement saying they believed that both boys had been taken, tortured, and killed by the same person. There were still no leads.

When Aaron told her the news, Kayla actually felt guilty for keeping the little boy and his family as far from her thoughts as she could. Here she was, spending the days helping Kate with Miren, or just being lazy, while a family's world was falling apart. Kayla had all her affairs in order and lots of spare time on her hands with no business to tend to. For the first time in her life, she chose to be selfish and just enjoy doing nothing.

She spent most of each day with Zach. They went for long walks on the beach, cooked together, took their turn watching out for all of the kids, and stayed up late into the night after the boys went to bed. Sometimes they talked for hours, and other times, they cuddled together for a movie or a favorite TV show. Eventually, Zach would start thinking about a job, but for now, they only focused on the boys and on each other.

Kayla became very good at compartmentalizing any thoughts, about a possible murderous kidnapper and her cancer, apart from the joy of her time with Zach. She didn't want any of that to encroach upon her happy little existence. Oh, there were still nights when she was unable to sleep, still times when she broke down crying at the uncertainty of her future, and still times when she worried about what Zach and the boys would do if something happened to her. But she tried very hard to focus on the positive. She wanted to enjoy every minute she had, especially the minutes with Zach.

But now, all she could think about was the safety of her boys. Where was EJ?

Zach and Kayla combed the park but didn't see him anywhere.

"Shannon, have you seen EJ? Is he with Sam?" Kayla asked when she saw Shannon and her husband, Lou, packing their chairs and blankets into their vehicle.

"No," Shannon said, looking around. "Billy has to write a paper, and Sam has a lot of makeup work to do after being sick last week, so they left right after the game. We stayed to see Cecelia's game."

Kayla saw the little blonde beauty peek her head out of the backseat and grin at them. Kayla tried to smile back, but her heart began pounding, and she felt dizzy.

"Kay, I'm sure he's fine," Shannon said, taking hold of Kayla's hand and looking around. "I'm sure he's off with his other friends."

"I'll help you look," Lou said to Zach as he pushed the button to close the back of the Explorer. "Shannon, why don't you and Kayla call the other boys' moms to see if he's with them."

"Good idea," Shannon said, leading Kayla to the open front door. "Take a seat. I'll call Marian. You call Anne."

"I already saw Anne," Kayla said feebly. "He's not with them."

"Okay, then who else can you think of?" Shannon asked as she listened to the phone ring. Kayla could hear Marian answer on the other end. "Hey, Marian, have you seen EJ? Kayla can't find him, and he's not at the park or with Anne's crew."

Kayla felt bile rise in the back of her throat when she heard Marian's response. Shannon refused to meet her gaze as she thanked Marian and said goodbye. "Marian is going to double check with her kids, but the last time she saw him, he was with Mr. Phelps, playing with his dogs."

Kayla's blood ran cold. Had they been wrong about the island's eccentric old man who loved dogs and kids? She could hear Zach and Lou shouting EJ's name which meant they were having no luck finding him. She looked around for the old man and wondered if he had EJ.

"I'm sure he's fine," Shannon said again, and Kayla began to wonder if that was the standard response that Ryan Graham's mother and Hank's sister had heard from everyone during those first twenty-four hours. Images of the horrors, rumored to have been afflicted on those poor boys, played through her head like scenes from a Stephen King movie. Her heart raced as she went into full-blown mode. She had to tell Zach about Mr. Phelps.

Kayla's phone buzzed. Startled, she fumbled to answer.

"Anne, have you—"

"He's fine, Kay. He's with Lizzie."

"With Lizzie?" Kayla repeated. "What do you mean he's with Lizzie? I thought Lizzie was with you."

"No, she went home with Susan McNally. And apparently, so did EJ. Didn't he tell you?"

Kayla groaned. "No, he didn't tell me. I've been worried sick. We've been combing the soccer fields, calling other moms, thinking he might…" A lump caught in her throat.

"Oh, Kay, I'm so sorry. I'm sure EJ didn't mean to worry you. They must have all assumed that you knew."

"Well, I didn't know," Kayla snapped at her friend. She closed her eyes and took a deep breath before continuing. "I'm sorry, Anne. I didn't mean to snap."

"No, I'm sorry. I guess we all need to be more conscientious about communicating to each other about the kids these days."

Kayla took a deep breath. "So, what is EJ doing with Lizzie and Susan?"

"They claim to be working on a school project."

"Claim to be?"

"Well, yes," Anne hesitated. "But according to Ben and Todd, EJ and Lizzie have been spending a lot of time together at school and online. I had no idea."

"Neither did I," Kayla said, as an image flashed through her mind of the Christmas pageant many months back, and the way Joseph, played by EJ, and Mary, played by Lizzie, looked at each other. She shook her head.

"Anne, thanks for letting me know. And please don't take it personally if Lizzie doesn't hear from EJ for the next week or so. His use of the computer and iPad are going to be severely restricted."

"I understand completely," Anne replied.

Kayla said goodbye and hung up as Zach and Lou walked up to the vehicle.

"I got your text," Lou said to Shannon. "He's okay?"

"Yes," Kayla responded. "And he's in a world of trouble. Thank you both for your help."

"No problem," Shannon said before encircling Kayla in a hug. "Never hesitate to ask for my help with anything."

"Thanks," Kayla said, knowing Shannon meant it.

"I take it we're picking up EJ on the way home?" Zach asked as they walked toward his truck.

"Oh, yes we are. I hope he enjoys his last fifteen minutes of freedom."

***

"What do you mean I can't go out tonight? It's Halloween," EJ protested on the way home from school a few days later.

"And you're grounded," Kayla reminded him.

"Come on, Mom, it only comes once a year. Please, let me go."

"EJ, I said no, and that's final." Though it pained her to say it, Kayla stood firm. EJ sulked the rest of the way home, but Kayla knew that she was doing what was best for him even though she felt like the worst mother in the world.

"Mom, is EJ staying home alone?" Todd asked later as he put on his Stormtrooper costume. He had dressed as Spiderman for the past three years, and Kayla knew that the whole island must believe she had no creativity at all when it came to Halloween. The truth was, Todd only wanted to dress as Spiderman or Star Wars characters, and she had no energy to fight it. She supposed there were worse things in the world he could want to imitate.

"No, sweetie," she answered Todd. "I'm going to stay with him."

Todd looked at his mother with wide eyes. "But who's going to take me trick-or-treating?"

"I am," Zach said from the doorway. He was grinning from ear to ear, and Kayla knew how much he was looking forward to taking on this most important role tonight.

"You are? Yay!" Todd cried before flinging himself against Zach. Kayla wondered for how much longer Todd would become so easily excited by childish things. He would be nine in January, and before she knew it, he would be in middle school and then high school and then a grown man. She still worried that he was immature for his age, but he had plenty of time to grow and mature. She was going to enjoy his youthful exuberance while she could. Thoughts of the unknown threatened to intrude on the night, but she refused to let them. She wasn't going to spend the next two weeks thinking the worst.

"Aunt Kate and Uncle Aaron are coming, too, and bringing Miren. I hope that's okay with you, buddy."

"Sure, Miren's too little to eat candy, so I can help."

Kayla and Zach laughed at the grinning lad whose eyes sparkled as he thought about the prospect of bringing home both his candy and Miren's.

"Uncle Aaron might have something to say about that," Kayla told him.

"I'm sure we can work out some kind of deal," Todd said as he picked up his candy bag.

"I'm sure you can," Kayla said. She had no doubt Todd was capable of charming Aaron into just about anything.

Zach gently took hold of Kayla's arm as they started to leave Todd's room. "Are you sure you're okay with this? I can stay home and let you go with Todd." Kayla smiled. "Thanks, but I think EJ and I need to have a talk, and I know how much you're looking forward to this."

"It's been a long time since I went trick-or-treating," Zach said, his excitement obvious by the twinkle in his eyes and the way his scar slipped into hiding inside the laugh lines above his cheek. "And I was almost eleven the first time I went. I have a lot of missed candy to make up for."

Aaron pulled Kate's SUV into the driveway thirty minutes later, just as Todd swallowed his last bite of dinner. Kayla made homemade perogies in the hopes that a filling meal would keep Todd from overdoing it on the candy. She knew it was a lost cause, but she felt like she had to at least try.

After they all oohed and aahed over Miren in her bunny rabbit costume and went over the rules with Todd, Kayla kissed Zach and Todd goodbye and watched the crew head out into the night. She knew that parents all over the island were on edge as well as on the mainland. The town of Stockton had canceled trick or treating. There had been much debate about the event on the island, but in the end, it was decided to allow the kids to have a normal holiday with increased police presence. Many of the Coast Guard members stationed on the island, as well as retired police and military, were volunteering to patrol the streets along with the local police. Nick and Megan volunteered to patrol together, and Kayla wondered what was going on there. She knew that Megan had a lot to work out, and she wondered if the girl had confided in Nick.

She watched as Kate's SUV pulled out of the driveway before heading to the kitchen to finish cleaning up from dinner.

"EJ, come to the kitchen, please," she called.

EJ appeared in the doorway with a sullen look on his face.

"Help me clean up, and then you and I are going to have a talk."

EJ didn't ask what the talk was about, and she didn't offer. She'd left him alone since Saturday when she and Zach had both tried to impress upon him that it was not okay for him to just go somewhere without permission, no matter whom he was with or where they were going. He argued that he thought it would be okay since they were doing homework, but Kayla made it clear, in no uncertain terms, that she must always know where he was.

As soon as the dishes were in the dishwasher and the table wiped down, Kayla suggested they have a seat.

"I have something for you," she said as she placed a bowl of his favorite candy on the table.

"Gee, thanks," EJ said with a scowl.

"If you don't want them, I'll give them to somebody else. The least you could do is say thank you." Kayla spoke sternly even though EJ responded exactly how she expected. She sympathized with him, but she wasn't going to let him think that his behavior was okay.

"Thank you," he mumbled. She watched him as he eyed the candy, but he exhibited great restraint by not taking any. She left the bowl there, hoping that he would loosen up during their talk.

"EJ, we need to talk about some things, beginning with what I'm hearing about you and Lizzie."

EJ's eyes widened. "What about me and Lizzie?" he asked, shrinking down into his chair a bit.

"I heard that you've been spending a lot of time with her at school and that you've been texting and snapchatting her on your iPad."

"Yeah," he said slowly. "We're friends."

"I'm glad you're friends. I like Lizzie a lot." She let that sink in.

"Her mom is like your best friend," he offered.

"One of them, yes. And you and Lizzie have grown up together. I guess you know her pretty well by now."

"Sure, I do," EJ said, sitting up straighter and becoming animated. "Like her favorite singer is Kenny Chesney. And her favorite books are the *American Girl* books. And her favorite TV show is some girlie show called, *When Calls the Heart*. I tried watching it once. You'd like it, but I thought it kind of su-uh, was boring." She cast a look at him to remind him that the phrase he started to use was off limits in their house. His cheeks turned red, and he looked down at his lap.

"Anything else you'd like to add?" Kayla found herself enjoying this new side of EJ.

"Um," he looked up and rolled his eyes toward the ceiling as he casually took a Snickers miniature and unwrapped it. "She loves ballet and puppies," he said with satisfaction.

"A girl after my own heart," Kayla said. "That's quite a lot to know about a girl. So, uh, does Lizzie know this much about you?"

EJ stopped chewing and looked at his mother. He moved his jaw to the side, puckering out his lips. "Gee, I don't know. She does most of the talking."

Kayla suppressed a giggle. "I see," she managed to get out. She pressed her lips tightly together as she watched her growing son lick his fingers. Why did he suddenly seem so old yet so young at the same time?

"EJ, are there boys and girls in your class who are…" How should she phrase this? "Who are *more* than friends?"

"You mean like boyfriend and girlfriend?" He asked without a hint of childish distaste. Kayla nodded. "Sure. Ricky and Molly have been dating for two weeks." He shrugged as if this was no big deal. This was obviously not a new topic of discussion among EJ and his friends. "Really?" Kayla was somewhat surprised. She never saw much interest in the opposite sex on the part of EJ and his friends. At least, not before now.

"And what does it mean for them to be 'boyfriend and girlfriend'?"

"Well," he puckered his mouth again as he reached for another candy bar. "It means that they sit together at lunch, and sometimes they meet to go to the movies."

"Alone?" Kayla asked, horrified at the thought of two eleven-year-olds being dropped off outside of the theater and left to do who knows what.

EJ shook his head. "No, pretty much with their families."

Kayla let out a sigh of relief. "And what about you and Lizzie? Have you ever talked about being boyfriend and girlfriend?"

"Honestly, Mom, she says that if she ever had a boyfriend, her dad would probably lock him up or something. So no, we're just friends."

Kayla smiled. It must be hard being the daughter of the police chief. And even harder on her pre-teen love interests.

"Good idea. But EJ, if you ever change your mind and decide to ask Lizzie, or any girl, to be your girlfriend, would you tell me about it? We might need to have another chat like this to make sure—"

"Mom, I know all about sex. We don't have to have that talk."

Suddenly looking every bit his age and then some, EJ looked at his mother. Kayla stared at him, temporarily unable to speak. After a moment, she asked, "What do you mean you know all about sex?" She swallowed as she waited for his answer.

"Uncle Aaron told me. One of the nights Todd and I stayed with Grandpa. He came over and saw me facetiming Lizzie and said it was time we had a talk. It was kind of gross, but Sam says that Billy talks about it all the time and that it's totally true. I mean, we did talk about where babies come from in school last year, but I wasn't sure what it all meant. It just seemed kind of weird."

Kayla didn't know whether to thank Aaron or kill him. If he wasn't going to ask permission, the least he could have done was tell her about the conversation.

"And did Uncle Aaron tell you that sex is something that you do not do until marriage?"

"Yeah, he said I have to love and respect a girl and show her that I love and respect her by waiting until we're married because it can be really bad for her if we did it and then we broke up. Like it could really break her heart or make people think she was a bad girl or something. He said it's not like that for the boy, so we have to make sure we're the responsible ones and always look out for the girl."

Kayla was impressed. Her brother had handled that pretty well. Of course, he was coming from the perspective of the father of a little girl.

"Very good," Kayla said. She'd have to talk to Aaron about what else he told EJ, but she didn't want to pry too much and make EJ not want to talk to her. So far, their conversation had been going pretty well. "EJ, you do understand why Uncle Zach and I were so upset the other day, right?"

"Yeah, and I'm sorry." EJ looked back down at his lap. His lower lip stuck out just a little before he raised his eyes back to meet his mother's. "Honest, Mom, I just wasn't thinking. I was talking to Lizzie and Susan about our project, and Susan said we could come over and work on it if we wanted, and before I knew it, we were in her car. I really didn't mean to scare you."

Kayla told Susan's mother that, while she appreciated her letting the kids work on their project at her house, she didn't appreciate not knowing about it. Erin McNally was shocked that Kayla didn't know. She assumed EJ had texted her. Kayla told her that her boys did not have phones. She wasn't sure if she was proud of or embarrassed by the look Erin had given her. It was clear that her boys were in the minority when it came to cellular devices.

"I know you didn't mean to scare me, but EJ," she paused until she knew she had his full attention. "Don't ever do that again. Do you understand?"

"Yes, ma'am," he nodded, and Kayla was glad that was over.

"Okay," she said, taking a breath. "We might have an hour left if you hurry and get your costume on."

"Really?" His face lit up.

"Really, but you have to stay with me. No going off with friends. You're still grounded."

"It's a deal," he said before racing out of the kitchen.

They stayed out just under an hour after meeting up with the rest of the family. The evening was pleasantly warmer than usual, but that was expected to change quite a bit in the next few days. Before heading home, Kayla walked with Aaron to Kate's SUV. She was sure Miren was well overdue for bed, but she wanted to have a word with her brother.

"So, Aaron," Kayla said quietly as she stood beside his vehicle, watching Todd and EJ climb into her SUV with their bags of treats. She turned to her brother. "I hear you and EJ had an interesting talk a few weeks ago."

Aaron's jaw dropped, and the guilt was written all over his face.

"Oh, yeah. I meant to tell you about that." He offered her a sad excuse for a smile.

"I would have appreciated the head's up. I'm glad you talked to him, but next time, let me know, please?"

Zach stood nearby waiting for Kayla. Aaron grinned at his brother-in-law.

"No worries, sis. I think there's a new teacher in town for the next talk."

"What, me? I don't think so," Zach said, waving his hands in front of his face.

"Good luck, Zach," Aaron said as he climbed inside, closed the door, and put the car into drive.

Kayla just turned to Zach and laughed. "Don't worry, I'm sure you'll know just what to say when the time comes."

She headed toward the car with Zach following behind her, coming up with every excuse he could think of to be spared from his newly assigned task.

Kanelbulle
Origin: Sweden

Nothing wakes you up in the morning like the smell of
fresh cinnamon rolls baking in the oven. It's a smell that
always reminds me of Christmas and New Year's, Easter
and birthdays. What better way to begin a day of
celebration than with a traditional cinnamon roll? Like
many of my recipes, I worked on this one until it
produced the perfect, aromatic, mouth-watering pastry.
Who can resist a hot-out-of-the-oven cinnamon roll?
Certainly not me.

From *Around the World in Eighty Meals*
by K.Z. Middleton

CHAPTER FIFTEEN

As predicted, November began with an arctic wind blowing in from the north. Kayla watched the Redskins game along with the rest of her family, snuggled up on the couch with Zach's arm around her while a roaring fire kept them all warm and cozy. She looked around the room and marveled at the odd collection of people.

Their family once consisted of just the four of them—Ronnie, Trevor, and the twins, Aaron and Kayla. Then, over the course of several years, Eddie came along, followed by the boys, and then Eddie was gone again. But in just one short year, the family had grown to include Kate and Miren, Zach, and now, it seemed, Megan and Nick, who, though they weren't exactly family, as far as Ronnie was concerned, might as well have been. She opened her door and her heart to everyone who needed a place to belong.

Kayla watched the two of them as they interacted. Megan played it cool, and Kayla wondered if she even noticed the way Nick looked at her. With whatever she had been through, she was probably constructing some pretty high walls around her heart, guarding her feelings like precious treasure.

Nick, on the other hand, wore his feelings on his sleeve. And whatever was on his mind, was on his lips. She prayed that he had some self-control when he was with Zach and the boys because she could see how hard it was for him to clean up his language around her and the rest of the family. One thing was for sure, he was totally infatuated with Megan. They seemed quite comfortable together and were arguing over whose team was better, her Redskins or his Steelers. At this point in the season, they were about even, but that didn't stop them from each claiming to have a better record in one stat or another. Kayla thought that Nick would debate with Megan about anything just to see the way her face lit up when she was engaged in an argument.

Kayla turned her attention to Kate and Aaron. They seemed totally oblivious to the football game as well as everyone else in the room. They were playing peek-a-boo with Miren, and Kayla had never seen her brother so happy, so content with life. Ronnie and EJ jumped and gave each other high-fives over the play that Kayla had just missed while she was surveying her family and friends enjoying each other's company. Todd looked up at her and smiled, and she smiled back, grateful to live so close to her family and be able to share Sunday afternoons with them. They were all going to need each other in a very short time, and she thanked God every day that she had them in her life.

As if reading her mind, Zach leaned in close and kissed her on the cheek. She tilted her head to smile at him and snuggled a little closer. She could hardly believe that her surgery was just over a week away. She was already registered and had been given all of her pre-op instructions. She had to have bloodwork done a day or two before the surgery, but she was ready for it. Not a day went by that she wasn't scared to death, but she refused to let the fear take over. And when fear did consume her, and it sometimes did, she put on a brave face for those around her.

She didn't realize she was crying until she tasted the tear that got caught in the corner of her mouth. She hastily wiped her cheek, and Zach leaned closer.

"You okay?" he whispered.

Pressing her lips together, she nodded yes. She was suddenly overcome with emotion and unable to speak.

"Do you need anything? Water? Wine? Do you want to go home?"

She shook her head. "No, I'm fine. Perfect actually," she whispered back. "I'm just happy. Really, really happy."

It was true. As the days on the calendar ticked by, she grew more and more anxious. But looking around this room, right here, right now, she couldn't ask for more.

***

It was nearly nine the following Saturday when Kayla heard Zach's knock on the door. The island's annual Veterans Day Breakfast was that morning, and everyone was ready to celebrate a good cause. While the kidnapper had not been found, and there were still no leads, things had been quiet since Henry's body had been found.

Kayla was used to seeing men in uniform. Her father served in the Coast Guard for most of her childhood, and then Aaron joined, too. There were Coasties all over the island, and Chincoteague had become a retirement playground for many in the Armed Services. She was used to seeing men and women of every age dressed in uniforms of all kinds. What she wasn't used to seeing was Zach in his uniform, an imposing figure who seemed so out of place on her deck when she opened the door. He looked handsome, tough, formidable, and... completely uncomfortable.

"You look about as happy as the general in White Christmas."

A bewildered expression lined his face. "What's that mean?"

Kayla laughed. "Never mind. We'll watch it next month. The boys will be thrilled that I have someone to force it on besides them." Ever since Zach had become a stable and stalwart presence in her life, she was finding it easier to look toward the future. No matter what happened with her surgery, they were all going to be okay. She refused to think otherwise.

"You look beautiful," he told her. Kayla looked down at the new blue dress she was wearing. Kate insisted they go shopping earlier in the week to find something festive to wear.

"Thank you," she said to Zach, almost giddy that they were appearing in public, for the first time, as a couple.

"Why are we doing this again?" He asked as he helped her into her coat.

"Because your sister asked us to. She's on the committee this year, and apparently they've planned something extra special."

Zach froze. "You don't think... I'm not going to be singled out or anything, right? She's not planning a big thank you for me taking care of her or anything like that, is she?"

"She wouldn't do that to you," Kayla said, firmly believing every word. "Besides, she insisted that Nick be there as well."

Zach nodded, feeling slightly relieved. They called goodbye to the boys who were engaged in a rousing game of Life with Debbie's oldest daughter, their sitter of choice.

"And don't eat all of the cinnamon rolls, got it?" Kayla added to their farewells

"Can we eat most of them?" Todd asked, his eyes gleaming with mischief.

"You may have no more than two."

"Only two? Can't I have three?"

"Todd," Kayla warned. "You heard me."

"Yes, ma'am," he said with a defeated pout.

"Honestly," she told Zach as they closed the door behind them. "You would think I starve the boy."

"You can't blame him. I had a hard time resisting them myself. This breakfast better be worth it."

***

The elementary school cafeteria was awash in red, white, and blue. Thank you signs, made by individual classes, dotted the walls. People of all ages greeted each other, some in uniform, some simply wearing hats or jackets that denoted their branch of service.

Zach had heard about the popularity of the annual breakfast, but he was still taken aback by the number of attendees. He searched the room until his eyes landed on his sister, looking beautiful in her bright red dress and red, white, and blue corsage. Zach led Kayla across the room and hugged his sister, being careful not to crush the flower.

"From Aaron?"

She shook her head. "No. It's a long-held secret. Apparently one of the vets orders them every year for the volunteers. Nobody actually knows who orders them. It's been happening for so long, we doubt the original sender is still alive. But what a wonderful thing to do, don't you think?"

Zach acknowledged the thoughtfulness.

"How are you feeling? You look good, really good."

"I feel great. I had an appointment with Dr. Sprance yesterday, and he says I'm the picture of health. My heart is strong, and I should be able to live a long, happy life without any further complications." She was beaming, no glowing was more accurate, but that made Zach wonder... "Kate, is there any other reason you were seeing Dr. Sprance? Are you and Aaron..."

Kate winked at her brother, a habit she had picked up from Aaron. "Not yet, but hopefully next year." Her eyes sparkled.

"Oh, Kate, how wonderful," Kayla said, hugging her.

Zach wasn't sure it was so wonderful. He would never forget how it felt to stand in the hospital, not knowing whether his sister and best friend would live or die. He spent the entire last winter taking care of her when she was put on bedrest to prevent a heart attack. He remembered watching Miren through the nursery window as he prayed that Kate's life could be saved by the emergency surgery she was undergoing. He sure hoped that Dr. Sprance knew what he was talking about. Having Miren had almost killed her, and Zach worried that another baby would be more than her heart could take. Shaking off his apprehension, Zach scanned the room.

"So, what's the deal? We eat, and then what?"

"We have a speaker this year. Oh, and recently discharged vets have special seating."

"Why?" He asked, immediately on edge. "We're not going to have to speak or anything, are we?"

"No, no. Relax. You'll see. It's all good. You're at our table. Just look for the spot with your place card." Kate spotted a man at the entrance and excused herself.

Zach and Kayla spoke to a few people before being waved over to their table by Aaron. Nick was already there, and he and Zach exchanged the awkward man-hug that many in the room had grown accustomed to. Kayla and Zach hugged Ronnie and Trevor and greeted others they knew.

When Zach found his seat, he discovered an ornate drinking glass. The glass was mottled with different colors and contained bubbles and dimples that marked it as a one-of-a-kind, handmade glass. He wondered what the significance was, especially after noticing that only a few of the attendees had them. He noticed that Nick had one in a different array of colors, but Aaron did not.

Once everyone was seated, Kate went to the podium and introduced herself. She welcomed everyone and signaled for the color guard. They all stood as the American and Virginia flags were brought in, followed by all of the Armed Forces and the MIA-POW flags. After the posting of the colors and the Pledge of Allegiance, Kate resumed her place at the podium and asked Father Darryl to lead them in an opening prayer and blessing. They bowed their heads as he led them in prayer, then Kate returned to the microphone.

"Thank you, Father, for the prayer and blessing, and for the prayers for the family of Henry Stevens." Kate's voice cracked as she mentioned the child's name, but she regained her composure and went on to explain the procedure for getting breakfast. Once they had all eaten, the special guest would be asked to speak.

When Kate returned to the podium after breakfast, she looked at Zach and smiled. His stomach lurched at the thought that she might single him out, but as she began to speak, he relaxed.

"Some of you may have noticed that you have a colored glass at your place. These glasses are not ordinary glasses. They are the inspiration of artist, Mac Singletary. They are a gift to you, our most recently discharged Veterans, and I would like Mac to come up and explain to us their origin and significance."

Mac approached the podium with the aid of a cane. Zach's trained eye realized instantly that Mac was missing a leg. A prosthetic leg peeked out from his pants' leg. He thanked Kate and stood before the crowd.

"Fifteen years ago, I was a broken man. I had returned from a fourth tour in the Middle East without a leg, a career, or, in my mind, a future." He talked about his inability to reconnect with his family and friends, his failure to find a job, and ultimately, his life on the streets. He told a story about being approached by a man in overalls, his hands calloused and worn.

"He asked me if I wanted to share a meal with him, and, for some reason, I said yes. He took me home to meet his wife and his family." Mac took a breath as emotion overcame him. "He treated me like a friend, like someone he'd known his entire life, not like a defeated waste of life he'd found on the street."

Mac told how the man, a Vietnam Vet, his wife and family welcomed him into their home for dinner and then helped him find a place to live—a small apartment above the garage of a family friend. He lived there, rent-free, in return for doing yardwork and handyman chores. The man, named Peter, helped Mac find a job, and most important, invited him to church. Mac found a whole new life with God as his most faithful companion. Eventually, he met Alison, his wife of ten years now. She was an art teacher at a local college, and she introduced him to other faculty, including a professor who taught students how to create hand-blown glass. Not long after, Mac became his apprentice.

"For the first time in my life, I felt like my hands had purpose. I could create, refine, remold, and reshape. I took all of the things I saw overseas, all of the blood that I shed, all of the nightmares and feelings stirred by PTSD, and I lit them on fire, literally." He chuckled. "And that's when it occurred to me that I could do more than burn those memories and feelings. I could take the actual sand that I walked upon, spit on, shed blood on, and turn it into something beautiful, something meaningful."

He picked up a glass from behind the podium and held it up for everyone to see. "We all came back with demons, some more than others. But I conquered mine by turning them into liquid and then refining them into a beautiful glass." He paused and looked at the crowd. Zach noticed that every person in the room was riveted by the man's story.

"A glass is an empty vessel until you fill it with water, or coffee, or whiskey, or whatever else you want to put into it. And then it's full, full of something life-giving. And that's how I felt. Empty until I found something to fill me up—a wife, children, a job I love, and most importantly, God." He moved his gaze around the room. "So, for those of you who recently returned from that place that nobody else can comprehend, here is your chance. Take these glasses, made from the sand of Mid-Eastern deserts, and drink from them, display them, do whatever you want with them. Just don't hide them or throw them away. Use them to remind yourselves that we aren't meant to be empty. Find the thing that fills you up. And cherish it with all your heart."

Zach stretched his arm beneath the table until it found Kayla's hand, lying in her lap. He squeezed her hand and hoped it conveyed what he was feeling right then. He continued to hold it tight as Mac said thank you, and he kept holding it as he and Kayla joined everyone else in the room in giving Mac a standing ovation, letting go only to show his appreciation through his applause. Zach had indeed been empty, but by the grace of God, he had found that someone to completely fill all of the empty spaces in his life.

***

"Why didn't you bring Megan today?" Zach asked Nick as they walked out together.

"I'm not sure she's feeling it," Nick said. He acted like it was no big deal, but Zach had seen the way he looked at her.

"Why do you say that? It seems to me like you two get along pretty well, and you hang out at her place a lot."

"Yeah, but it's not going anywhere. Don't get me wrong," Nick held up his hands. "I like her, I really do, but she doesn't even act like she wants me to touch her. I have no idea what's going on with her. One minute, she's looking at me like maybe there's something there, and the next, she's putting up some kind of invisible shield. Like, the other night, I tried giving her a goodnight kiss when she walked me out. But when I leaned in, she turned her cheek to me before hurrying back inside. It was weird."

"Be patient, Nick. I don't know what kind of demons she's hiding from, but you and I both know that it takes time to bring them into the open."

"You're sure as hell right about that," Nick said. "Anyway, I've got to get to the station."

"Still helping them look for the kidnapper?"

"Yeah. I think there's a job for me there if I want it. I'm seriously considering it."

"Good luck. Let me know if you need help with anything," Zach said.

"Will do," Nick called as he got into his truck.

Zach watched him drive off before going back inside. Kayla had urged Zach to walk out with Nick while she helped Kate with some of the cleanup. Zach went back inside to help and found Aaron stacking chairs.

"Need help?" Zach asked, lifting a chair onto the stack.

"Thanks. Kate has a crew that's coming in to clean, but she's not ready to go, and I hate to stand still."

"I know what you mean." Zach thought about Nick. "Hey, Aaron, what's the deal with Megan? What's she running from?"

At first, Aaron looked at Zach in surprise, but then he shook his head. "I guess you know what you're talking about. Hard not to see it when you've spent a good deal of your life running from something, too."

"So, I'm right," Zach said.

"It's not my place to tell, Zach, but she has a tough decision to make."

"Just please tell me she isn't married," Zach said.

Aaron laughed as they continued stacking chairs. "Been there, done that," he said. "But no, she's not married, and she's not pregnant, either. Been there, too."

"Nick's kind of hung up on her."

"You think?" Aaron asked. "I'm tempted to tell him to steer clear, but the truth is, she needs someone she can trust. Just tell him to be there for her. Is he capable of that?"

"Nick's all talk as far as the love 'em and leave 'em stuff," Zach said. "In truth, he's all heart. He'll be there for her. I'd just hate to see him get hurt. Nick hasn't had many people in his life he could count on."

"I don't think Megan has either. Maybe they're both just what the other needs."

"Or the last thing each other needs," Zach said warily.

"Or that," Aaron agreed.

***

The call came early on Monday morning. It was barely dawn when Zach picked up his phone and hastily answered, his heart already racing.

"Aaron, what's wrong? Is Kate okay?"

"Yeah, it's not Kate."

"Kayla?" Zach said as he jumped out of bed and reached for his jeans that were draped on the nearby chair.

"It's Ethan. Tammi's son. He's gone."

"Gone?" Zach's stomach clenched at the thought. "do they think…"

"Yes, they do, but that's all I know. I'm not sure right now exactly what happened. Tammi and Rob are a mess. Can you get Kayla and take her to their house? I'm headed over there now."

"Sure thing," Zach said, disconnecting the call. He looked at his reflection in the mirror. "How the hell do I tell her this?" When he got no answer back, he went to the bathroom to clean himself up before heading to Kayla's.

***

Kayla collapsed into the overstuffed chair in Zach's living room. She had never seen Tammi so distraught, and her heart was breaking for her dear friend. The boys were still at school, and Kayla had no idea how to tell them the news.

"I don't even know what to say. Or think. Or feel."

It was the second worst day of her life, next to the day Eddie died. Even worse than the day in Dr. Zink's office. She had thirty-five years of ups and downs. Ethan was only eight.

"I know." Zach said, glancing at a text on his phone. "It's Nick. He's been asked to join the Chincoteague Island Police Department. Which is good since Rob isn't going to be able to touch this one. They were going to be a man down."

"Do you think that's why his application went through so quickly?"

"I suspect so, but he'll be a great addition to the department. He'll work hard and leave no stone unturned."

"Paul said that the FBI is taking the lead on the case."

"It's officially being looked at as a serial killer case." He winced as he said the words. That was giving into the presumption that Ethan was another victim. Kayla knew that Zach hated, as much as she did, the thought of any kid, but especially one of Todd's closest friends, being among that exclusive group.

"How are we going to tell Todd? It was all I could do not to say anything this morning. I had a hard time letting them out of my sight when we dropped them off after you called. Do you think the kids already know? Would the school have told them?"

"I doubt it. They're going to leave that to the parents." Zach opened a cabinet and took out a bottle of Scotch. "I know it's barely noon, but do you want something?"

"No, thanks. You go ahead. I'm not sure my stomach can handle it."

Zach poured himself a drink and downed it in one gulp before pouring another. He sat on the couch across from Kayla.

"Are you okay?" he asked.

"I'm not sure any of us will be okay ever again. How could this happen? We've been so diligent. We haven't let the kids out of our sights. How could Ethan have disappeared?"

"I wish I knew. What was it his brother said about a dog?"

Kayla sat up and looked at Zach. "He said that they saw a dog running down the street on their way to the school. Ethan said he recognized the dog and wanted to catch it, but Alan told him no. Alan turned his back for just a few minutes, and Ethan was gone. Tammi is blaming herself. She says she never should have let them walk to the school without her, but it's so close to their house, and she was running late for work."

"Maybe they should look into that old guy again, the one with the dogs?"

"But Mr. Phelps is just a harmless old man. He's been around as long as we've lived on the island. I can't imagine that he would do something like this." Kayla shook her head at the thought.

Zach finished his drink and looked down at his glass as if debating whether or not to have another.

"Go ahead, I won't judge," Kayla said.

"No, I'd rather have some semblance of coherence when we hear from Paul. The whole town is going to want in on finding Ethan and whoever is doing this, and I'll do what I can to help with the search."

"Are you going to go back to work at the police station? Do you think they need you?"

"Do you want me to? Would that make you feel better?"

"Zach, I know you weren't really happy with your job, working with guns all day long, teaching other people to shoot. I don't want you to have to do that, but do you think they could use your help on this?"

Zach shook his head. "I don't know. It's certainly not my area of expertise. If they need me, I will go. It's just that…" He looked away.

"You're afraid of the task they might want you for." Kayla got up from the chair and went to him. She sat on his lap and wrapped her arms around his neck. "You aren't the bad guy, Zach. He is. Whatever happens to him, whether you do it or not, it's not a reflection on you."

"God, I love you," he said, burying his face in her neck. "Why didn't I come clean with you sooner?"

"Because you're a man," she said playfully. "It will always take you longer to see what's right in front of your face."

"Not if it's you that's right in front of me," he said before claiming her mouth with his own. Kayla lost herself in his kiss but not before wondering how she had managed to live so long without it.

***

After three days, there was still no sign of Ethan. Zach wrestled with his conscience. Should he go into the police station that the FBI had commandeered as the new command center in the investigation and offer his support? It wasn't like he hadn't been helping. Like most of the men on the island, he had joined law enforcement officials on the organized searches and had combed the running trail, waded through the marsh, and walked every road and back lot between the Chincoteague Bay and the Assateague Channel. The island was not very big. How could Ethan have disappeared without a trace?

Pouring himself a cup of coffee, Zach looked at Kayla's house and thought about Todd. He hadn't stopped crying since they told him the news. He had moved into Kayla's room at night, afraid to sleep alone in his own bed. Tranquil places like Chincoteague Island weren't supposed to have to deal with these kinds of things. They were supposed to be havens, refuges from the outside world.

Zach and Kayla had spent the last three days at the small community center on the island which had been turned into a command center for those wanting to help the Warren family. Their friends made calls, printed flyers, and took turns aiding the police and FBI on the search. Since only a few days had passed since Ethan went missing, there was high hope that he would be found alive. If only they had a solid lead as to where to look.

"Mornin' Zach. You're up early," Nick said. Zach turned to see the younger man fastening the necktie of his new uniform. Though he had been part of the search for the past three days, while his paperwork went through, this was his first official day on the job.

"Wow, you clean up really nice," Zach mocked his friend. "I hardly recognize you."

"Hey, I know how to dress right when the situation warrants it."

"Yeah, well get used to it. That pretty blue shirt and fancy tie are now your regular day-to-day clothes."

"I'm gonna hate wearing this thing," Nick admitted, holding the tie out and looking at it with disgust.

"Better you than me," Zach said, taking another swallow of his black coffee.

"How's Todd?" Nick asked.

"Not good. Any leads?"

"Not that I know of. Maybe I'll know something by the time I get back here this evening."

Zach nodded. "Let me know how to help. I'm sure Kayla and I will be at the community center most of the day."

"There's not much you can do that you aren't already doing."

"Still, I'm here if they need…anything."

A pregnant silence hung between them. "If it comes to that, I'll shoot the animal myself," Nick said before walking away. "I'll grab a doughnut and coffee at the station," he called before heading out.

"Good luck, Nick," Zach called. "I hope you catch the SOB," he said quietly as the front door closed.

Stroganoff
Origin: Russia

I've always thought of stroganoff as a man's meal. It has the perfect ingredients for a fall or winter night – meat, pasta, mushrooms, onions, and sour cream. Growing up in the desert, in the rainforest, and on mountainsides, there was never a traditional meal of meat and potatoes, but this sure comes close. It took years for my sister, Kate, to warm up to the flavor, but I think we both agree that there are few things in life better than cozying up on the couch with a good book or long movie and a hearty bowl of stroganoff.

From *Around the World in Eighty Meals*
by K.Z. Middleton

CHAPTER SIXTEEN

Four days before her surgery, and just over a week after Ethan's disappearance, Kayla went to the island clinic to have her bloodwork done and sent to Dr. Zink. She was walking through the clinic's waiting room, on her way to the community center, when pandemonium broke out. Several personnel from the clinic were running down the hall, at least two doctors and a few nurses, with other staff joining the pack. A small crowd gathered in the waiting room as the local news was turned up on the big-screen television. A 'Breaking News' banner floated across the screen.

"...bloody jacket, fitting the description of the one Ethan Warren was wearing, was found in the dumpster behind the Chincoteague Library." The voice of the local newscaster was drowned out by a sudden roaring in Kayla's ears. She reached for the nearest chair and lowered herself down. She looked for a trash can, knowing she would never make it to the bathroom in time. As she fought down the breakfast she had eaten earlier,

Island of Promise

she looked back at the television. Hot tears sprang to her eyes, and she realized that the pulsing she thought was her racing heart was her phone, buzzing inside the pocket of her jacket.

Swallowing hard, she answered the phone. "Zach," she breathed. "The jacket." It was all she could say.

"Where are you?"

"I'm at the clinic."

"Stay there. I'm on my way. We'll go to Tammi's before we pick up Todd."

Kayla nodded.

"Kayla, did you hear me?"

"Oh, yes. Sorry. Zach."

"I'll be there soon. Wait for me at the clinic."

Kayla disconnected without saying goodbye. She was in a daze and wondered what it meant that the jacket was in the dumpster. Where was Ethan?

Acting on autopilot, Kayla made her way outside. She watched two police cruisers fly by, their sirens blaring. She needed to know more. Even though she knew Zach was on his way, she fought the people standing on the street, ogling at the disappearing cruisers, and headed toward the center. She went inside and looked around. Every face was turned toward the television. Nobody moved or spoke. Anne's face showed a mixture of horror and pain. Debbie's oldest daughter, a babysitter to nearly every young child on the island, collapsed in tears. Shannon gripped one of the tables, her mouth open, her eyes wide.

Kayla couldn't take it. Rather than go to her friends, she fled. She fought back tears and nausea as she made her way outside and onto the sidewalk. She gripped her coat, pulling it more tightly around her, and her scarf whipped in the wind. She was having a hard time focusing and couldn't tell if it was the circumstances or all of the blood she had just had drawn.

"Kayla," Zach shouted, his voice straining against all the other noises on the street. His truck was illegally parked in front of the clinic, but he made his way toward her. She melted into him as he reached her. Though she could have walked to the truck on her own, he gathered her in his arms and carried her back through the throng of people. If anyone wondered why, they didn't ask. Everyone was too caught up in the horror of what was happening.

***

"You need to eat something," Zach said as he put the truck in drive. "How much blood did they take?"

"I have no idea," she answered. "I don't usually feel this shaky afterward. I guess it's a combination…" she let the rest of the sentence trail off, and Zach anxiously looked over to make sure she was still conscious.

"Maybe going to see Tammi is too much for you."

"No, I have to go. I need to be there for her," Kayla said, holding her head as if to steady it. "What if his body—"

"Kayla, don't. So far, nothing else has turned up. We're not going to make assumptions." Turning the wheel, he headed in the opposite direction from Tammi's.

"Where are we going?"

"Home," Zach said. "I'm making an executive decision. You're going to get something to eat and rest." He was prepared for her to protest, but she leaned her head back on the seat of the truck and closed her eyes.

Zach watched the road while continuing to glance her way. A host of emotions played across her face. He wanted to punch the steering wheel. Why was this happening? Didn't she have enough on her plate already?

Gravel spewed as Zach came to a flying halt in her driveway. He put the truck into park and turned off the engine, jumped out and ran to Kayla's side as she opened the door.

"I'm fine," she told him. "I can walk."

"I know you can," he said. "But I'm going to help you anyway." He closed the door to the truck, put his arm around her, and led her to the house. Man, she was stubborn. And beautiful. And tough. And vulnerable at the same time. He wondered again why she had to go through this.

As if reading his thoughts, she stopped at the base of the steps that led up to the house.

"Why is this happening? I don't understand why all of this is happening?"

"I wish I knew, sweetheart," he said as he wrapped her in his arms. He held her close and then leaned down to kiss her, hoping to assure her that, no matter what, he would be there to help her get through all of this. "Come on. Let's get you out of the cold. You take it easy, and I'll get the boys from school."

Kayla gave in to Zach as he led her into the house and helped her get settled on the couch. He poured her a glass of ginger ale without ice, just the way she liked it.

"I'm going to heat you some food and call Aaron to see if he knows anything."

"Zach, wait," she called, getting up from the couch.

"What is it?" Zach asked, going to her side and wrapping his arms around her. Kayla pulled back and looked at him. Her jaw was set, and her eyes were wide and clear.

"Let's get married," she said. "This week."

Zach was stunned. This was out of nowhere. Kayla wasn't thinking straight. *Maybe she's in shock and doesn't know what she's saying.*

"Kayla, are you okay? Where did that come from?"

Kayla shook her head. She looked as surprised as Zach felt. "I don't know. I just suddenly realized how much time we're wasting."

While Zach had every intention of marrying her, this was not at all how he pictured the proposal—no ring, no bended knee, no lunch with her boys to ask permission. He knew this was her second marriage, but he wanted to do it right.

"Kayla, let's not rush things."

The determination on her face turned to panic. "I," she stammered, "I thought you'd want to…I'm sorry," she said turning away.

Zach took her arm and turned her back to face him. "I do. Believe me, I do. I just thought I'd be the one asking." He tried to reassure her with a smile. "I'm kind of old-fashioned that way."

"Zach, I need you. I need you physically and emotionally. I need you to be here with us all the time. I need to feel like something in my life is going right, like there's still joy in the world. I need…" She turned away, a pained look on her face, and then turned back. "I need you to be here with us. I need you to help me deal with all of this, everything. I need you—"

Zach crushed her to him and held her as tightly as he could before forcing her to face him. "I love you. I love every part of you and always will. I will be here for you through all of this—the sickness, the heartache, looking for Ethan, helping Tammi, protecting your boys. Whatever you need, I'm here."

Kayla nodded and sniffed. She wiped her tears with the back of her hand.

"I know, but…please, I need this," she implored, her voice barely above a whisper.

"I'm not sure we how fast we can make it happen."

"Can we at least try? I don't want to wait," she said, and in that instant, he knew that he would do anything for her, anything, no matter the cost or the lengths to which he might have to go to accomplish it.

Maybe there was a way to make this happen. And he thought he knew just the man to ask.

"Is this what you really want? Right now? With all of this going on?"

"More than anything," she said, gripping his hands with all her strength.

"Okay. I'll see what I can do. I've got some things to look into, and then I'll pick up the boys from school. Call me if you need anything. I have a feeling this is going to be one heckuva roller coaster of a week." He gave her a powerful kiss before he left, leaving them both hungry for more.

***

Father Darryl's smile didn't quite reach his eyes when he opened the door to see Zach standing on his threshold.

"Zach, come on in. This is a welcome treat after the day I've had."

Zach winced. "I take it you've been to see Tammi and Rob."

The young priest's face fell. "It's so sad. I baptized Ethan and gave him his First Holy Communion. I just can't believe this is happening." He shook his head as he ushered Zach in and closed the door.

"So, what brings you here today? No nightmares, I hope."

"They're still there, but I'm learning to cope with them," Zach said, taking a seat. He and Father took their places in the comfortable chairs that faced each other in the cozy office. "I know you're busy, and I won't keep you. It's about Kayla."

"Is something wrong?" Father asked.

"No, not exactly. She's worried about the boys and distraught over Ethan."

"Yes, I'm sure. We all feel the same. But the cancer, is that causing her any pain?"

"Only emotional pain," Zach answered with a wry smile.

The priest nodded, took off his glasses, wiped them with a handkerchief, and motioned to a small refrigerator nearby. "Water?"

"No, thanks," Zach added. "I actually don't have a lot of time either. I'm heading to the school to pick up the boys. Kayla wants us to tell them about Ethan before they hear it from someone else."

"Understandable. So, let's get right to the point. What do you need to talk about?"

"Father, Kayla and I want to get married."

"How wonderful," Father Darryl said, reaching to shake Zach's hand. "Congratulations. I'm glad to hear some good news for a change."

"Thanks," Zach said, his smile spreading across his face. Realization hit him as the words sunk in. He and Kayla were getting married.

"I take it you talked to her about your past."

"I did, and you were right. I wasn't giving her enough credit. Of the two of us, I always thought of myself as the strong one. Over the course of the past several months, I've realized that Kayla is stronger than I am by leaps and bounds."

"She comes from a good, strong family."

"She does," Zach agreed. "Only now, she's worried. Maybe even in a bit of shock. I think all this stuff with Ethan and the other boys is getting to her. Plus, her surgery is just four days away. She wants to have things right before it happens."

"And what do you mean by that?" Father cocked his head to the side and looked at Zach for clarification.

Zach took a deep breath and exhaled. "Father, I know this sounds crazy, but she wants to get married right away. Maybe even before the surgery if that's possible. Before anything else bad happens. I know it's fast, and I know it's not ideal in the eyes of the Church, but it's what she needs. Is there any way to make that happen?"

Father's bright blue eyes twinkled. He broke into a wide grin and nodded.

"I think, under the circumstances, we can find a way to work this out. There are some things we will need to discuss, and some things you and Kayla will need to discuss. Children, for one, the boys and any future—"

"I understand," Zach cut him off. "Tell me what we need to do, and we'll do it."

"Do you have a few minutes to talk over some logistics with me, about the wedding and the marriage? I have maybe a half hour, and then I want to go back to Tammi's. I want to be there in case there's news."

"Sure, Father. I can give you all the time you need if it means we can make this happen." Relief washed over Zach. He felt as if he'd been holding his breath for the entire meeting. Saying 'thank you' didn't seem adequate in light of what the priest was doing, so he hoped the tears in his eyes conveyed the full measure of his gratitude.

***

Kayla braced herself as she watched Zach and the boys climb out of the truck and head toward the house.

When they walked inside, she looked at Zach, trying to read the expression on his face. When he grinned at her, his scar disappeared into the folds of skin beneath his eye, and she knew everything was going to be okay.

"Mom, we did the most awesome experiment in science today. Mr. Palmer is the best teacher ever. He lets us use the middle school science lab just like EJ's class. And next week, we're going to—"

"Todd, slow down. I want to hear all about it, but Uncle Zach and I have something important to tell you." She looked toward Zach.

"Boys," he said. "Your mom and I have some good news and some bad news."

Kayla took a deep breath as she bent down and took Todd's hands. She hated to tell Todd about the jacket, especially when they weren't sure what it meant. But it was a small town, and word was traveling fast.

"Todd, the police found something today," she told the little boy. "Something that might mean that Ethan is badly hurt."

As she spoke, Kayla continued her internal prayer that Ethan would somehow be found alive and unharmed.

Slow Roasted Fish with Rosemary and Citrus
Origin: Australia

Barramundi is my favorite fish, but it's not easy to find outside of Australia. Luckily, you can use this traditional recipe with almost any kind of flaky, white fish. I like to slow roast it, just like we did when I was growing up in the wilds of the Land Down Under. Almost everything we ate, in that small village in the bush country, had to be cooked over an open, slow-burning flame. That's precisely what allows all of the flavors in this recipe to stand out. It's a welcome home, life is going to be okay, kind of dish.

From *Around the World in Eighty Meals*
by K.Z. Middleton

<u>CHAPTER SEVENTEEN</u>

Three days later, Kayla sat at her antique dressing table, which had belonged to her grandmother, and watched the transformation in the mirror. Kate fixed Kayla's hair so that it formed soft curls above her shoulders, and Megan was working magic on the dark shadows and worry lines on her face. She felt like a movie star being prepped for her big scene.

"All done," Megan said. "Do you like it?"

Kayla batted her eyes, noting how the blend of smoky grey and rose-colored shades on her lids highlighted her hazel eyes. Her lashes were curled and heavy with mascara for the first time since before EJ was born. Her cheeks were rosy, and her lips were perfectly kissable. She smiled.

"It's beautiful," she said. "Thank you."

"You're beautiful," Kate said. "Come see."

The three women gathered in front of the oval, full-length mirror that matched the dressing table. Kayla stared at the reflection, feeling like the ugly duckling in spite of the makeup and hair. To her left, Megan stood, tall and lean, her raven hair gleaming as if it had been polished. She wore jeans and a pale pink sweater but still managed to look beautifully exotic. To Kayla's right, Kate towered above her in a royal blue dress and the first pair of high-heels she had worn in a year.

Kayla eyed her own reflection. Her dress was a cream-colored one that had always been a favorite of hers but hadn't been worn in over ten years. It was a little too big now, a result of stress, lack of appetite, restless nights, and the disease that was eating away the tissue inside her body. Despite the looseness in her shoulders and waist, the dress looked good. It had full-length sleeves made of lace and a lace overlay that hung over the bodice.

"I never imagined that, if I ever married again, it would be in a quick ceremony without all of my friends present." She suddenly felt weak and grabbed Kate's hand, meeting her gaze in the mirror. "Do you think we're making a mistake to do this? In this way?"

Holding Miren in her arms, Ronnie came up behind her daughter. "You're doing the right thing," Ronnie told her. "There's not time for a big wedding, and everyone is at the center or helping with the search. Your friends will all understand."

Turning toward Ronnie and blinking back tears, Kayla wrapped her arms around her mother. Miren batted her away in protest, and the women all laughed.

"Those had better be tears of joy," Ronnie said, handing Miren to Kate and reaching out to carefully wipe the tears from Kayla's face. Kayla managed to laugh as she looked back in the mirror. She assessed her appearance once more before lowering her gaze to her right hand. With a tear in her eye, she slid the small gold band from her finger. Someday, if he wanted it, Todd would be allowed to slide the ring onto the hand of his own bride. Until then, she would keep it tucked away beside her engagement ring, which she hoped EJ would want for his fiancé. She kissed the ring before gently laying it in her jewelry box.

"I love you, Eddie," she whispered as she closed the lid to the box. She then nodded to her mother, Kate, and Megan. "Okay," she breathed. "Let's go."

As the four women walked down the hall, EJ gasped.

"Mom, you're beautiful," he said, and Kayla's heart swelled as she gazed upon her fast-growing son in his dark suit. Thankfully it still fit though he had already grown since Kate and Aaron's spring wedding.

"Thank you," she said, laying her hand on his cheek, remembering how little he once was.

"You are beautiful," Todd agreed before wrinkling his nose and twisting his mouth. "But I don't understand why this is a secret and why there's no party like the one Aunt Kate and Uncle Aaron had."

Kayla bent down and gently kissed her son's cheek.

"There will be," she said. "When Zach and I get married again in a few months, we will have a giant party with all of our friends, and we'll dance all night long."

It was a promise that she and Zach had made to each other. No matter what was to come, they would have a traditional wedding and reception to celebrate the love they were so blessed to have found.

"Are we ready to head to the church?" Kate asked. "Aaron, Dad, and Zach should be there already."

"I'll lock up here and see you all after the ceremony," Megan said. She hugged Kayla. "You are truly a beautiful bride. I am so happy for you."

"Thank you, Megan. We'll see you shortly."

When the group walked out from Kayla's house and onto the deck, Kayla stopped and gazed over the water. So much had happened since the day she saw her neighbor, Kate, and the good-looking stranger beside her, walking arm and arm along the water's edge. She smiled remembering how jealous her brother had been when she told him that Kate was out walking with another man. My, how their lives had changed. Today, she would be the one walking beside Zach, arm and arm, beginning the first day of the rest of their lives. It was cliché, but she didn't mind. She just prayed that God would grant them a long life together.

***

The ceremony was brief, and Kayla regretted that there had been no Mass, but they were grateful that Father was willing to marry them under the circumstances. He waived the traditional pre-Cana requirements, saying that he already knew that Zach and Kayla had faced more together over the past year than many couples would face in a lifetime. There had been an uncomfortable moment when they broached the topic of future children, but they made it through that discussion without too much worry.

If they were lucky enough to someday think about having children together, then they were lucky enough.

Zach and Kayla had made a hasty trip to the courthouse on the mainland to file for the marriage certificate, and all of the other necessary provisions were taken care of in record time. Of course, it helped that there was no Mass, no reception, and no honeymoon to plan. And, since they had kept the wedding a secret from everyone but their family, there were no invitations to send out or any if the other frills that usually accompanied such an occasion.

After a few quickly-snapped pictures, Zach and Kayla walked back down the aisle, hand-in-hand. Kayla looked down at their hands. They wore Ronnie and Trevor's wedding rings, on loan until they would be able to pick out their own. She liked the way their hands looked, bound together for better or for worse. Kayla glanced up at Zach and smiled.

"Happy?" he asked, squeezing her hand.

"Very much so," she answered, leaning up for a kiss.

"Wait until tonight," he promised, and she felt her insides melt as a wave of heat shot through her.

***

Zach and Kayla spent afternoon of their wedding day at the community center. Nothing had been found since the jacket was discovered, and the search for Ethan continued. Kayla found it hard to concentrate on the calls she made. Every time she looked over at Zach, who was giving instructions to each new search team that gathered, she felt the heat rise in her cheeks. Each time their eyes met, Kayla felt a jolt inside of her abdomen. She felt like she was sixteen again and falling for her first crush.

Only Anne noticed the rings on Kayla and Zach's hand, and the way they looked at each other. Kayla nodded at Anne's questioning look but put her finger to her lips. *Later*, she mouthed, and Anne's tear-filled eyes conveyed understanding. They were there for Tammi. Everything else could wait.

***

"Goodnight, my sweet boy. I love you," Kayla said to Todd as she tucked him into the big queen-sized bed he was sharing with EJ at the Baltimore hotel. Kayla's surgery was early the following morning, but it was still her wedding night, so the boys were staying in Ronnie and Trevor's room to give Kayla and Zach some privacy.

"I love you, too," Todd said, hugging her fiercely.

She moved around the bed to EJ.

"I love you, EJ," she said, folding him into her arms. "Take good care of your brother tonight."

"I will. I love you, too, mom." Kayla pretended not to see the tear that rolled down his cheek.

She and Zach thanked both of her parents and hugged them good night at the door.

"We'll see you in the morning." She blushed as she glanced toward Zach and quickly looked away. Though she was grown and now married twice, she felt bashful saying goodnight to her parents and leaving with Zach. "I hope the noise from the street doesn't keep you awake."

"We'll be fine," Ronnie assured her as a car horn blasted from the busy Baltimore street below. "Everything will be fine. We love you, and we'll see you in the morning."

Kayla nodded, unable to respond as she turned to leave her family after their emotional day.

Once Zach and Kayla were in the hallway outside her parents' hotel room, Zach put his arm around his bride and led her to their room at the other end of the hall. As he unlocked the door, Kayla felt warmth pool in her abdomen. She followed him into the room but avoided his gaze.

Eddie was the only man she had ever made love to, the only man to ever see her naked, the only man to ever touch her intimately or hold her afterwards. But theirs was a love of youthful romance. She remembered feeling shy and awkward on their wedding night, unsure of what to do or how to act. She let Eddie take the lead then.

Raising her eyes to meet Zach's she saw the uncertainty in his eyes.

"Are you okay?" he asked in a whisper.

"I'm better than okay," she replied, taking his hand. "I was just thinking about how right this feels. I'm not afraid. I'm not unsure or apprehensive. I'm not shy or embarrassed. If tomorrow I find out that I'm dying, I will know that we had tonight, and know how it feels to truly live and love."

"I love you, Kayla," Zach said, his voice filled with raw emotion and yearning.

"I love you, Zach. Let me show you how much."

Zach turned back to the door and slid the chain across the channel before taking his wife to bed. It was a night of tenderness and passion, of laughter and tears, of two bodies and two hearts joining as one. A day that blended both the best and the worst that life had to offer, was transformed into a night that held hope and the promise of tomorrow.

***

The waiting room became crowded with people as the hours ticked by. Zach looked around and wondered how many other surgeries were taking place that morning. He crossed the floor to the window and looked out across the city. He felt Aaron at his side but didn't turn in his direction. After a few minutes, Aaron spoke.

"It seems like yesterday that our roles were reversed."

Zach remembered it well. His sister was the one in surgery, and he and Aaron were both nervous wrecks. Kate's life hung in the balance after a heart attack the night Zach killed her ex. As soon as her heart was stabilized, Miren had been delivered more than eight weeks early by an emergency C-section. Then Kate was rushed into heart surgery. Zach and Aaron had stood by a window then, too. They had watched Miren in the nursery and prayed for Kate to be okay.

"I can't believe everything we've all been through over the past fifteen months," Zach said. "Yet here we stand, once again not knowing what tomorrow will bring."

Aaron was silent for a moment before placing his hand on his brother-in-law's back.

"But isn't that always the case?"

Zach turned his gaze toward Aaron.

"We really don't ever know what tomorrow will bring," Aaron continued. "We live each day the best we can, hoping that we will have tomorrow to make up for anything we didn't get right today. But we never really know if tomorrow will come or what new challenges it will bring. All that matters is that we have today. Kayla knows we're here. She knows we love her. She's a fighter. We all know that. She has a lot to live for, just like Kate did. She will hang onto that, to your love, and the boys' love, and all that she has to look forward to. She knows that tomorrow might be tough, but she's ready to take it on."

Zach just nodded, too overcome with emotion to speak. It wasn't merely the words that Aaron spoke. It was the knowledge that he and Kayla would take it on together. For so long, Zach had been alone. Even when he was surrounded by his brothers in arms, their bunks so close they were almost touching, he had always felt alone. His world was one that he tried to keep others out of, as if getting close to him would cause them to feel the guilt that he carried around with him for so long. Meeting Kayla and the boys had changed that. From the first night they met, he let his guard down. He allowed himself to feel like a human when he was with them rather than a detached robot following orders to kill. They made him feel alive. That was the gift Kayla gave him. He just needed more time to show her how much it meant to him, how much she meant to him.

"Mr. Reynolds?" A nurse called from the doorway.

"That's me, I mean, I'm Zach Middleton, Kayla Reynolds' husband." Zach nervously rushed to the nurse as Ronnie and Trevor, Kate, EJ, and Todd rose to their feet. Aaron reached for Kate's hand.

"Your wife is in recovery. She should be awake within the next half hour or so, and I will come back to get you then."

"Is she okay? What did they find? Did they remove her—"

"I'm sorry," the nurse interrupted. "I really can't answer any of that. The doctor will have all of that information for you shortly. I'll be back to take you to your wife as soon as she wakes up." She smiled and retreated back through the double doors.

Zach breathed a sigh of relief. He had no answers, but Kayla was out of surgery, and he would see her soon. That was enough for now.

***

"Kayla, can you hear me?"

The voice sounded far away, and Kayla was having trouble responding. She tried to place it, but there was no recognition.

"Kayla, can you open your eyes?"

Slowly, and with great effort, Kayla managed to open her eyes. The room was dim and smelled of antiseptic. She could hear muffled voices and faint noises from somewhere nearby. She blinked a few times and began to focus on the face above her. A woman she vaguely recognized was smiling down at her. A nurse. She was a nurse. What was her name? Candy? Sandy? Mandy? Kayla couldn't remember.

"Very good, Kayla. You have a lot of people waiting to see you. Once we get you sitting up and able to drink something, we can call someone back. Try to stay awake, and I'll get you a drink. Okay?"

Kayla slowly nodded as her memories came flooding back. Tentatively, she reached under her gown and felt for her breast. It was heavily bandaged, but it was there. Relieved, she closed her eyes and said a prayer, asking for the presence of her breast to be a good sign.

"Here's some ginger ale," the nurse said, placing the cup on the swingable-arm that acted as a table. "Let's get you sitting up a little."

She helped Kayla sit up as comfortably as she could and held the cup to Kayla's lips so that her parched mouth could relish some of the bubbly liquid.

"Very good," the nurse said. Kayla glanced at the name tag—Sandy.

"Thank you, Sandy," she whispered.

"You're welcome. Any pain?"

Kayla thought about it. There was some discomfort but no actual pain at the moment. She shook her head.

"Very good. I'll go get your husband, if you're ready."

Husband? Kayla tensed and felt a small stab of pain. She tried to take a deep breath, but it caused discomfort in her breast.

Eddie is…oh, wait.

She relaxed with a smile. Everything had happened so fast she could hardly believe it was real. But as memories of the night before surfaced, she knew that it was, indeed, real.

"Yes, please," she managed before closing her eyes and resting her head back against the pillow.

When she opened her eyes, she wasn't sure whether she was still remembering her wedding night or staring into the green eyes of her husband.

"Zach," she said quietly, feeling as if she were in a dream. "Are you real?"

Zach laughed. "I sure hope so," he said as he leaned down and kissed her. "Does that help?"

"You're real," she said, absent-mindedly licking her lips to savor the taste of him.

"Dr. Zink said everything went very well," Zach told her, taking her hand. "She said they got everything they saw and didn't see any signs that it had spread farther than the lobe where we spotted the cancer. It will take a week or so to get the biopsy from the lymph nodes, but she was confident enough that they got everything that she didn't remove your breast. She left as much of it as she could anyway."

Kayla lazily nodded.

"How do you feel?"

"Like Rip Van Winkle." She blinked her eyes to relieve the dryness and reached for her cup. Zach understood and handed her the drink.

"She said that the effects of the anesthesia will wear off soon. Your mom is anxious to get back here. Would you like her to come alone, or do you mind if I come back, too?"

"Bring the whole gang," Kayla said. "I want to see the boys. And Kate and Aaron. Tell everyone to come." She was starting to feel more awake and was craving her family.

"I'll see what I can do," Zach promised before leaning in for another kiss. "I love you, Mrs. Middleton."

"I love you, too, Mr. Middleton." She smiled at Zach. The love in the room was palpable.

She watched him go and slowly leaned back. In spite of the multi-hour surgery, the myriad of stitches, the now-emerging pain, and the new odd shape of her breast, Kayla felt blessed.

***

Zach helped Kayla up the steps to where EJ held open the front door. The three-and-a-half-hour ride home was rough, and Kayla was feeling the full force of the pain that the anesthesia had kept at bay. She had been prepared to stay a night or two, assuming she would be having a mastectomy, and was pleasantly surprised when she was released late in the day following the surgery.

"Bed or couch?" Zach asked.

Kayla thought for a moment. "Couch, for now, please."

Zach and the boys led her to the couch and helped her get comfortable.

"What can we get for you?" Zach asked, and Kayla realized he was nervous.

"I'm fine. Are you okay?"

"Yep. Never better," he said quickly.

"Zach, relax. I'm home. I feel good. A little sore, but I'm okay."

She watched him expel a long breath and nod.

"Okay. Do you need some pain medicine?"

She considered her pain and the amount of time since she last had anything. She was more than a little sore.

"Yes, I think that's a good idea."

"I'll get some water," EJ said, going into the kitchen.

Zach opened the bag from the doctor and read the labels on the various vials. When EJ returned, Zach gave her the appropriate pain killers.

A couple hours later, Kayla awoke to the tantalizing but unrecognizable aroma of food. Todd was on the floor beside the couch playing with his Legos, and it was dark outside.

"Hey, sweetie, what's Uncle, uh, what's Zach making for dinner?"

"Some Australian thing. It smells good, but I have no idea what it is."

Kayla smiled. She inhaled the aroma and caught the scent of fish.

"Can you get mommy some water, please?"

"Sure, I'll be right back." Todd jumped up and ran into the kitchen, but it was Zach who brought her a cup of hot tea.

"I can bring you water if you want, but I thought you might want some of your favorite tea."

"That's perfect. What are you cooking?"

"Fish for us, but chicken noodle soup for you. I hope that's okay."

Kayla groaned with disappointment, but Doctor Zink had cautioned her that the anesthesia could upset her stomach. "I guess I don't have a choice, but your cooking smells heavenly. Todd said it was Australian?" She looked at Zach with a raised brow. He laughed.

"Kind of. I'd be hard pressed to find barramundi here, but I did have some local fish in my freezer. So, this recipe uses Chincoteague fish but has an Australian flair."

Laughing, Kayla shook her head. "You amaze me," she said.

"Then it doesn't take much," Zach said, brushing his lips against hers. "Gotta get back to the kitchen. Dinner in five? We'll eat in here around the coffee table, Asian-style."

"Sounds good," she answered.

Todd returned from the kitchen and resumed his spot on the floor. Kayla thought about the phrasing of her earlier question and wondered when would be a good time to bring up the matter with the boys. She supposed now was as good a time as any. The boys were thrilled when she and Zach announced that they were getting married even though the timing hadn't been ideal. Todd was distraught about the disappearance of his friend, and the news brought a welcome smile to his face. Even EJ was visibly happy for his mom and his 'uncle.'

"Todd, sweetie," she began.

"Yes, Mommy?" he said without looking up from his toys.

"Can I ask you a question?"

Perhaps sensing the seriousness of her question, he stopped playing and faced her. "Sure."

"Well, Zach has been part of our family for a while now. He's Aunt Kate's brother, so it was natural for you and EJ to call him 'Uncle Zach.' But now, things are different, and I wasn't sure, since he's your stepfather, what you wanted to call him."

"That's an easy one," EJ said, coming into the room. Kayla hadn't expected him to appear and felt self-conscious. She knew that EJ and Zach had a bit of a rocky relationship. EJ sat on the couch next to his mother. She pulled her legs in toward the back of the couch to give him room.

"Mom, I loved dad. I was five when he died, and I remember thinking he was the greatest guy in the world. But lately," he looked away, and Kayla thought she saw him wipe his eye before looking back. "Lately, I've had a hard time remembering what he looked like." He swallowed and blushed just a bit. "I have to look at a picture just to see his face instead of closing my eyes like I used to."

"That's very normal, EJ. You don't have to feel bad about it."

EJ nodded. "Yeah, I know. I talked to Uncle Aaron about it."

For the millionth time, Kayla thanked God for her brother and the bond he shared with her boys.

"Anyway, last night, I was thinking about it. I've been alive for longer than I had a dad."

Kayla's heart broke at his words.

"And it's not fair for a boy to not have a dad, especially a kid as young as Todd."

Hoping she understood where he was going, Kayla pressed her lips together and waited for him to continue, holding back her own tears.

"I think Zach should adopt us." He looked at his mother. Wow. That was not what she expected. Calling Zach 'dad' was the most she hoped for, but now that EJ had said it...

"It's not that I don't love dad," he continued. "I do. But dad's gone, and Zach is here, and you're married, and I just..." His voice cracked, and the tear he had been trying so hard to contain escaped from his eye.
As always, she felt Zach nearby. Their bodies had a way of communicating with each other that left her amazed and grateful and longing to touch him.

"There is nothing I'd love more," Zach said quietly from the doorway, holding a tray with Kayla's soup and a small vase that held a rose from one of the bouquets that had greeted them when they got home from the hospital. Tears escaped from his eyes as Zach walked to the coffee table and set down the tray. Todd jumped from the floor and went to him. Zach knelt down and wrapped his arms around the little boy.

"I love you, Dad," Todd said, his voice cracking, too.

"Me, too, buddy," Zach managed to squeak out as he held Todd. When his teary eyes met Kayla's, her heart melted with joy. EJ beamed at his mother, tears still trailing down his cheeks.

"I guess that settles that," EJ said proudly.

"I guess it does," Kayla said, reaching over to muss up her son's hair.

"Hey, Mom." Todd said. "Next week, when we all say what we're thankful for at Thanksgiving dinner, can I thank God that I have a dad?"

"I'd say we all have a lot to be thankful for," Kayla told him. "You boys having a dad is one of the things on the top of the list."

Despite having just had surgery for cancer, Kayla had a mountain of things to be thankful for. She felt like she must be the happiest and most grateful woman in the world.

Nathan's Famous Chili
Origin: San Antonio, Texas

I would be remiss if I didn't include a favorite recipe belonging to a friend. Rich and savory, Nathan's chili is a favorite among my friends. Whether it's eaten plain, with sour cream and cheese, or topped with Fritos (my children's topping of choice), it's a versatile comfort food like no other. If you don't like beans, you can omit them. If you want it spicier, shake that chili seasoning into the pot a little longer. Do you want chicken, beef, or vegetarian? The possibilities are limitless!

From *Around the World in Eighty Meals*
by K.Z. Middleton

CHAPTER EIGHTEEN

The room was dark when Kayla was jolted awake. Zach slept peacefully by her side. Though almost two weeks had gone by since their wedding night, Kayla was still delighted every time she opened her eyes and sensed him next to her. But this time, her heart pounded, and Kayla wondered what had roused her from sleep. Her heart beat wildly in her chest as she breathed slowly and tried to get her bearings. What was that noise?

As the buzzing of her phone continued, Kayla's heart beat even faster. She reached for the device and squinted as her sleepy eyes read the number. She reached over to nudge Zach and answered the call.

"Aaron, what's wrong?" she said, her voice catching in her throat. Zach rolled over and stared at her. In spite of his light snoring just a few seconds earlier, he was fully awake, his eyes wide and waiting.

"They found him, Kay. He's," Aaron's voice cracked. "Oh, God, Kay, it's awful."

There were only a few times in their adult lives when Aaron cried. One was the day Kate delivered Miren. The second was on his wedding day. The third was the day of Kayla's surgery when she and Aaron shared a few minutes alone together before she was released. Kayla wanted to reach through the phone and hold her brother. He and Rob were close, as close as she and Tammi were, friends since grade school. She felt every bit of her brother's pain.

***

Kayla looked around the little island church where she had been married just a few weeks prior. Closing her eyes, she swallowed and prayed that this nightmare would come to an end. She gripped Zach's arm and willed herself not to cry. Not yet. There would be more than enough tears as the Mass progressed.

"I have to go," Zach whispered, squeezing her hand before gently slipping his arm out from her hold and walking to the back of the church.

Kayla watched her husband and her brother exit through the open doors that ushered in the cold, December wind. She shivered and grabbed Kate's hand, knowing that her sister-in-law shared her grief.

The congregants stood as Zach and Aaron, along with the husbands of their friends, Anne, Marian, Shannon, and Debbie, walked down the aisle beside the small casket. Tammi, Rob, and Alan followed the casket to its place at the front of the church and then sat in the first pew. When Zach joined her in the pew, Kayla took hold of his hand and allowed his strength to flow through her.

She looked around the packed church. It seemed that the entire island was amassed inside the small building. All of her closest friends and their families were there to support Rob and Tammi—Anne, Marian, Debbie, and Shannon. The principal, Mr. Urbansky, was there as were all of the teachers, including the famed Mr. Palmer. She saw the faces of Marge from the local paper, an attendee rather than a reporter, Henry, the owner of the local grocery store, Jane, from the deli, and all of the owners and employees of the Creamery and the island museum. Uniforms dotted the scene—police and military, including many from the Coast Guard. Kayla marveled at the turnout and wondered if the entire town had shut down for the day to say goodbye to a boy who so easily captured the hearts of those who encountered him.

It all seemed surreal to Kayla. How could this have happened to Ethan? A boy she had known since the day he was born. She wondered if there could be anything worse than this—watching a mother say goodbye to her child.

***

Standing in the shower on a late December day, Kayla let the water run over her. She was feeling healthy and looking forward to spending Christmas with her family. They all longed for something to celebrate and to the few days when they could just be a happy family.

The chemo treatments were rough, but after a few days, she felt stronger and more like herself. She reached for the shampoo and poured a small amount into her hand. As she lathered her hair, she felt an odd sensation in her scalp. She ran her hand through the shampoo and pulled it away with a handful of hair.

She was so shocked to see the brown tendrils lying limply in her palm, that it took a moment for reality to hit her. She dropped the hair and ran her fingers through the wet strands, pulling away more and more with each swipe. Tears ran down her face as she watched clumps of hair fall inside the shower and slither toward the drain like a nest of snakes. Even though she knew it was coming, the reality caught her completely off guard and blindsided her with grief. Collapsing in the shower stall beside her hair, she sobbed, oblivious to the voice calling from down the hall.

When the door to the bathroom opened, she heard Zach's gasp.

"Kayla, are you all right. Why didn't you wait for me to get back?" He tore open the shower door and stared at her, sitting naked, surrounded by strands of hair.

Quietly, Zach reached for the handle and turned off the water. He took her towel from the top of the shower door and wrapped it around her. He gently lifted her from the floor and carried her into the bedroom.

"Shh," he hushed her cries. "It's okay. We knew this would happen. It's okay."

Knowing it would happen, and seeing it happen, were two very different things, but Kayla didn't quite know how to explain that to him. He had been so patient, so understanding. She just had to accept that there would be some things that were beyond his comprehension, beyond hers even.

"Did you get the boys to school?" she asked between sniffles as her sobs began to subside.

"Sure did. They're safe and sound."

"Thank you," she whispered into his shirt, now damp and rich with the smell of him.

"I'm sorry," she said.

"For what?" he asked, pulling back to look at her face. "For losing your hair?" He surveyed her face and her patchy scalp. "You're still the most beautiful woman I've ever laid eyes on."

Smiling, but feeling self-conscious, Kayla pulled the towel tighter around herself.

"Oh, no, you don't," Zach said, standing up and sitting her on the bed. He took the towel from around her and took her in, naked and shivering. She shrunk away from his stare, folding into herself to cover her lopsided breast with still-visible scars. "Kayla," he said, kneeling beside her and enfolding her in his arms. "Do you know how beautiful you are? When I look at you, I don't see your breasts or your scars or your hair. I see you. I see your inner beauty *and* your outer beauty, your strength, your compassion, the love you have for me and for the boys, the way you go out of your way to help others. I see far beneath your skin, your tissue, or your lymph nodes. I see the you that only exists in your soul. And I have never known a more beautiful person."

Kayla reached her arms around his neck and pulled him more tightly to her.

"How do you always know the right thing to say?" she asked him.

"Easy," he said. "You taught me how."

They kissed, and for the next hour, Zach managed to make her forget about her hair.

Lying under the covers, her head on his chest, Kayla inhaled the scent of his sweat, his deodorant, and the shower soap they shared. She was content to stay there all day.

"Hey, I have something to talk to you about," Zach said, turning to face her.

"What's up?"

"I've been doing a lot of thinking about Second Helpings. Have you ever heard of Plated?"

Kayla searched her memory but came up with nothing. "No, what's that?"

"It's a company in New York City that was started by a former Marine. I read an article about them in Forbes. He designs easy, healthy, and affordable recipes that anyone can cook. People place orders online, and someone delivers all of the ingredients and recipe directions right to their doorstep. It's similar to those mail-order meals that are becoming increasingly popular."

"So, like what I do but without all the cooking involved on my end." Kayla sat up and tucked the sheets under her arms, very interested in the possibilities that were now stirring in her mind.

"Exactly. Between the two of us, with your traditional family recipes and my international recipes, I think we could create a menu that would satisfy anyone's palate while tweaking everything to make it easy for busy families and even those who don't have any cooking skills."

"We could run the business, design the menu, and create the recipes and, once we're established, hire people to do the shopping and deliveries," Kayla said. Her mind raced with ideas. "And, like those other businesses, people could sign up for their meals ahead of time, so there's no last-minute prep for us and no rushing to the store every day to come home and throw together the meals."

"I think it's perfect for us. And, when EJ is old enough to drive, he could do deliveries. He'd love the extra cash, and it would teach him responsibility."

Kayla threw her arms around Zach's neck. "I love the idea."

Kayla kissed her husband, ignoring the hair that lay in clumps on her pillow.

She may be losing her hair, but she was alive. She had two wonderful boys and the sexiest, most attentive and adoring husband a woman could pray for. He had made many promises to her over the past several months, and he had seen them all through. It hadn't been a smooth path to happiness, but it was a road that led them here, to this moment in time, and to each other. They promised to never look back in the rearview mirror again. Their eyes would be on the road that lies ahead, and they would travel into the future together.

***

Christmas Eve found Zach and Kayla at Mass, alongside the rest of their family, including Zach and Kate's parents, Mitzi and Walter. Kayla smiled at Nick and Megan when the pair entered the pew behind them. She glanced at Zach with a raised brow. He answered her with a shrug, and she wondered if he knew more than he was letting on.

Kayla looked around at the familiar faces. Across the room, her eyes settled on Mr. Urbansky. The school principal seemed to have aged ten years since the beginning of the school year. Kayla imagined it was a hard time for many teachers and principals in the area with everything going on.

After Mass, Megan and Nick left, saying they were going to celebrate together that night, but would be at Ronnie and Trevor's for Christmas dinner the following day.

Rather than staying up all night, as was their family tradition, Kayla slept in her old bedroom from the time after dinner until midnight when she heard the door creak open.

"Mom," Todd whispered. "It's Christmas."

"Are you sure?" she teased. "Maybe it's still Thanksgiving."

"Don't be ridiculous, Mom. It's time to open presents, but Grandma said, if you're too tired, we can wait until morning."

Unwilling to disappoint him, Kayla sat up in bed. "Just let me brush my hair and teeth, okay?"

"Mom," Todd said with exasperation, "you don't have any hair."

"I don't?" she gasped in mock surprise. "Oh! You're right. Then I just have to brush my teeth, and I'll be all ready." She smiled at her son.

Todd giggled. "I'll let everyone know," he said before rushing from the room.

All the lights in the house were off when Kayla headed down the hall. She could see the faint glow of the Christmas tree coming from the living room, and she wondered why it was so dark and quiet.

When she entered the room, everyone yelled, surprise. Zach, still dressed from church, was on bended knee before the tree. Their families looked on as Zach held up a small, velvet box.

"Kayla Elizabeth Reynolds, would you make me the happiest man in the world by agreeing to be my wife?"

"I'm so sorry, Mr. Middleton, but I'm already quite happily married," she said with a smile as she kneeled down beside him.

"Then say you'll at least wear this ring and take me for who I am for better or worse and in sickness and health, for the rest of our lives?"

"Now that, my dear husband, I can say yes to."

Everyone cheered as Zach took her hand and removed her mother's ring from her finger. He slipped the new ring onto her finger and put her mother's ring in the box. He tossed the box into the air behind him, and EJ expertly caught it, handing the ring inside to his grandmother. Kayla laughed.

"How long did the two of you practice that?"

"A long time," EJ said.

"I love you," Zach said, looking deeply into her eyes.

"I love you back," Kayla said as Zach took her into his arms and kissed her while everyone cheered and whistled around them.

***

Zach and Kayla sat in Kayla's office going through her recipes. Since Christmas, they had looked up the company Zach mentioned and gone through every inch of the website. They talked to Kate about re-designing the website for Second Helpings and looked into the logistics of when and how food would be delivered. They hoped to launch the company by the end of February, but there was still so much to do. And though it had been a mild winter, January and February were often cold, and snowfall was truly unpredictable. Most years, the island saw no snow at all. But every now and then, a nor'easter hit the area hard, turning the marshes and nearby beaches into layers of ice and snow.

When Kayla's phone buzzed, Zach watched her smile as she identified the caller.

"EJ, again," she said. "I swear, he's finding every excuse to use the Christmas present we gave him." She slid the button to answer the call. "Hey, hon, what's up?"

Zach suggested they give EJ the latest model of the hottest smartphone for Christmas. Zach spent a lot of time going over the rules of having the phone, including the biggest stipulation that EJ's location services were to be on at all times. If he ever hid his location from them, the phone would be gone. Zach made sure that EJ knew how to click the lock button three times to display the emergency screen that allowed his location to be tracked by the 911 center. Today was the first day back at school, and Zach was sure that EJ was enjoying being able to show off his new phone to all his friends.

Zach's thoughts shifted abruptly when he saw Kayla's face drain of color.

"What do you mean, you can't find Todd?" she asked in a panic, reaching for Zach's hand. "And they've checked everywhere?" She met Zach's gaze with fear as she listened to EJ's response. "We'll be right there," she said, standing and reaching for her purse before disconnecting the call.

"Todd didn't show up at the meeting place after school. EJ, Lizzie, and Sam waited for ten minutes before heading out to meet Anne. They looked everywhere around the school but didn't find him." Her voice cracked as they hastily pulled on their coats and closed the door behind them before racing out to the truck.

"We'll find him, Kayla. I'm sure he's fine," Zach assured her, but his mind roared with the possibility that the killer had struck again.

Anne's husband, Paul, Chief of Police, was with Tammi's husband, Rob, his second in command, back at work and looking determined to find this monster. They met Kayla and Zach at the entrance to the school. Mr. Urbansky, the principal, was with them and shook their hands. Zach felt the sweat in the man's palms and resisted wiping his own hands on his jeans.

"Go ahead, tell them what you just told us." Paul motioned to the principal.

The well-liked man wrung his sweaty hands in despair. "As soon as we heard Todd was missing, we locked down the building. All of the teachers were supposed to be performing their afternoon duties." He shifted his eyes toward the officers and back to Kayla. "They should have immediately followed the lockdown protocol, but that doesn't seem to have happened." He swallowed and pulled at his necktie.

"What do you mean?" Zach asked. "What didn't happen?"

Mr. Urbansky closed his eyes and shook his head, obviously too overcome with emotion to speak.

Rob took over. "It appears that one of the teachers left the building. He slipped out the back door of his classroom and hasn't been seen or heard from since."

"What does this have to do with Todd?"

Rob continued. "According to one of Todd's classmates, the teacher, Mr. Palmer, told Todd to meet him in his room after school today. The boy overheard them when he went to get a book he had left in the classroom. He heard Mr. Palmer tell Todd that it was going to be their secret." Rob didn't try to hide the contempt in his voice, or the heartache.

"I don't understand," Kayla said. "Todd loves Mr. Palmer. He's his favorite teacher. Todd would do anything for…" She covered her mouth, and Zach put his arm protectively around her.

"You said he hasn't been seen or heard from since he left the school. Have you all checked his house?" Zach asked.

"As you know," Paul began, "the FBI is in charge of the investigation. They have a team on their way to his house now. They're going to treat it as a crime scene.

They're working with some of our guys to go over the classroom."

"Mom!" Kayla and Zach turned toward EJ's voice. Followed by Nick, the boy ran down the hall and threw his arms around his mother. Looking up into her eyes, he shook his head. "I'm so sorry. I promised I'd take care of him. I'm so sorry." EJ broke down in tears. Zach put his hands on the boy's shoulders.

"EJ, it's not your fault. You did everything right."

"But Todd, he's missing, and I was supposed to watch him."

"EJ, listen to me," Zach said forcefully. "We're going to find him. We have a lead this time. We're going to find him before it's too late."

Kayla grasped Zach's arm and held onto him for dear life, her pleading eyes burning into him. "Do you really think so?"

"I do," he said, looking toward Paul.

"I do, too," Paul agreed. "He messed up this time, and we're going to take advantage of it. We've got a roadblock set up at the causeway, so no car can leave the island without being searched. And the Feds and state police are already interviewing the faculty and staff as well as the people who live close to the school."

"Why don't you all go home and wait to hear from us," Rob said. "I know how you feel, and I will do everything in my power to bring Todd home." The look in his eyes would haunt Zach forever. It was the look of a man who had seen the devil but was trying to find a way to climb out of the hell that he lived in day and night. Zach had seen the look before in the eyes of his comrades after they lost one of their own.

"We're going to question all of the teachers and the kids who had Mr. Palmer. We're going to find him," Nick promised. "Go home. I'll call you when I can."

The officers turned to leave. Mr. Urbansky looked at Zach and Kayla, his face contorted in agony.

"I'm so sorry," he said before turning and following the other men down the hall.

***

When Zach saw Nick's name appear on his phone, he walked into Kayla's office to answer the call. Kayla had been fielding calls all afternoon and evening. Debbie, Anne, and Marian called, offering support. Shannon delivered homemade chili and cornbread. Tammi texted but did not call. What could she say? Her story offered no comfort for Kayla.

"What have you got?" Zach asked without greeting.

"The Feds ran Palmer's prints and Social Security number. They didn't match."

"What do you mean?"

"The prints belong to a known pedophile, Adam Henderson. The Social Security number does belong to a person by the name of Martin Palmer, a teacher, but he's been dead for three years."

"Homicide?"

"Doesn't appear to be, but we're still waiting for the autopsy report."

"So," Zach said walking back into the kitchen where Kayla was trying to convince EJ to eat something. "Do they think this guy, Henderson, was impersonating Palmer?"

"Seems that way," Nick answered. "They're still checking everything out. But Zach, there's something else."

Zach braced himself for what sounded like more bad news.

"The Feds finished the search of the house. They found things that I can't even say out loud. What he did to those boys is worse than anything you and I ever saw in all our years of combat. There was blood and body fluids and signs of unthinkable horrors inflicted on those kids. The stuff in those autopsies don't tell half of the things that happened in that house."

Zach felt weak in his knees. They had to find Todd, and they didn't have a moment to waste.

"I'll give you a call when I know more," Nick said when Zach didn't respond

"Thanks," was all Zach could say before disconnecting the call.

When he relayed the information about Palmer to Kayla, she looked even more vulnerable than ever with no hair, a thin frame, and the mixed emotions of shock and grief showing in her eyes and on the lines on her face. Zach spared her most of what Nick told him. He knew that eventually news about the contents of the house and the things that were done to those boys would come out, but until they knew that Todd was back home safe and sound, he was going to shield Kayla from the rest of the gruesome details. Those were things she didn't need to dwell on right then.

Zach wished there was some way to ease her pain, but he knew that, in truth, she would rather have died from the cancer than to lose her son.

Sensing movement outside, Zach turned toward the window in time to see Kate's SUV pull into the driveway. She climbed out of the driver's seat and opened the back door to retrieve Miren. Ronnie climbed out of the passenger side door. She opened the back door, and Zach watched as she pulled several grocery bags from the backseat. He went outside and took the bags from her as she neared the house.

"How is she holding up?" Ronnie asked.

"How would you be?" was Zach's response. Ronnie nodded and rushed up the steps and into the house.

"Dad and Aaron are helping with the search," Kate told her brother as they walked up the stairs. "I wish there was more that I could do to help."

"Kayla will be grateful that you're here," Zach told her. "I'm not sure how she's able to keep standing. It's all I can do to walk past his room."

"They're going to find him," Kate assured her brother. "Aaron texted me. They already have a ton more information than they did when any of the other boys disappeared. They've got to be closing in on him soon."

"That's what worries me the most," Zach told her as they stood on the deck outside the house. He glanced inside to be sure that Kayla was not within hearing distance. "He has to know by now that we're onto him. The other boys were gone for weeks before he killed them and dumped their bodies. He took his time with them. He knows that he won't be able to do that with Todd."

His sister looked at him in horror, her mouth agape.

"You're not sure we're going to find him alive, are you?"

Zach shook his head. "I pray to God that I'm wrong."

***

The house was almost dark, lit only by the single lamp beside the couch where Kayla held vigil. She refused to sleep even though her body needed rest more than ever. Zach paced the floor to keep himself awake for her sake, but every so often, he pleaded with her to close her eyes even if only for an hour.

"I can't," she finally said. "Every time I close my eyes, I see Todd's beautiful smiling face, and then I see those other boys and imagine what that monster did to them." She shuddered and blinked back tears.

"I keep…" Zach began before shaking his head.

"What?" Kayla asked, her eyes searching his for more information.

"I keep asking God why this is happening. Why He's putting you through this." Zach ran his hand over the top of his head as he continued to pace. "How much pain has to be inflicted on you?" He stopped and faced Kayla. "Haven't you suffered enough?" Even in the shadows, she could see the tears glistening in his eyes. "There's never an answer, and though I know that God does not inflict pain or harm, and He doesn't want you to go through this any more than I do, I can't help but ask, why?"

Kayla understood what Zach was going through. Those same thoughts had kept her awake many nights over the past few months.

"I wish I had answers," she told him. "My mother keeps saying that we can't lose our faith. That God will come through for us. And I think, like He came through for Tammi? For Hank's sister?" She shook her head. "I just don't know how to reconcile it all."

Car lights illuminated the night, and Zach and Kayla turned toward the window, watching in silence as the lights turned into the driveway and shined on the house, casting an unnerving glow on the dimly-lit room. They glanced at each other, both holding their breath, preparing for whatever news was about to be thrust upon them.

Before the visitor could knock, Zach flipped on the porch light and opened the door, casting Nick in an eerie spotlight.

"I wanted to be the one to tell you the news," Nick said, stepping into the room and closing the door. Zach switched on the overhead light, causing Kayla to blink several times as her eyes adjusted to the change.

She tried to stand but she was too weak, from worry or loss of appetite, she didn't know. Perhaps both. Zach, always able to sense when she needed him, went to her side.

"They found Henderson's car. It was registered in Palmer's name, just like everything else was. The guy knew what he was doing. He had all the right credentials. Anyway, the car was found by a park ranger in the Assateague parking lot. As you know, it has limited operation hours this time of year. He was able to get past the guard without being recognized, probably before the

APB was put out on him. It wasn't until after hours, when the ranger was doing his rounds, that he came upon the car. The Amber alert hadn't reached him." He shrugged. "No cell service out where he was patrolling that afternoon."

Zach and Kayla listened intently. Kayla had so many questions, but she allowed Nick the time to finish.

"Instead of calling it in, he went back out to the seashore to try to find whoever was still in the park. By the time he finished searching, it was well after dark. He took down the tag number and called his superiors. They alerted us, and we sent a team over. By the time I got there, they had confirmation that it was Henderson's car, and they'd managed to get it open. They found this inside."

Nick reached into his pocket and pulled out a plastic bag containing a small glove. Kayla gasped.

"It's Todd's?" Nick asked.

"Yes," she whispered. "He got it in his stocking," she said, her voice breaking with emotion.

Nick nodded. "I thought so. We had to get it confirmed."

"He's close by," Zach said. "There's no place for him to go if he's on Assateague Island."

"Well, he could theoretically have an inflatable boat stashed somewhere on Assateague, but it's highly unlikely. The ocean is unforgiving when it comes to small vessels, especially at night. And the Coast Guard is on high alert. He wouldn't be able to get as far as Ocean City without being spotted, and there's no possibility he could go farther than that in a small boat."

"Do the authorities believe he still has Todd with him?"

Kayla tensed at Zach's question. Had he already killed Todd and left him behind in Chincoteague? Had he disposed of him in the cold, rough waters of the Atlantic? Her heart raced as her mind conjured the possibilities.

"There was no blood in the car, not even a trace, and no signs of struggle anywhere near it. He had to be in a hurry to ditch the car. And killing right away is not his MO. We're fairly confident Todd is still alive."

Kayla breathed a sigh of relief, purposely ignoring the word, 'fairly.'

"Do you have a search team out there?" Zach asked.

Nick nodded. "They're just getting started. It took some time to round everyone up and get them to the shore. The good news is that there aren't many places for him to hide. It's almost all sand, and the grassy areas are pretty flat with few trees. The dogs are on the way, and they'll have no problem sniffing him out if he's hiding in any of the bushes or wooded areas along the western side of the island. In fact, that's one of the reasons I'm here. We have this glove, but it's pretty new. We need—"

"I'm on it," Zach said without letting Nick finish. He stood, hurried down the hall, and returned with several articles of clothing.

"These were in the laundry basket, so they should have plenty of scent on them."

"Thanks," Nick said. "It's still dark, so it's not ideal for searching. Once it starts to get light, if we haven't found them already, we should be able to zero in. If you want to be there—"

Again, Zach cut him off. "We'll be there. Is Aaron part of the search team?"

Nick hesitated before answering. "He's leading the water search," he answered quietly.

Kayla's heart lurched. She knew what that meant. Closing her eyes, she prayed that Aaron and his crew would not be the ones to find Todd. If they did, it would already be too late.

***

Kayla stood on the Assateague beach, the cold January wind slapping her tear-stained face. There was a ribbon of red across the horizon blending into a brilliant orange sky. The rising yellow sun seemed to sit on top of the water, causing the waves to take on the appearance of a perfectly designed painting. The water closest to the sun was pink but changed to purple as it flowed toward the shore, ending in a deep blue as it lazily rolled onto the beach. The sand glowed yellow in the early morning light.

The magnificence of the scene was a stark contrast to the dark turn of events that Kayla's life had taken in the past twenty-four hours. The irony didn't escape her as she watched the sun rise over the ocean. Even having cancer, and all that the diagnosis could have meant, could never have prepared her for standing on the beach at that moment waiting to hear if her son was dead or alive.

Without warning, men began running down the beach. Kayla looked at Zach, and, as if reading each other's minds, they took off after them. After only a few yards, Kayla was winded and had to stop. She gasped for air, clutching her chest beneath the heavy winter coat, and readjusting the pink hat that Tammi knitted for her for Christmas. Even through her own grief, Tammi continued to think of others. Zach stopped and put his hand on her back.

"Go," Kayla told him. "I'm coming. Go get our son."

Without a word, Zach began running down the beach, fear, hope, and whatever else he was feeling at the moment, propelling him ahead of other runners. Kayla watched as he zipped in and out of the Feds and police officers, making his way to the front of the pack and out of her sight.

She felt another hand on her back and turned. Ronnie gave her an encouraging smile and took her hand.

"Let's go," she said. "We can walk fast. Running won't change anything. Zach will make sure he's okay."

Unable to answer, Kayla silently prayed that her mother's words were correct. *Please, God, let Todd be okay.*

***

Zach was hardly out of breath when he spied the circle of uniformed and suited men ahead. He trampled the terrain quickly, ankle deep in marsh grass and slimy water. He broke through the circle as they lifted the small, lifeless body from a sandy bog.

"Out of the way," one of the men yelled, and the circle opened enough for a Maryland park ranger to carry Todd out of the marsh and onto the beach where they could lay him down on solid ground.

"He's blue," Zach cried, his chest on fire.

"He's just cold," Jimmy, a Chincoteague EMT said, kneeling beside Todd. Zach tried to go to the boy, but Nick grabbed him by the sleeve.

"Let them work," he said as Jimmy's partner, Tori, knelt by Todd and searched for vitals.

"His pulse is weak, and he's suffering from hypothermia," Tori said, "but he's breathing."

Jimmy wiped the slime off Todd's face and placed an oxygen mask over his mouth.

Zach thought his heart would explode. *Thank you, God,* his mind played over and over, like a scratched record from his youth.

"Zach!" Kayla's scream was carried by the wind. Zach turned, scanning the crowd for her. Seeing her and Ronnie making their way down the beach, he fought through the onlookers and search teams, clearing a path between Kayla and her son.

"Kayla!" he yelled. "He's alive!" He didn't recognize his own voice, a mixture of pain, relief, and joy all rolled into one. He had experienced so many emotions in such a short time, he didn't really know what he was feeling.

As Kayla made her way to him, Zach heard Tori call in Todd's information.

"Eight-year-old boy, unconscious and unresponsive. Pulse weak, breathing thready, pupils dilated. Signs of hypothermia present."

"Roger that, helicopter en route."

As if on cue, they heard the hum of the engine.

"Brace yourself, and cover your face," Zach said to Kayla, recalling many sandstorms caused by an incoming chopper.

The sand began to whip around them. A blanket was laid over Todd's body as he was carried to the open door of the helicopter. Zach and Kayla followed.

"Only room for one," the state police informed them.

Without another thought, Zach helped Kayla climb aboard. When their eyes met, he tried to convey a message over the thrumming of the rotors. *I love you. Take care of our boy. I'll see you soon.*

He watched the chopper lift off the ground, oblivious to the swirling sand.

"Let's go," Nick said. "Paul's letting us take his cruiser. We'll have the lights and siren on the whole way."

Without a minute to lose, Zach and Nick began their run down the beach. The farther into the sky the chopper went, the more Zach felt the all-too-familiar void. He couldn't get to Kayla fast enough.

Best Ever Homemade Ice Cream Cake
Origin: England

Birthdays were always causes for big celebrations in our home. No matter where we lived or what was going on, my mother always made sure we had homemade ice cream cake, and she would tailor it to our favorite ice cream flavors. Today, I am the creator of the ice cream cakes for the family, and there isn't anybody I know who can eat just one slice. Ice cream cake can turn any occasion into a celebration.

From *Around the World in Eighty Meals*
by K.Z. Middleton

EPILOGUE

"Happy birthday, dear Todd. Happy birthday to you."

Everyone in the Kelly and Middleton families gathered around Todd's bed along with Megan, Nick, several nurses and doctors, and even Dr. Sprance, Kate's obstetrician, who was at the hospital that day checking on patients. Kayla noticed a shift in the way Megan and Nick were with each other. Had Nick finally broken through Megan's wall? She'd have to ask Kate later.

Todd blew out the candles, and the small crowd cheered. The effects of the drug he'd been given took several hours to wear off, but Kayla and Zach were assured that it would have no lasting effects.

Kayla cut a large slice of Todd's favorite birthday treat, homemade birthday-cake-flavored ice cream cake, and placed it in front of her son. The room was quiet as they all enjoyed their cake. When Todd was halfway through his slice, his eyes widened. Kayla followed his gaze.

Anne, Paul, Ben, and Lizzie stood in the doorway along with Tammi and Rob. "Are we in time for the party?" Tammi asked, a melancholy smile on her face.

"Just in time," Kayla said, walking over to her friend and enfolding her in her arms.

"I know this is hard for you," Kayla whispered, hugging her friend.

Tammi didn't respond, but Kayla felt the small intake of breath as Tammi sniffed back a cry.

Kayla hugged Anne as well and, from the corner of her eye, saw Lizzie go to EJ's side, and take his hand.

"We're just having ice cream cake. Would you like a piece?" Kayla took Tammi's hand and led her to the cake without waiting for an answer. She cut enough slices for all of the newcomers and handed them out. Todd and Ben grinned at each other, ice cream dripping from their mouths.

"Mom?" Todd asked, wiping ice cream from his chin with his arm. "What's going to happen to Mr. Palmer?"

The room stilled as the adults looked from one to another. Zach stepped over to the side of the bed.

"Todd, Mr. Palmer will probably spend the rest of his life in jail. It's where he should be so that he can't hurt any more boys." Palmer, AKA Henderson, had been found farther down on Assateague after Zach, Kayla, and Todd were all en route to the hospital.

"But he was a really good teacher. We all liked him a lot," Todd said, unwilling to accept the fact that his teacher was not the man he appeared to be.

"I know, Todd. We all wish he hadn't been the one, but sometimes people just aren't who we think they are," Zach told him, glancing at Kayla with a sobering look.

Kayla went to Zach and took his hand. "And sometimes people are exactly who we think they are, and more." She squeezed his hand and looked up at him with admiration.

"So, who's ready to open presents?" Aaron said.

"I am!" shouted Todd.

"Mine first," said EJ, handing his brother a wrapped box containing a photo of the two of them. He made the frame himself in art class.

Once the presents were open, Zach took Kayla's hand and led her into the hallway.

"We haven't had a chance to talk since I got here this morning. I brought the mail with me. I thought you might want to look at it."

"Okay, but I'm sure it can wait until after everyone is gone."

"It can, but there's something I thought you might want to share with Todd."

Kayla eyed Zach curiously. "What is it?"

Zach handed Kayla an opened envelope from the Clerk of the Court. She looked up at him and raised her brow.

"Just read it," he said, his scar disappearing as his smile widened.

Kayla read the document. The court had waived a home visit and set a date for the adoption.

"March seems like a long way away," she said, though she grinned back at Zach.

"But we have a date," Zach said. "On March fifteenth, just a couple days after you finish your treatments, we will officially be a family."

"We already are," Kayla said, entwining her arms around his neck.

"Yes, we are," Zach answered back before kissing her. He pulled back and gazed into her eyes that matched the greens and browns in the scarf wrapped around her head. "The house has been awfully lonely the past couple days without you. I've missed this." He leaned back down for another kiss.

"It's been a rough few months," Kayla said once they came up for air. Laughter filled the room behind them. "I'm ready to be at home with you and the boys, starting our business, doing normal family things."

"That's all I've ever wanted," Zach said.

"Mom," EJ called. "Can I have the last piece of cake? It's melting."

Kayla laughed. "Sure, EJ, go ahead." She grinned at Zach "Shall we get back to our family?"

"I like the sound of that," he said, taking her hand and leading her back into Todd's room.

Kayla looked around the room. Once again, she felt the contentment that came with knowing that everyone she loved was together and happy. She looked from her parents to her brother and his wife, over to Anne and Paul and to Lizzie and EJ. She gazed at Tammi and Rob, grateful they had come to the hospital despite their grief. She stopped as her gaze came upon Megan and Nick.

Who knows. God brings people together under the most mysterious of circumstances. We'll see what the future brings.

She smiled at the thought. A short time ago, she wasn't sure she would have a future. Now, she had so much to look forward to. But no matter how much she looked forward to March, with the end of her treatments and Zach adopting the boys, she was content to live this moment as fully as possible. The future was bright, but she had learned that the *present* is what matters most.

Island of Hope
Coming 2019

About the Author

Amy began writing as a child and never stopped. She wrote articles for magazines and newspapers before writing children's books and adult fiction. A graduate of the University of Maryland with a Master of Library and Information Science, Amy has resided on the Eastern Shore of Maryland for 23 years. She worked as a librarian for fifteen years and, in 2010, began writing full time.

Schisler's first children's book, Crabbing With Granddad, is an autobiographical work about spending a day harvesting the Maryland Blue Crab. Sarah Book Publishing released Schisler's novel, A Place to Call Home, in August of 2014. A revised second edition was released in March 2015. Picture Me, A Mystery was released in August of 2015 and won a 2016 Illumination Award as one of the top three ebooks of 2015 among Christian writers. Schisler followed up her success with the critically acclaimed, Whispering Vines, a 2017 Illumination Award winner as one of the best Christian romance novels of 2016.

Amy is the author of a weekly blog which has over a thousand followers around the world. Her topics range from current events to her daily life with her husband, three daughters, and two dogs.

Follow Amy at:

http://amyschislerauthor.com
https://amyschisler.wordpress.com
http://facebook.com/amyschislerauthor
https://twitter.com/AmySchislerAuth
https://www.goodreads.com/amyschisler

Book Club Discussion Questions

1. Zach was fighting powerful demons, but he leaned on his faith and his vision for the future to help him overcome his PTSD. What would your suggestions be for him to help further his recovery?

2. Kayla was reluctant to pursue a relationship with Zach, in part because she worried about how it would affect her children; however, her boys encouraged her to love again. What advice would you give to someone in her shoes? Is there a right way or time for a widowed mother to start over?

3. Kayla's true strength came to light when she learned she had cancer. Though naturally frightened, she was determined to beat the disease. How would you react to the things that Kayla had to face: the diagnosis, the realization that you might leave your family behind, the change in your appearance, the need to rely on others?

4. Ronnie is always the Kelly family's pillar of strength. She credits her faith with her ability to stay positive. Who, in your family, is the pillar of strength? What is it about that person that makes him or her the person everyone feels they can lean on?

5. Kate and Zach share a strong sibling bond, solidified by their many years growing up in remote parts of the world. Kayla and Aaron share a twin connection. Coming together as couples seemed inevitable. Have you experienced that same kind of closeness with siblings or other members of your

families? Was there an event, or series of events, that helped form that bond?

6. Kayla worries that Todd is immature for his age. EJ, on the other hand, shows signs of being quite mature. How does the reader use these traits to form their sibling bond and relationship?

7. The Eastern Shores of Maryland Virginia have seen their share of violence throughout their history, yet there is still the common mentality that "bad things can't happen here." In *Island of Promise*, there was a gradual heightening in the panic that ensued on the island over the kidnappings. Have you ever experienced a gradual, growing terror like the one in the book? How was it handled by the community?

8. Ronnie and Trevor knew from the start that Zach had a violent past, yet they accepted him without question and prayed that he and Kayla would find their way to each other. Has there ever been a time when you saw beyond someone's past and accepted them into your circle? How did that transform you and that person?

9. At the Veterans Day Breakfast, the speaker used a glass as a metaphor for how he found good things to "fill" his life with passion and purpose. How would you use your story to tell others how they, too, can find their passion and purpose in life?

10. Nick and Megan are the newcomers to the island and, like Zach and Kayla, were welcomed with open

arms. But Nick has his faults, and Megan has a past of her own she refuses to face. Zach and Aaron agree that Nick and Megan are just what the other needs, or the last thing the other needs. What do you think? Is there ever an ideal time to think about what the future holds?

CPSIA information can be obtained
at www.ICGtesting.com
Printed in the USA
LVHW051511240521
688342LV00002B/167

9 781732 224209